The Anubis War

*Tales of Vasco
Alcazar al Madina
del Goya*

Book One: Sema – The Listening

By
David R Packer

This is a work of fiction. Names, characters, places, and incidents either are the product of the author's imagination or are used fictitiously. Any resemblance to actual persons, living or dead, events, or locales is entirely coincidental.

Copyright © David R Packer, 2021

All rights reserved. No part of this book may be reproduced in any form on or by an electronic or mechanical means, including information storage and retrieval systems, without permission in writing from the publisher, except by a reviewer who may quote brief passages in a review.

ISBN 978-1-7776078-0-7 (paperback)
ISBN 978-1-7776078-1-4 (ebook)

First Edition: Oct 2021

ACT ONE
MURIDI - DISCIPLESHIP

Chapter One: Divine Essence

It was fitting that the Valkyrie came into his life with the howl of a Banshee.

The Banshee was a reminder of Vasco's past. The big jet engine had been a fixture in his old life, a comforting presence on the battlefield. When the dirigibles were around, you had all the support you could ever want. On Francisco, they were never needed, but never wasted. A big battleship of the air made a fine freighter.

Vasco had heard the howl and glanced into the street in reflex, and his eye caught on the tall woman cutting across the road. She was in an unfamiliar uniform with an unusual triangular patch on the shoulder. Her bearing wasn't quite military but stiff, formal... and somehow just a bit feral. She vanished into the crowd almost as soon as he noticed her.

Something had made him look a moment longer, lingering on the spot even after she was gone.

Funny that the memory of that moment was coming to him again. It had been months ago, the first time he saw her. Before he enlisted again.

He should have known better, but when had he ever? Not the first time he signed up, not the second... maybe when he'd finally resigned and opened his fencing school, but now here he was. Up the well of gravity again. And heading for another Long Drop. Vasco was headed back across the stars, on a light-years-long dive, then he would go back down the well of another world, where he would find new dust under his feet and death to come. Maybe his.

He sighed and looked out the port. The *Alexi* was hours past being a bright shining bar in the black. When the shuttle had first broken free of atmosphere, the now completely built ship had been just a bright dot. Bigger than any star, but still just a distant dot. The steady rumbling acceleration had inched them closer and closer. Vasco could make out details now, and his mind filled in what his eyes couldn't see.

The spaceship was a heavy cylinder in appearance, kilometers long and thick. One end was the thick base for the drive plate. It was a squat and ugly assembly with struts and pistons as big as buildings connecting it to the main body. The entire ship had cooling spars coming off at all angles. Blisters all over for weapons and external communications. Tatar-class ships like the *Alexi* were a cylinder within a cylinder, the outer cylinder responsible for cooling, spare reactor mass, and armor. The inner carried the crew, propulsion, cargo, and other goodies. In the space between the two cylinders, the *Alexi* held an armada of smaller ships.

The bio-warfare blister on the outside of the big ship always gave Vasco shivers. He hated the damn things. The bio-warfare blisters were safe. Supposedly. Only accessible from the outside of the ship. Only connected to the ship with thin spars—just enough to keep it attached in normal orbital conditions.

The theory was that almost nothing but hard vacuum would ever come between the blister's hell-contents and the inside of the ship. Vasco knew for a fact that some of the hardest armor in the ship was under that blister. The slightest breach of the blister's hull, or disruption of contact with the ship, would cause an instant immolation of the contents. No worry about losing personnel—no one ever entered the blister.

If the time ever came to use bio-warfare, the appropriate bombs would be attached to the correct loading points and filled with the required contents. The outer shell of the blister held the non-lethal infectious agents. The inner, the pure terror weapons. If the Timariot of the mission required them, the captain would release them... and some lucky planet would learn that the Polity didn't play fair. Terror was a tool, and when it came to Reconnect missions, no tool was left behind.

On the whole, Vasco thought it a pretty smart policy. Hard-nosed, for sure. Fair? If everything went wrong, you'd be stuck a thousand years from home. The Long Drop drive was only a two-way trip if you could replicate the math to follow the same hole back you came in. If you couldn't do that, you could still go home but relativity would have its say. Depending on the length of the drop, a thousand years might pass before you returned...or more. Every soldier knew the risk, as did the Polity.

No backup for possibly years, and no idea what you would face when you announced your intentions to a new planet? The Polity sent Reconnect missions to succeed, not fail. The purpose was the highest goal in the Polity, the ultimate mission: Reach out to the scattered and lost remnants of Humanity and bring them back into the fold. And in two thousand years, not one mission had failed. The bio-warfare blister was one reason, but only one. It was really only a minuscule part of the ship. Tatar-class ships were the biggest things humans had ever created, and their only purpose was to make a world submit to the heel of the Polity. One ship to conquer one system.

Vasco watched the big ship grow in the viewport. The *Alexi* would be his home for at least the next two years. Like every other drop he'd been on. Not every system was two years away by Long Drop drive, but the Polity had planned the expansion out to be as regular as possible, to keep the tightest connection to the once-a-decade Tech updates. So the drops Vasco had been on tended to be two years out and back, and it wasn't unusual.

He should be able to disembark after the fight to orbit, if one happened. The Gyrenes—the Polity's fighters—always had a solid betting pool going about what kind of welcome to expect when they reached the world they were meant to Reconnect, but as often as not, there was no winner.

Sometimes Unconnected worlds regressed right out of spaceflight, either from some belief system or, more normally, because the populace had fallen to war or other focus and lost the economy or drive to maintain a space presence. Sometimes they regressed further, into complete barbarity. Sometimes a Tatar arrived and slid into orbit, sending landings without a touch of resistance or recognition. Sometimes.

Vasco had made the Long Drop twice, and both times, they'd seen hard fights to get to orbit. The first had been so bad the Timariot had dropped the gloves for real and had dropped rocks on the planet until only the small cities were left. Wasteful, but it had made Vasco's job easier. Almost no one was left to fight by the time the Gyrenes made landfall. No Timar—the planet by default always became the governed property of the Timariot—of value left though. The Timariot had pretty much had to build up the planet from scratch, which put him in huge debt to the follow-up forces. But at least the world was Reconnected to the Polity, her future children safe in the arms of New Ottoman Empire.

Vasco's second Long Drop had been a little better. The Unconnected had held out until the orbitals were taken, and then they called it quits. Vasco's job at that point had been a few years of cleaning up insurgents and bitter holdouts. Hard work, but he'd been able to show his worth and earn good shares. He could have stayed and settled down on a nice claim, but... there was still a universe to see. That voice inside still called him on. He still had that need to move forward.

So there he was, watching another Tatar loom, wondering if he would come back in ten years or twenty. Vasco was pretty sure he'd come back to Francisco. It was the closest to home he'd ever felt. Eventually he'd be back. Maybe not too long. He'd heard of drops that had brought troops home after just five years. Rumors, really, but still. Possible.

Or maybe this would be one of those screwed-up missions with a botched return tunnel. It hadn't happened in a few hundred years, but every Gyrene wondered if he'd come back from a ten- or twenty-year mission to find a thousand years or more had passed.

Vasco found he wasn't really watching the *Alexi*'s approach all that much. The new kids would be. The veterans were mostly watching the new kids. Or mentally reviewing old mission habits as they found them kicking back into gear. Vasco was glancing out the port every few minutes while playing a game on his Pet, trying to figure out how much time he had before docking.

The hours passed. An old friend had dropped by for a bit but moved on to catch up with other companions. A little wistfully, Vasco watched her go. It wasn't that he was an outsider; it was that he always felt like an outsider. Gyrenes came from all the worlds of the Polity, from all the myriad races and cultures, and once down the drop, they mostly tended to stay, to try to make the new world home. Vasco had as well, but somewhere deep in him was the longing for another home—an unknown one. Maybe it was because of his birth.

His hand ached for his sword. Steel was such a comfort. No matter what the world brought him, at least when he had a sword in hand, Vasco felt he could handle it all. Maybe his home was in the blade. He felt a little lurch at the thought of what he had given up. His school! So much work and effort to create the best school on Francisco. Such glorious students! But he knew they were in good hands, just as he knew his place to be was elsewhere.

Neruda came for him after turn-around, as the shuttle flipped end over end and started to brake as it approached the *Alexi*. Vasco had pointedly not been looking for her since he'd arrived on the pinnace. His oldest friend had been the one who talked him into signing up for one more Long Drop. She'd made some hints about the location of the drop. Probably too many. It was no secret that the *Alexi* was being built in the system, obviously. Tatar-class ships built at the edge of the Polity sucked in resources from every nearby system, and were only built when a mission was planned. But as a matter of policy, almost no one knew what the next Timar mission was going to be. You really didn't want a system knowing in advance it was about to be forced into becoming a highly taxed and regulated province. That didn't always go over well. But it was the only way to unite humanity back together into a cohesive whole.

Vasco had never known Neruda to be any good with secrets. The real kicker, months before, had been her subtle brag about an actual Laconian being along for the long drop. The same day he'd first seen the Valkyrie. It had been a momentous day for many reasons. At the time he'd thought he was wrapping up his old life, and finally settling down.

He had just promoted his top two students to their overdue status as masters and turned his school over to them. He planned to retire, but he didn't really have a retirement plan. He was still too young to do nothing, though. But he was ready to put himself to the wind again, and this time maybe settle somewhere. Then Neruda came by, her timing almost coincidental, and asked Vasco to join her for a private meeting.

"They've put up a call for veterans this drop," Neruda had said. "Something's going on this time. This one's special."

"Special? Aren't they all?" Vasco had replied.

"It's not just rumors. I've seen the first call up list of troops. The new meat is all top notch. The Timariot had his pick, and he has cherry-picked the absolute best. Top of every class. He even skimmed out an entire shipload's worth of Samarkand-qualified."

"Jesus!" Vasco was surprised. Samarkand Station was the major Polity special-ops training facility. The Polity was rich in material, but not in trained personnel. A few hundred systems were still classified as In Transit, which meant there was a real need for those troops.

"Probably recruited him too. I have to admit, the recruitment bonus being offered…"

"Uh huh. So this isn't just a friendly visit?"

"Hey, I would have made the trip down the well just to see you, you know that. But if I could get the Polity to cover my fare, why not? They asked about you. The Timariot's got a thing about martial arts. He's heard about you. Had his adjutant chat with me."

Vasco snorted. "Bullshit. My rep's not that good. I've seen my file."

"Better than you think, apparently. Only five guys ahead of you on their list. None of them were available."

"Five! There are at least two dozen better than me, and that's just the guys I've met."

"I wondered about that. Apparently the adjutant was in the mood to brag. The Alexi has been fitted with a Helot, and a Laconian adviser came along for the install. She's going to be catching a ride back on the Long Drop. The Helot made the list. According to its needs, you're number five."

"A Laconian! Christ, I thought they never left their world. I've heard they aren't even human…"

"I used to think so too, but she's as human as us. Not bad looking either. I guess that's what we get for listening to folk tales."

"You met her?" Vasco was shocked. Laconians were known for being inaccessible, and the Helots—their special computers—were lusted after across the Polity. Only the Laconions had the knack of producing the sophisticated AI that drove those computers. The original Laconian colony was still the farthest point in human space. They'd gone that far on purpose. It was only a hundred years or so ago that they'd made themselves known again, offering their computers to the Polity. An exception to the Tech updates had been made, but only for Tatar ships and the densely populated core government worlds.

"She came down the well with me. I invited her to come along and meet you, but she had some things to do. She's human. Kinda formal, but not bad. Some kind of officer."

"Neruda, you ever wonder why you never got a security clearance?"

She snickered. "Not really. Never could be bothered to watch my tongue. I hate secrets. What I let loose this time?"

"About the only thing we know about Laconia is roughly

where it is. If she's catching a ride back… we're gonna unify the Sami, aren't we?"

"Got it in one. Not sure it's that much a secret. Aren't a lot of colonies left, are there?"

"Nope. Samis, huh? All right. I'm in."

And here he was, on his way to *Alexi* a few short months later. He shook his head a little to put the memories back where they belonged.

"All caught up?" Neruda asked as she approached Vasco. "I figured you'd like a little time down here with the proles, but you know your shiny new Evocati rank has its perks. You should be up in officer country."

"I'm not sure I can breathe the air up there. Don't I need special breathing gear for the rare air?"

"Usually. I'm pretty sure you don't have enough brain cells left to worry about losing though. You should be fine. The mess is stocked with Francisco ales."

"After you, old lady."

"Fine, but you're buying…"

They had just settled themselves into the officer lounge and ordered their first drink when they were interrupted. Vasco was trying to fight the awkwardness he was feeling. He had the same rank as before, Centurion, but coming back as an Evocati Centurion, a soldier recruited out of retirement for their expertise, meant he was now seen as an officer of enough rank for special privileges. He would have never come to this lounge had Neruda not come and pulled him in. But now that he was here, he meant to enjoy the privilege. He had seen the woman approaching as she entered the lounge from the other side.

She was a tall woman who looked thin at first glance. As she moved down the narrow aisle, Vasco saw she wasn't actually so thin; she just had very broad shoulders. Her uniform accented the look, being mostly plain black, except for the shoulder flash Vasco recognized. She was the woman he had noticed outside his school.

Neruda got up from her seat. "Sigma! Good to see you again. I hope your visit planetside was pleasant?"

"My duties were fulfilled." She was looking at Vasco.

"Great!' Neruda continued. "May I present my friend, Vasco al Madina del Goya? He—"

"Is the instructor we requested," Sigma interrupted. "Centurion del Goya. I am pleased to meet you. I am Walkure Sigma." She held out her hand for Vasco to shake.

Her grip was interesting. Her skin was dry and tough, but oddly smooth. Vasco had expected calluses. She carried herself like a martial artist, but there were none of the tell-tale marks. He had the impression she was holding back much of her strength as well. Vasco, on a whim, decided to test her. He squeezed back a little harder, as a warning, then put all his strength into it.

Vasco had a formidable grip. Years of fencing with all sorts of weapons had added a lot to his strength, but he had been born with more strength than most men. He'd broken the hands of hard men with this trick before. He was confident he could stop before breaking her bones though. He'd developed better control and sensitivity as he'd gotten older.

She didn't react at all. Her hand didn't grip harder or try to pull back. She kept a neutral grip and smiled politely at Vasco. Vasco felt as though he were trying to squeeze a metal statue. Her hand didn't give one hair.

"You are very strong, Centurion. That's why we chose you," she said.

Vasco released her hand, curious. "Chose me? Eventually, you mean. I know there were five others ahead of me."

"No. That was a ruse. You were chosen because you were born on a Creche world. We wished to see what you had become."

Vasco was dumbfounded. He felt himself falling back into his chair in shock.

No one knew his background. The Polity had written the Creche worlds out of its history. Five Tatars had been lost in the attempted unification of Creche worlds, and those worlds were now little more than radioactive wastelands. It wasn't a historical tidbit the Polity wanted as part of its legacy.

During the time of separation, the Creche had become masters of genetic engineering. The things they had done were abominable. Vasco had only been a baby when the last surviving nursery had been liberated. Of his entire world, only Vasco and a few dozen other babies had made it off the surface before final quarantine.

He and his siblings had been scattered throughout the Polity. They'd been fostered, given a chance to be raised as normal children. It was a gift Vasco would be forever grateful to the Polity for. But it was also a secret. The foster parents knew—they had to, in case of genetic triggers buried in the children—and the children were told when they were old enough to understand, so they could hide their differences and fit in. But the official record showed them as nothing other than normal kids. Normal people. The Creche worlds were unknown now.

Vasco glanced at Neruda, but his friend was looking on with a grin, amused at the sudden turning of tables on her friend. Vasco gave himself a little shake to gather his wits. Another of Neruda's games, maybe? She might have told Sigma his secret. Probably let it slip in her usual loose-tongued fashion.

But he knew how to turn the tables back. Any fencing master worth his salt knew how to find his opponent's deeper strategy, the hidden motivation behind the tactics, and exploit it for his own gain. Neruda wanted to one-up Vasco, as usual. Their friendship was built on the constant competition. Best to deal with it directly, Vasco decided.

"How did you know that?" he asked Sigma. And then it came to him. The uniform was unfamiliar, and the Polity prized standardization. He'd assumed she was wearing some sort of corporate uniform and was some sort of technical specialist on hire to complete work on the Alexi. Civilian contractors were known to ape military dress to fit in a little better. It often had the opposite effect, but Walkure Sigma seemed to pull it off naturally. Unless her pose and habits meant she was from a different culture. Which in the Polity means she was either Sami, or..."You're the Laconian, aren't you?" he said.

"Yes, I am. The Helot has access to almost all Polity records. I am the installer and trainer of the Helot. Timariot Smith asked me to help him crew his Timar, as a calibration exercise."

That made sense to Vasco. Helots were rare and extremely powerful AI's. The rumor was that they needed to spend time getting to know their chief operator's thought patterns in order to function at their utmost. Their main power and use came in their ability to take complex data and reduce it to simple metaphors, so humans could make swift decisions. Crewing the more than hundred thousand members of a Tatar-class ship would be a worthy exercise.

Something made Vasco feel uneasy about this line of discussion though. When he was younger, he felt only anger toward his creators. But as he got older, he had developed a curiosity about the Creche. The Laconian, being out of the Polity, might know more about Vasco's home world. It wasn't something he was comfortable talking about in front of Neruda though, so he decided to change the subject.

"I don't know anything about Laconia," Vasco said. "Until now I didn't even know if you were human or alien. I gather from your uniform you have a military."

"We do, of a sort. I am a Walkure, an officer. It's an observer rank though, not a combat position. You could think of me as a sort of civilian contractor. After the Helot is calibrated, I will be acting as an observer for your Unification efforts on Rumi."

"Rumi? Is that where we are going?" he asked.

"Yes, Rumi is the Sami homeworld, in the Anubis system. The Sami are our agents for the sale of Helots," Sigma answered.

Vasco frowned. "How do you feel about them becoming unified with the Polity? It might affect your trade relations. No more middlemen?"

"The Sami have been working with the Laconians since our mutual foundings. We are very interested in observing the process of unification. Aside from my journey here, this will be the first chance Laconia will have to see and understand what the Polity really is, and what it offers in Unification."

Fair enough, thought Vasco. Trying to avoid the real question. Time to be more direct. "Do you think the Sami will fight us? Or will they accept unification?"

"Do worlds often accept unification?" she replied. Toneless. No change in her facial expression at all. Nothing there to read.

Vasco found himself wondering if she fenced. "Depends. The more backward worlds do, sure. Hard to say no to free technology, medical care, education, and industrial infrastructure. Some worlds don't see the benefits though. They'd rather their children suffer for their 'freedom.'"

"By your standards, the Sami are backward. They don't have an interest in technology or industry the way you do," Sigma said.

"Honestly, I don't know much about them," Vasco said. "I know we buy Helots from them. Hell, all we know about Laconia is that you guys make the Helots."

"We do. The Helots run our world. They take care of everything and leave us free to pursue our leisure in the way we prefer. The Sami have no use for Helots but are not as private as we are. They are willing to act as agents for a sizable commission," she said.

"I can imagine," Vasco said. "I've heard a Helot costs as much as three Tatars!"

"That is about your cost, yes." She added a short nod. "They are far superior to your own AI though."

Their conversation was halted by the steward walking down the aisle and making sure everyone was strapped in for final approach to the *Alexi* and docking. Neruda gave up her seat to the Laconian in order to deal with some message that required her attention. Sigma sat silently for the remainder of the flight, staring ahead and not responding to any further questions.

Vasco was starting to wonder if he was right to think Laconians weren't human. And Neruda was up to something.

She'd been silent the entire conversation, but Vasco had recognized her subtle shifts of attention. Neruda was usually the talkative one, but she'd been the quiet watcher in Vasco and Sigma's brief conversation. Something had changed in his old friend.

-Rumi, Anubis System

Nils woke in time to see the Weta clamber up the windowsill. The insect stretched its foreclaws down inside the window. There was no moonlight for Nils to see the creature's grey carapace and sightless face by. The cat-sized, mantis-like bug with a featureless mannequin head was just an angular silhouette. Up the windowsill it had come, and down the wall outside it turned to go.

It was a quiet companion to his lonely night, but it was still a presence. Nils resigned himself to being awake. He had no idea what time it was, but it was obviously time to be up.

The bed was warm, but the air coming in through the open window had a bit of a chill to it. Not much—just enough for his animal mind to grumble about hibernating. The floor was chilly on his feet too. The only sound was the faint whisper of wind.

There was no one else in the house to disturb. Still, he moved with care as he shambled outside, pulling on his threadbare bathrobe. He moved around the tiled walk, out to the back where the garden was and where the Weta had come to sit.

He stopped in the middle of the garden and rolled his head around on his big neck. His belly grumbled.

The air was still.

He turned to look at the Weta, and it seemed to be looking at him. That was impossible, of course, but also the only possibility.

It was time to Listen, and Nils did.

The world was still.

He was still.

Something was missing.

He looked up into the sky.

A star was missing, only it was a star that wasn't there yet.

It was a yet-to-be star, and it was missing. It was coming. A star was coming. There was an empty hole in the sky waiting for it.

Nils sighed. He turned to look at the Weta, but it was already climbing up and over the wall, off to wherever the Weta went. He thought about going back to sleep. Some part of him truly wanted to go back to sleep and forget. But he was a Listener, and he had work to do before he could fall asleep.

And he would never forget. Not even death would free him from remembering.

By dawn, his horse was saddled, all his meager belongings packed into the saddle bags. The house had served him well the last few years. He'd miss it, but there was always the next one. The morning sky was turning fresh and warm and full of life.

He set off to spread his message.

Chapter Two: The One Who Calls Forth

Vasco was mildly surprised on arrival at *Alexi*. The pinnace landed in one of the boat bays, not on a utility dock as Vasco had expected. The pinnace crew were all straightening their uniforms as they cracked the seals and opened the VIP unloading doors. Neruda motioned Vasco and Sigma up while the rest of the passengers conspicuously stayed seated.

Following Neruda, Vasco drifted from handhold to handhold. It had been years since he'd been in zero-g, but he'd never forgotten the first ripping wrench on his shoulder when he'd built up too much momentum and thoughtlessly grabbed a handhold. Gravity may be gone, but mass wasn't. He'd worry less when he was fitted for ship's armor, but that was probably days away.

After Vasco, Neruda, and Sigma drifted up to debark, the pinnace crew clipped ship slippers on them. The combination of magnets and Velcro would help keep them oriented when they needed to be. Neruda was first out, then Sigma, and Vasco followed… and nearly flew off into the boat bay when he saw not only a landing party waiting for them, but also the Timariot himself.

Timariot Emil Smith was a bear of a man, and a legend. This would be his eighth Long Drop. Most Timariots made one drop. Eight drops was an incredible feat of endurance if nothing else, considering a Timariot could expect to be committed to a drop for ten years at a minimum.

More incredible when you considered that a Timariot's pay for a Long Drop was effective lordship over the newly unified planet. Timariot Smith had been planetary governor of seven worlds. He probably had enough income from his estates to purchase his own Tatar. And he was waiting to greet them on his ship.

Vasco resisted the urge to try to reverse course and head back into the pinnace. They'd obviously been mistaken for another party. Two centurions, even if one of them was an Evocati, did not rate a landing with the Timariot. He and Neruda would be expected to report to a tribune, and a particularly eager one might want to meet them on disembarkation. Unless it was the Laconian the Timariot was there to meet, they'd just blundered ahead of someone important.

"Walkure Sigma!" the Timariot said, giving a short bow and a broad smile. "Welcome back aboard. Your Helot has been missing your skill at chess. I fear I've only bored her."

"Timariot, it's not possible to bore her. I know she loves the distraction of chess, and if she's winning, it's only because she believes you are capable of improvement. Worry when you win— that's when she's letting you," Sigma said. Vasco could have sworn she almost smiled.

"Ha! Laconic Laconian my Baltic ass!" the big man said.

Obviously the Timariot had formed a friendship with Sigma during the Helot installation. That meant this was an informal greeting. Now that he had a moment to focus, Vasco could see the Timariot had only brought minimal staff. It was a friendly greeting party, and Vasco could relax. Thanks to his father, he'd been raised with a certain amount of comfort in high society. He could play the game.

"That's flattery if I've ever heard it," the Timariot continued. "I see you've brought my fencing master on board. Maestro al Madina del Goya, it's a pleasure to finally meet you!"

He held out a great paw for Vasco to shake. Vasco swiftly masked his surprise while putting on a pleasant smile. Apparently

Neruda had not been kidding when she'd told Vasco the Timariot was an eager student of the sword. Vasco also recognized the look in the Timariot's eyes. He was testing Vasco already. As Vasco reached out his hand, the Timariot's face was all smiles, wrapped in a gregarious shroud. But the eyes were the eyes of, if not a predator, a serious competitor. Some men might have been thrown off by such a mighty personage acting so down to earth, but Vasco knew the tactic. Disarm before the tanks move in…

"It's a pleasure to meet you as well, Timariot Smith. I look forward to serving under you," Vasco said.

"Ho! I'm going to make you earn every penny of your Evocati pay, don't worry about that. I've already scheduled our private sessions. Have you finished that interpretation of Marozzo yet?" the Timariot replied.

Vasco's eyebrows rose. If the Timariot knew about that, then he was no dabbler. Vasco had been talking about his work with only a few select maestros, and they were all tight-lipped. "Not yet. I've had to revise some of my thoughts. I managed to get a new set of swords made by a local bladesmith who specializes in old earth designs. The balance shift suggests some things I'll have to play with."

"Excellent!" he replied. "I will see you tomorrow morning! Have you had a chance to meet Centurion Neruda Always, my intelligence Primus?"

Vasco was a little immune to shock at this point, which was a good thing. It appeared he had been played by his old friend.

Neruda was hardly even looking smug. Intel Primus? On a mission like this, that put Neruda right at the top of the food chain. Neruda must have been busy in the years since they had last spoken. And she'd apparently been hiding much of herself even when she and Vasco had been inseparable friends.

"We've served together previously, Timariot," Neruda said. "Catching up with Centurion Vasco was actually one of my other goals down the well."

"Excellent! I don't suppose you fence as well, Always? This might be an excellent voyage!"

Vasco was starting to think it certainly *would* be an interesting voyage.

The Gyrene was already too far away to hear Vasco. Corporal Cave was a pleasant and buxom woman at first glance, and Vasco was looking forward to working with her. If he could ever catch up to her.

She'd obviously been onboard long enough to get used to the lack of gravity. Vasco might have thought she was an old hand, except for the lack of service marks on her ship's armor. The armor itself hadn't changed since Vasco had last worn a set. No surprise—the next Tech wasn't due for another few years. It was still the same sleek arrangement of rigid panels and discrete rods and cords.

Ship's armor was designed to keep a body safe in space, in or out of combat. It provided a good bit of impact resistance through rigid materials and impact gels, but its main purpose was to be a solid exoskeleton. Combat ships had to pull high g's for a long period of time. The limiting factor for spaceships was always the humans inside. You could only maneuver, accelerate, and decelerate so much without turning the humans inside into decorative interior paint.

The Polity wanted as much performance as possible. A combat ship was rated for 8gs of acceleration for up to three months before overhaul. The only way for a human to survive that and still function was to have better bones, skin, and internal organs than they were born with. Barring a genetic redesign, which was as likely as artificial gravity, the exoskeleton was the way to go.

Crew and Gyrenes had it the worst. Passengers and non-essential crew could get by with a plain suit of tight-fitting armor and minimal movement. But for those who had to function and survive under high-g? They'd start by shaving all the hair off their bodies. It would regrow no matter how much depilatory you applied, but you had to make do. Once you shaved off all your hair, you'd break out the tape.

A heavy mylar-style tape was tightly applied to the skin. Gyrenes were taught the universal pattern, but most learned to adjust it to their own body. The tough tape would act as support to the ligaments. Every major ligament in the body had some exterior tape backup. Extra tape to hold the tape in place. It took real toughness to endure having tape stuck to you for months at a time.

The tape acted as the first layer of support for the armor. It restricted your movements somewhat, but it let you do a lot more and endure a lot more. Vasco had once worked with a special forces group that had undergone surgical modification. The only bit he had been cleared to know about was the most obvious physical one.

Most of the ligament insertion points in their bodies had been reinforced with steel pins buried into the bone. They had used some sort of heavy canvas strapping instead of tape. It clipped into the steel pins. Attaching those straps took enough force that Vasco knew the bones themselves had to have some reinforcement as well. Spinal attachments too... straps across the belly. The special forces troops were expected to put up with killer gs.

For everyone else, just the tape. After the tape came the armor. It was custom fitted to everyone from generic size sets. Hydraulic and pneumatic pistons, joint protection, control equipment, the works, all added on after. In space, it wasn't needed for zero-g, but it was convenient once you got used to it. Under high-g, the armor meant you could move and live almost like normal. Your guts knew different, but you got used to that. Space wasn't for everyone.

If used on a planet's surface, the armor would triple your strength and make you almost bulletproof. Using it in ground combat would be a Gyrene's dream, except it was far too complex and sensitive to function outside of the sterile atmosphere of a spaceship. Dirt and dust would shut down the joints within a few days... and the suits were expensive enough that even the Polity balked at using them up that fast.

Thus, they were restricted to ship use only. Special ops used them for groundwork from time to time, but they always had spare armor. Vasco had heard rumors that advanced suits for ground use were due in the next Tech, but he wouldn't bet on it. One of the Polity's foundational principles was slow, predictable, and non-disruptive introduction of new technology. Powered ground armor didn't fit the pattern.

Cave's armor was either brand new or she'd never had to use it in earnest. It still had some packing grease on it. Grease that would collect every random bit of dust and dirt, letting that grime work its way into the joints—or worse, under the armor and next to the skin. Under acceleration, dust became pinpricks of pressure that rapidly turned your armor into a horrible sandpaper trap.

Bad training, inexperience, or laziness. It didn't stop her from moving down the corridor as if she had been born in the suit though. Vasco picked up his pace as best he could, but he couldn't keep up with her. She was bouncing down the ship like a bowling ball.

Well, Vasco thought, time to teach the pup a lesson. Enthusiasm was okay, but there was no excuse for not paying attention. And absolutely no excuse for intentionally showing up a senior officer, if that was what she was doing. A less experienced officer might have tried to shout her down, or at least rehearsed a rage-filled explosion to put her in her place. Vasco was going to be working with Cave though, so it was time to use an old trick.

Vasco had made Centurion at the end of his first Long Drop. Despite his title on this drop, he wasn't expecting to be in any kind of command. As far as he knew, he wouldn't even see real combat. Again. The billet had been for a senior combat instructor, not an assault company captain. But it was still good policy to act as if he would be in command of combat troops. He always started by building trust and letting the troops make small mistakes. At the start anyway.

He slowed his pace, letting Cave rocket out of sight. She'd

eventually figure out she'd left her charge behind and come back and look. Probably at great haste, imagining the trouble she'd get in. Probably already rehearsing the barracks bitching she'd do and gloating about the sympathy she'd get. Maybe. Or maybe Vasco was being terribly unfair to her, and she was just young and excited. Either way, he'd find out when she came back and found him missing.

It had been years since he'd been on a Tatar, but the *Alexi* had the same Tech as his last ship—so there should be a muster station back one turn and down the next corridor. Vasco turned back to go find out. Sure enough, there was. The clean and empty muster station was a perfect place to clip up for a minute and orient himself. In the usual spot, he pushed off and grabbed the handles on the map console. It lit up with the local map. He zoomed out for perspective.

He'd forgotten how immense the damn ships were. The interior layout was color coded to match the walls. The center of each section was pure color, gently shading toward the color of the next section you were heading for. Grey was for hull. He was in a dark grey section, heading for the white of the Ring. About a half kilometer to go before he was in mostly white.

The internal layout was the same. Kilometer-wide Ring in the front quarter. Forward of that was the Crypt, where most of the crew would hibernate during the two-year Pod space trip. Forward of that, all the way to the bow, was the Landing zone. Gyrene territory. The big Orion landers, collapsed dirigibles, ground combat vehicles... an entire invasion package. Back of the Ring, System zone. Combat space patrol. Cruisers and frigates, resupply ships, and the central weapon stores for the *Alexi*'s space weapons. Farther back were the gigantic donuts of the reactors, the Pod drive, and the drive plate. A full third of the inner ship was fuel: reactor mass or drive charges.

And that was just the map of the inner ship. The outer hull contained all the fun stuff and was armor and radiator all in one. It was also crammed to the gills with the extra goodies that might be needed but either didn't need protection or nobody wanted in the ship. Most of what was out there was unlabeled, and Vasco knew he'd sleep better if he pretended it was nothing but unused storage space.

"Centurion?" Relief mixed with frustration but stayed well contained. Cave had taken less time to find him than he had expected.

"Ah! Corporal Cave! My apologies, I wandered off. It's been some years since I've been on a Tatar, and I got lost in reverie. My last drop was the *Madonna*," Vasco said.

"The *Madonna*! You were on the Alois drop?" Cave asked.

"I was. I was just checking... this line here, not far from here, see this?" he asked, pointing at an area about a hundred meters behind where they stood.

Corporal Cave nodded, glancing back up the corridor. Vasco thought she was doing a good job of not looking too anxious to get moving again. He could almost hear the muttering in her head about doddering old men.

"This is where I was stationed when they fired their main laser banks. The mirrors put that beam right here. Cut the *Madonna* in half. I was following my drop team at the time. They just happened to be in the wrong place at the wrong time. I watched them evaporate in front of me," he said, his voice flattening against his will. He was remembering as if it were happening all over again.

Bouncing down the ship under 3gs of acceleration, alarms everywhere, his drop team had been tasked for ship-to-ship action. Their assigned frigate was on the hull for only ten more minutes before it was back out into the fray. They could easily make it to the dock before launch, but they were eager to get into the fight. Faster... they had to get there faster. Vasco dimly recalled urging everyone to pick up the pace.

The Alois had made great use of their single gas giant and dense asteroid belt. They had a solid infrastructure in place—mass drivers, refineries, multiple space habitats, and about a million small crafts. They weren't a system that wanted to be rooted to a planet. To them, gravity was the tides and islands in space caused by the dance of the planets, not a background constant.

Unification had come hard to the Alois.

There was an Alois woman Vasco remembered so very well... tall and willowy, she'd never felt gravity. He'd almost loved her, but she was Alois to the core. One day she'd just kissed his cheek, smiled, and moved on without explanation or care. A fickle people.

They had no compunctions about turning their industrial backbone into weapons.

It was so quick. The corridor had just blended from orange into solid grey. At the hull, only two minutes from the frigate. Vasco had paused for the slightest second. A last-minute order came in. He slowed long enough to acknowledge...

The beam was bright and soundless. At least in his memory. It was too quick for screams—that was the merciful part. One second his teammates hurried down the corridor, the next second there was no corridor. He had the afterimage of Cordoba, his sysop, seeming to smear into nothingness. Instead of the jackleg turn to the frigate, Vasco found himself staring across a twenty-meter gap into the astonished face of an armored sailor.

He couldn't stop moving. He'd sailed across the gap. In retrospect, he'd been screaming. At the time, it had seemed silent. Vasco was flying through space, between what had been one ship and was now two.

The sailor had no arms anymore. Just red stumps, not so neatly cauterized, pointing toward Vasco. Vasco had slammed into him, knocking them both over. Even with ship's armor, at 3gs acceleration, it was the last thing Vasco remembered for a while. He never found out who the sailor was.

"It was nasty surprise," he continued, coming back to himself. "But it didn't stop us. That's why the particle beams are where they are, between the reactors. They got their shot off, then it was our turn."

He was silent for a moment. Whatever else he was in life, Vasco wasn't immune to ghosts. Cave waited quietly.

"The point man on my drop team was a Rod Cave. Any relation?" he asked.

"No, Centurion. Not that I know of."

"Ah. Well, he was a hell of a Gyrene. Just atoms now, spreading through Alois. Try not to get too far ahead of me again, hm?"

"No, Centurion! I won't."

"Let's continue, shall we? I'm looking forward to reviewing my class schedule."

Vasco tried not to smile as Cave moved on at a more normal pace. There were probably more subtle ways to let her know he wasn't a fool. If she hadn't figured out yet that centurions weren't like other officers, she might have a streak of fool going on herself.

He remembered being a fool like that, back in his first drop. Polity training was good… damn good. You came out of it feeling as though you could single-handedly conquer a world. With the right resources, you almost could. That kind of confidence had a tendency to make you think everyone who hadn't—immediately, in front of you—conquered the world had to be an idiot. Especially if they were older. God knew you were ready to overcome any odds and hold the stars, so if you'd dared to get old and didn't hold all the stars in your hand? Must be something wrong with you.

Heady days. They'd been burned out of Vasco with a steady stream of dead friends. He'd been slotted up the command brackets early. He'd made the mistake of showing proficiency in hacking and been bounced into a Tactical Sysop role for what should have been his first combat drop. The Long Drop itself hadn't been too bad, not like Alois, but there had been good shooting to be had.

Instead, Vasco had had the joy of sucking up all his fears and hearing artillery bounce around and blow up his friends while he was safe in the bunker, trying to get the bad guys to hit their own forces. He'd been safe, but he'd been ready to run out into that fire and fight, maybe even die, with his friends. He'd been ready, but he'd stuck to his job. He'd wanted to charge out there and show that he could overcome that clenching, overriding fear... fear so powerful that his stomach seemed to vanish, leaving him a hollow, shaking spine and little else.

More than anything, Vasco had wanted to move to quiet that whisper of "coward" in the back of his mind. But orders were orders, and every key stroke he typed was saving a life, saving a friend, and striking back far more surely than they were. He'd managed to not only penetrate the enemy's artillery net, but also to find a backdoor into the command group. He'd rooted their main server and found an active login to the municipal network.

In twenty minutes of work, he'd won their battle. It took the enemy over a month to catch all the damage Vasco had done to the city infrastructure. It had been a significant blow and helped end the war. He had the medal to show for it.

But when it was over and he ran out to help the wounded, he still felt like a coward. He swore to himself that he would prove himself in the next battle. He'd get someone else to man the signals station... but he got bumped up, shuffled over to other duties, and his chance never came. The need to prove himself burned hot enough in Vasco that he'd signed up for his next Long Drop almost immediately.

He'd thought, over the years, that he was over that kind of thing. But as he watched Cave moving down the corridors and remembered another Cave smearing out of existence in a blast of light... he knew why he was back again.

"Extortion," the junior centurion said. "I'll take my two spice." She reached across the table and nimbly plucked two of the stylized tokens from the miffed-looking Triari. The junior centurion could have called Autonomy, which blocked the Extortion card, but the look on the Triari's face clearly showed he wasn't holding that card.

Not that it would matter. Golpe Spicio was a game that required bluff and deduction. There were only six kinds of cards in the deck, and each player got two cards per hand. Each card gave you certain powers in the game, either allowing you to take an action or block someone else's action. It was a game of diplomacy and influence. You lost when everyone knew what your hand was and used some of their actions to force you to reveal your cards.

Vasco knew the junior centurion was bluffing. There were only three extortion cards in the deck, and he had two of them. The third one was sitting face up in front of the grumpy Triari, who was trying to play the game straight. Vasco had been pretending to hold an Assassin and Protection, and so far, had only been forced to bluff protection once. The bluff had gone uncalled, which might mean the other player wanted people to think she maybe didn't have the Assassin she did have... or maybe she wanted everyone to think she did when she didn't. It wasn't a game for simple people.

Vasco figured the junior centurion was sitting on Stockpile and Protection, which was a damn fine hand. She'd only been playing Extortion so far, and Vasco was waiting for her to try it on him so he could call it. He'd be out an Extortion, but he'd get to exchange for a new card which would just get him a better hand... at the cost of taking out the junior centurion's much better hand. Just a win all around.

Which was probably why the junior centurion had been avoiding working Vasco over for most of the game.

Or not. Vasco hadn't played Golpe since his last drop. He tended to overthink games, and the headache creeping up was reminding him of the consequences of trying to be cleverer than he was. Still, getting back into the company of Gyrenes was good. The military wing of the Polity was sometimes seen as a home for the more simpleminded, and that was somewhat true. Cannon fodder was still useful, but even with a vessel the size of a Tatar to ship them, the truly simple were far too expensive to ship across the stars.

Everyone had to hold their own and then some on a Long Drop. Even the dullest troop was someone with a flair for self-sufficiency. You just had to dig to find it sometimes.

Chapter Three: The Hidden

The next time Vasco saw Neruda was at the end of a fencing class for Gyrenes.

Gyrenes were quite proud of their dress sabres, but a Gyrene hadn't ranked in a Decan championship in almost a hundred years. Timariot Smith took that as a personal affront and had encouraged Vasco to work with the *Alexi*'s coaches to change that.

Vasco had started by having the coaches bring their top students in for a small tournament. One at a time, all the students against Vasco. He'd wiped the floor with each of them.

He didn't bother to fence the coaches, but they'd gotten the message. They had all tried to book private lessons with him, but there wasn't time in the last month and a bit before the drop, and their sleep. He'd arranged a once-a-week group session for them in the meantime.

So far, they'd proven to be a driven group of students. He had hopes for a few of them, and the rest would be vastly improved coaches by the end of the voyage. It would be a shame the Polity wasn't trying to unify the Sami at sabre point!

Neruda was with Sigma, watching the tail end of the class, and they were now chatting. Neruda was making fencing motions with her hands.

Vasco decided it was time for a little payback. "Primus Always! Let's see if you've remembered anything from your old training sessions!"

He tossed his blunt training sabre to Neruda and turned to look for another. A grinning Gyrene offered Vasco one. The students had stopped their cooldown to watch the new entertainment. It was bound to be a good show. They'd either see the unbeaten instructor upset or see one of the highest ranked officers on the ship lose. They all looked at Vasco as if they had already placed bets.

Neruda looked amused as she grabbed the sabre out of the air. The ship's engines weren't due to be online for another day and the gym was in the Ring, the spinning section of the *Alexi*, so no one wore ship's armor. Vasco seemed to have lost his old loathing for the centrifuge and had not only moved his quarters to the Ring, but also hadn't been out in zero-g since the day he'd arrived. Neruda had been all over the ship, but she must have stripped out of her armor for a workout.

"I've kept up my training." Neruda said. "Do you want to go by the old rules? Or are you too old for that now?"

"Ha! I think, old lady, that I've aged enough to pay you back for your trickery!"

Neruda replied with a wicked grin, "I never said what my job was. You made an assumption! Still angry about that, eh?"

"Not angry, no, but I can't let you think you can get away with that sort of thing. I'd hate it if you had to have your armor refitted for your swollen head…"

"My head would never swell enough to match that ego of yours. I guess I'm going to have to knock you down a notch."

"My God! I think I wet myself in fear! I am so ashamed. I'll just have to make you pay for the cleaning."

"You should be used to wetting yourself by now."

Vasco was doing his damnedest not to laugh as he settled into guard far outside of Neruda's range. "Old rules" meant no rules. It was how they had learned, many years ago. Neruda had once started a match by throwing her sabre at Vasco…

"I learned from watching you learn to drink," Vasco said. "How many suits of armor did you rust out?"

"My name is Neruda Always! You killed my bladder! Prepare to die!"

Deceitful as always, Neruda waited until Vasco was actually laughing to launch her attack. She burst across the gym floor with a fleche, a running attack. It was quite good, Vasco thought. Neruda had been training.

Neruda stretched out as far as she could, ramming her sword forward in a desperate attempt to touch Vasco's chest. It was a blisteringly fast and aggressive attack that would have landed on any of the students Vasco had been training.

But Vasco was a maestro, and this was where he lived. He contemplated for a moment. He could parry, sidestep, and rap Neruda on the back with a clean cut. He could accept the attack with a close block and let the game turn into the vicious kind of infighting he and Neruda had both loved when they were younger...

Or he could show Neruda what it really meant to be a maestro.

Vasco dropped his weight and stuck his left leg out to his right. Pivoted, he shifted his weight onto his left leg, driving his buttocks toward Neruda... and scything his right feet right into Neruda's. Neruda was good—very good. She stumbled, hopped, and managed not to fall. She turned and whipped her blade up.

And stopped as she felt the cold kiss of Vasco's sabre cupping her chin. Vasco smiled at Neruda down the length of his blade.

"Best two out of three?" he asked.

"No. Good God, Vasco. No. How about a nice game of chess?"

Vasco laughed. It felt good. He'd always been better than Neruda, but he had been wondering if he was getting old. If he was, it was certainly a case of older and better.

"Might I try?" Sigma asked.

Vasco turned, surprised. Sigma already had a sabre in hand.

She wasn't in guard yet, but her grip looked confident. Practiced.

Neruda chuckled. "Go ahead, Vasco. I think I need to go change my shorts anyway."

"You've trained with sabre? I didn't think that would be the sort of thing a Laconian would do," Vasco said. From the rumors he had heard, they were a world run by computers. No crime, no war, nothing to do but laze around all day.

"We are more than our Helots, Centurion. Our leisure is expressed in many ways." She gave him a crisp, sharp salute. "We are also comfortable fencing without masks and using the 'old rules' if you prefer."

Vasco had the odd and unpleasant feeling of not being sure about this match. Everything he'd been taught about Laconians was that they were a hidden, private planet of intellectuals. They didn't even have a military as far as anyone knew. But her salute was old—a classical salute from the oldest days of sabre fencing on Earth. Vasco hadn't been actually challenged by a student in a long time.

"I think… we can do old rules. First touch or…?" He would leave it up to her. The practice sabres were blunt, but a strong cut could still split skin. A determined thrust in the right place could kill. He was laying everything on the table.

Vasco was surprised to feel his pulse hammering, and he realized that this, no matter what it might look or sound like to others, was going to be a duel. An actual duel, and he'd let her decide the conditions.

"First touch. With sharps—that's the one that matters, isn't it?" she asked. That was true enough. When facing a sharp blade in expert hands, you had to expect the lightest touch would be opening arteries. That was why Vasco always drilled his students to never be touched.

"Indeed. Shall we?" he said, saluted, and settled into guard.

This wasn't a show-off bout like the one with Neruda. Every sense was keyed up. His muscles were locked, and he felt every inch of his blade as if his nerves ran right down the steel to the tip.

Sigma stepped forward, moving like a panther. She threw back her shoulders, thrust out her chest, and extended her foot forward smoothly. Her sabre swept around from her side in a low hanging parry to guard. She inched forward, settling her hips and hands in a deep and wide guard. Vasco had never seen its like before, but he saw the threats immediately. She was no master fencer, but she clearly had some weapon training.

He dropped his right shoulder slightly. Enough to ease a forehand cut into a slight opening he saw. Her elbow was just enough out of position that her reaction would be slowed down, and he might be able to land a cut. She moved her elbow as he moved his shoulder.

She shifted her hip a little, threatening a low lunge. Vasco dropped the tip of his sabre a hair, so he could retaliate with a slip and a cut to the head. She flared out her pinkie and leaned back a bit, setting up a parry for that cut. Vasco sucked his belly in a hair so he could pull the downward cut a little short and thrust into her belly.

The students, and Neruda, saw them staring at each other in guard, unmoving except for small adjustments. No one could look away. They felt the intensity but couldn't see why neither of the fighters were moving.

Vasco and Sigma were almost sweating with the effort of the mental battle. One of them would break. One of them would move first, either as a sacrifice or to exploit an undefended weakness. Vasco's thighs ached.

Sigma exploded. Vasco barely saw the cut whip at his face. All that saved him were his Creche muscles and reflexes—reflexes he had never used, not in twenty years of fencing. He riposted immediately after his parry, hammering a blow at the top of her head. Shocked into instinct, he had thrown the shot with every ounce of muscle, power, and speed he had. It would split her skull in two, even with the training blades.

Incredibly, she not only managed to parry, but stopped his blade cold. Vasco saw the wide, thick blade actually bend almost enough to touch her back. Her riposte was as fast as his.

For almost a minute, they slung blows at each other from arm's length. Incredible, shattering blows. It was like listening to a room full of blacksmiths. Vasco had never in his life used all his genetically modified ability as he was now.

He desperately reached for more speed, more strength, while his mind raced to come up with some stratagem. He could think of nothing else he could do... he had to keep up the incredible pace. The slightest change and he would never be able to react fast enough to her hammer blows. And then he focused on her face.

She was serene, peaceful. This was no effort to her at all. She was actually smiling. Then she winked at him, dodged his incoming cut by just a hair—for a mad second, he actually saw one light stray hair peeking out over her ear, bending aside as his blade cut past it. She twisted her body, changing her cut into a massive chop at his defenseless left side...

And she stopped just short, frozen in place, as the general quarters alarm rang out over the ship.

The Ring ground to a slow halt. Some of the energy would be dumped into the enormous flywheels that sat deeper in the hull. If the situation warranted, some of that stored kinetic energy would be kicked right out to the hull. There were times when the captain might want to use the eccentric rotation it would give for fast maneuvers from start.

The *Alexi* was an Orion-capable ship, so she could move instantly. A single drive charge could be pumped out in a blink, and its shaped charge would be enough to hammer even the giant mountain of *Alexi* into instant action.

The Ring was the worst place to be in action. It was meant to be used for the long trips in Pod space. It was a wide ring right at the outer hull, that spun to create an artificial gravity. As such, it was oriented toward a "ground" on the floor of the ring. Years in zero-g weren't healthy, so during Pod trips, the crew lived and worked as much as possible in the Ring. The Ring was setup to be a living and working space in that time and had no real setup for zero gravity. There was no risk of collision or conflict in Pod space. Real space was considered a high-risk action space, where the crew would be in ship's armor at all times. *Alexi*, outside of the Ring, was built for zero-gravity orientation as well as rapid acceleration in many directions. Pre-launch *Alexi* was considered to be in home space, so the rules were more relaxed. *Alexi* played no role in system defense pre-launch, so there was no reason for her to go to general quarters.

Which didn't stop Vasco or any of the other crew from sprinting to stations. If they actually had to accelerate or maneuver, there would be casualties, if not fatalities. Crew that didn't have actual jobs to do ran for the nearest safety stations, where they could at least hope to survive a brief high-g run.

Vasco was a training officer, so his only duty was backup TacOps. He wasn't far from his assigned station. He was off the Ring in just over a minute, moving hand-over-hand through the corridors. His station was a self-contained pod between the inner and outer hull. It had limited connection to the inner ship but full access to the communications gear on the outer hull. They had their own dedicated array and spares container to go with it. In action, they were meant to be an autonomous unit, so they had to handle their own repairs.

Vasco swung into the pod. It was fully crewed already. Corporal Cave had already configured the screens, tailing multiple log files and grouping them onto clustered screens. Cave was snugged into her station, only her upper body visible. TacOps was a little more cramped than other technical stations because the others had to have more space for old-fashioned paper and slide rule work. TacOps had no job if systems were compromised, so their stations had no redundancy. Nothing but screens and keyboards positioned for efficiency and density.

The observer chair was the only space left. It wasn't really a chair—just a back pad and a series of straps to keep Vasco in place. It had a small arm with a keyboard and integral tablet doubling as a monitor. Vasco locked himself into place and logged in to catch up with the scrolling log files. He was anxious to find out what was going on, but old combat habits kept him focused. At the moment, nothing mattered past grasping the gestalt of the current system. Diagnostics of all the sensors. Performance specs, lists of attached and active equipment, active processes and users, dormant and background services. The regular operating space of his station was his battlefield, and situational awareness was life-and-death for everyone on the ship.

Cave hadn't even looked up when he came in, but she'd sent him a sitrep already. He'd open it when he was done. One more check of queues—all empty, buffers clear—and he was ready to go. Time to pull his head out of the sand and work. His job—the Tactical System Operations pod's job—was to hack enemy systems and protect the ship's systems from enemy hackers. Observation was the bulk of the protector's job. You watched everything, looking for anomalies. Anything out of the ordinary could be a sign of a successful or attempted penetration. Software could handle most of it, but software always had flaws. In something as complex as a Tatar, there was always something...

Vasco had already split his tiny screen into quadrants and opened the sitrep, the situation report, over his personal menu. It was a system map showing a simplified diagram of the solar system. The alarm trigger was obvious, shown as a shining gold icon. A Pook ship had arrived in system.

The Pook were friendly, if enigmatic. So far, all aliens were friendly... to a point. Skirmishes happened, but no wars. The Pook were the reason.

When mankind had first gone to the stars, they'd assumed they were all alone. They'd colonized dozens of worlds before they found the first ruins. Hundreds of worlds after that, they found more and more ruins. A pattern of destruction emerged. So many worlds with strange geological formations. That was what had provided the first real clue. Geologists realized that some of the strange formations, and the low level of life on planets, were best explained by impacts... near light speed impacts.

There had been a war. An enormous war that had sterilized life all across the galaxy so far explored. When humans encountered the first Pook ship, the Pook were stunned. Even more stunned than humans were to discover that the galaxy was teeming with life…

It turned out that humanity had been born in a dead zone, a galactic graveyard. Millions of years earlier, the Pook had survived a relativistic war. A war with weapons that moved at the speed of light meant there was no possibility of warning. You would not know you, or your world, was a target until it was too late. And a weapon-sized mass moving at the speed of light could cleanse a planet in a heartbeat. Whole planets and systems would be wiped out with no possible defense. Our section of the galaxy had been the battleground, and Earth had actually been a Pook planet. The Pook had been seriously upset when they saw the first pet cat. It was only too easy to imagine humans feeling the same if they found aliens had pets that looked and acted just like brainless humans.

The relative peace in the galaxy was born out of fear. The Pook had survived an unimaginable war, and no one knew how. And nobody at all wanted to risk upsetting a race capable of that. The Pook were pretty clear about one thing too—any use of relativistic weapons, anywhere, by anyone… and your race is gone. No exceptions.

Every sentient race was in agreement and support. If you used relativistic weapons, you went to war with every living thing in the galaxy.

It kept everyone fairly peaceable. There were some nasty races out there, but the spirit of cooperation on that one thing helped keep a damper on things. Multi-race coalitions were happy to stomp out any troublemakers if they got out of hand.

The Polity was starting to pay renewed interest in the Pook. The final Unity of humanity was on the horizon, and that put humanity right at the edge of Pook space. The Sami were on the border of Pook space, and the rumor was the Laconians might actually be in Pook space. The Polity was only focused on unifying humanity… so far.

The reason for the alert was related to one aspect of the

Pook that the Polity had the hardest time dealing with. A small percentage of Pook were insatiable hackers. Insatiable, and incredibly talented. They never committed any harm, but Vasco had been training with a battlegroup once when a Pook ship came through the system. While the Pook were in transit, not a single weapon in the entire battlegroup would function. They were dead until the Pook left, then the weapons worked again. No one ever found out the reason. When the Pook had been later asked about it, they just said it was a joke by a junior crewman.

The Polity had been excessively paranoid since then. The Helot mounted on *Alexi* was a sign of how paranoid they were. They had actually broken Tech to install Helots in ships as opposed to running solar systems, and *Alexi* was amongst the first dozen ships to have one installed. The Laconians had guaranteed that Helots could withstand Pook hacking. It hadn't been tested yet. Now might be the first test.

Sure enough, Vasco noted that his TacOps pod had been cut off from the *Alexi*, except for a dump to a log file in an external server. The server itself was connected to nothing but could be accessed by the Helot later. If things went bad.

Vasco's TacOps pod was being set up as bait in a honeypot trap. It was Polity standard practice. Hacking was an excellent tactic. Ships needed computers, needed to sense, needed to communicate. Computers ran everything on a modern ship. A hacker who could get in and get control could cause a lot of damage.

The honeypot mimicked an opening in the ship's firewalls—subtle or not, depending on the operators. Once a hacker had been lured in, the hacker would think they were in the real system. Honeypot operators had the job of keeping the hacker busy as long as possible by maintaining the illusion. They would fight the hacker and win or lose as they judged correct. It was a huge bluffing game and took serious technical smarts and human knowledge.

Vasco was never sure if he was good at being a TacOp because he was a fencer, or if being a TacOp made him a good fencer. Both required the ability to read an opponent and react to what you read on a subconscious level. You had to be able to act almost before you knew why you were acting. It was a game of instinct, and only the best could play.

It helped that TacOps wasn't required to counterattack. Other teams would do that. The honeypot teams built profiles and collected information, but it would only be used forensically. Modern hacking was dangerous enough that you really didn't want any connection between a honeypot and the active system.

The *Alexi* had one honeypot team, five penetration teams, and twenty defense teams. Her main defense was in trained personnel. Bridge, engineering, and fire team crews were all chosen for their basic math ability before anything else. At the first sign of enemy attack, the entire ship went offline, and the nomograms and slide rules came out. Whatever a computer could do, the crew could do... slower, to be sure. But slow was better than dead, and a hacker could easily steer a ship into a gravity well while making the crew think everything was fine.

The first subtle sign showed up on his screen. Vasco saw the smallest variance in a sensor log. And then another, and... a cascade. It looked as if some sort of particle beam was drifting across the ship. It looked like a standard Pook active scan, but... not all the sensors reported the same thing. The logs spilled across his little screen, but it wasn't big enough to hold all the info he wanted. He looked up on the main screens. Cave was tracking the same thing, almost a hundred logs running simultaneously. You could see the pattern showing up just in the report length of the log entries.

Vasco had a strange feeling. The pattern looked familiar. It was... yes, it was a code. The little hairless felines were trying to hack Alexi! Vasco itched to open the right electronic ports to let them in, but that wasn't his job. Cave was on it... and she was fast. She'd set up a fake sensor server and had it open as an incoming port for the expected packet.

And there it was, a HILO packet. The server popped a LOHI in reply, then there was a flurry of ACK packets. It hadn't taken the Pook long to find the hole and lock in. Finally they would see how the little devils operated.

Cave swore. Vasco looked at her. She was typing like mad and pulling data from one screen to another faster than Vasco could keep up with. The kid had talent.

But it was already too late. The Pook was into the system and locking out all the users… and suddenly Vasco figured out the problem.

He cleared his screen. "Cave!"

"Busy!" she shouted back. Her fingers were a blur. She was good, but in this case, her focus was betraying her. She was so intent on solving the problem, it hadn't occurred to her that the problem couldn't be happening.

"Cave! Fold it! Light speed lag!"

Cave started to yell back, then she swore and leaned back in her console. "Dammit, I'm an idiot. Thanks for the heads-up. You think it was a test?"

She'd caught on. The Pook was in the system, but even at light speed, there would be hours of lag in communication. If the Pook were really trying to hack the *Alexi*, TacOps would have just noticed the first pass on the sensors. It would have been a few more hours until they responded. They'd been had.

"I think Primus Always wanted to keep us on our toes. Good job, Cave. Start the diagnostics, but I think you'll find you were going up against a Helot."

That probably wouldn't make Cave feel better. She'd let the hacker…probably someone with the same job as her but on another shift, working from one of the auxiliary systems…root the honeypot in record time. She'd never live it down. She was supposed to make it look hard to keep up the illusion. Time to limit the damage.

"Open a line to TacSys command, let them know we're compromised," Vasco said. "You can get some points back by letting them know before they let you know."

"Thank you, Centurion. I've been doing that while we've been talking."

Fast indeed.

The Pook ship, on the best scope the Alexi had, showed up as a shimmering golden cluster of spheres. Neruda knew they had a central structure—a drive train and power plant—but all the spheres were individual ships. A Pook ship was a collective of common interests clustered around the beliefs of the main Pook. Neruda always thought of the top Pook as a queen, but she knew that wasn't right. The Pook had a bizarre but rigid hierarchy. The top of the Pook food chain was an unknown to any source the humans had access to.

What the Polity did know was that each main "ship" was, for all intents and purposes, a unique Pook nation. There was a central political structure to the Pook as a whole, but how it worked was beyond anyone's reckoning. It wasn't that the Pook kept it secret; it was that the language they used about it was obtuse enough to be useless. Much like their talk about how their drives worked.

"Well, Primus Always?" the Timariot asked.

His tone was light and amused, but Neruda answered carefully. Timariot Smith played the jovial big man, but he was a hammerhead shark when you turned your back on him. "I would hazard a guess they're just passing through, Timariot. They arrived just above the plane of the system, and their course is leading them out on a tangent. They should pass near Rubicon at the midpoint. Refueling perhaps?"

Rubicon was the gas giant in this system.

"Walkure Sigma," Neruda asked, "do you concur? Do the Pook use gas giants for fuel?"

"No, not for fuel. They do have an interest in the giants though," she said.

"We have noticed they're always approaching them, but we've never figured out why."

"You Laconians deal with the Pook all the time, don't you?" asked Timariot Smith. "You're neighbors, aren't you? You must know far more about them than we do."

"We know a bit more, yes," Sigma answered. "They appreciate the ecosystem of the giants the way we might a forest or a mountain range. This group may be sightseeing or recovering a science pod."

"A science pod? We haven't noted any such thing." Smith said. "There hasn't been a Pook ship in this system for almost a hundred years!"

"The Pook plan millennia in advance, Timariot. And they have more kinds of communication than we know about. It's possible a pod is deeper than your sensors would detect, but still able to converse with passing Pook ships."

"It's a good thing they aren't our enemies." Neruda shot a warning glance at Timariot Smith.

Sigma had not only deftly evaded the question about the unknown whereabouts of the Laconian homeworld, but also seemed to be about to goad the Timariot into talking about Polity plans for the Pook. That wouldn't do.

"The Pook are no one's enemies," Sigma answered.

The three of them watched the Pook ship for a while. It was moving at an incredible pace. The Pook had figured out artificial gravity, and that let them crank up the acceleration. It took them less than two hours to reach the outer radiosphere of Rubicon, and they took up a station-keeping orbit on the far side, keeping the bulk of the gas giant between them and the *Alexi*. It appeared the honeypot crews wouldn't be getting a real workout this time.

Vasco was itchy in his armor. One of the tape edges must have come slightly loose and rolled, and the damn thing sat just under the edge of a plate on his thigh. He had been trying to surreptitiously scratch since the lecture started. He'd fix it as soon as the lecture wrapped up. Under high g, that little itch would rapidly become a bruise, a burning scratch, and finally a ragged wound. No fun at all.

In the meantime, he was trying everything he could to soothe the agonizing itch. But between the plate and the compression fabric, there was no way to get to it. At least, not without making a spectacle of himself in public. He finally realized he couldn't do anything about it and decided to listen to the briefing. He'd have more than enough time to catch up on everything during the two-year Pod space trip, but the rest of the crew was being briefed now. It would probably be a good idea to know what they knew.

"The Sami," said the briefing officer, "were originally a settlement of Quakers with Odinist leanings. They took a group of Sufi with them, who were apparently fleeing one of the era's Islamic cleansings. The two groups found quite a bit in common and unified into the Sami within a few generations. They began as an aggressively agrarian series of communes with a bias against advanced technology, borrowing some teachings of the old earth Amish. Basically, their goal was to become farmers who practiced complete self-sufficiency and independence.

"Over the two thousand years since the colony was founded, fragmentation has taken place. Rumi, the Sami homeworld, has a large highland plateau on the central, inhabited, continent. Due to the heavy mountainous nature of the rest of the continent, farming is concentrated on this plateau. As anyone who has done any farming knows, cooperation and technology are somewhat inevitable. The plateau Sami developed a stable collection of towns and cities, eventually embracing space travel again. They have colonized another two systems, with apparent help from the Pook and the Laconians.

"Not all Sami agreed with this turn of events, and a splinter group migrated off the plateau and into the mountains. The conditions in the mountains are much harsher than on the plateau, and the so-called 'Outlander' Sami have not been able to come even close to the population levels of the plateau Sami. The Outlanders continue to embrace their own ignorance of technology. The two groups have no conflict with each other, and the Outlanders are regarded favorably, if not enviously, by the rest of the Sami. Any questions so far?"

One of the officers held up their hand. "How disconnected are the Sami? How are we getting intel on them?"

"Thank you," said the briefing officer. "Sami trade off planet has been limited. There is only one known tunnel to Polity space, and the transit on that tunnel has been Polity traders only. Until about three hundred years ago, the Sami only traded local goods and luxury items. Since then, they have acted as agents for the Laconians, selling Helot AIs.

"Polity visitors are mostly rare on Rumi. Aside from anthropologists and a small trade embassy, the only tourists are occasional climbing expeditions. Sami almost never leave their systems. So we have to rely on some fairly dated information. We expect to update when we are in system."

"What are we looking at for Unification?" asked another officer. "Do we have any idea of if they are strongly biased towards us, or resistant?"

"We expect the plateau Sami to put up token resistance to Unification," said the briefing officer. "The Outlanders will resist strongly, but with limited resources or technical ability, we expect them to be a non-factor. Sami resistance should be minimal once their space-based defenses are taken out. The defenses they do have in place were purchased from the Polity, with what we assume are the agent fees collected from Helot sales.

"The Laconians are an unknown factor. The Walkure Sigma is the first Laconian ever seen in the Polity, or by any member of the Polity. We continue to assume the Laconians are peaceful scientists with no military beyond basic self-defense needs. They have no influence or contact with any Polity world, or any non-Polity world aside from the Sami. We can therefore safely assume they are still a minor, if scientifically advanced, planet. Neither Walkure Sigma's presence nor her discussions have given us any reason to alter our intelligence estimates. We have assured her our unification of the Sami will not affect our Helot purchases or business channels in any avoidable way, and on behalf of the Laconians, she has accepted our assurances.

"In short, we believe the Sami will be mildly resistant to

unification, but the benefits will be seen by the population to far outweigh any negatives. A swift reduction of space-borne forces, a rapid seizure of ground assets, and a visible presence of ground troops will quickly quell any desire for standing battles, and the prospects of extended guerrilla resistance are low. We expect to begin unification protocols within six weeks of landing.

"Weather on Rumi is…"

Vasco tuned out when the officer moved on to more predictions of how things would go. Projections never meant a damn thing. He'd learned that on his first Long Drop and was already a cynic by his second. If the Sami didn't fight, he'd enjoy getting to know the locals. Maybe set up another fencing school. Maybe see what sort of martial arts they did on Rumi. It was always good to learn new things.

If they fought… well, maybe that was why he was on this drop. He had one last chance to prove to himself that he could be useful in combat, that all his training was for something. He'd been born with unique skills and been trained in their use—trained far more than most—and was more capable than anyone he had ever met. All of that had to be for some purpose, some reason.

All his dead friends, and he was left behind to deal with the consequences. Left to deal with the what ifs, to wonder if he hadn't had to do his job, if he wasn't in the place he had to be, if he could have saved them. If he could have really made a difference.

It wasn't even about being a hero… just… the chance to maybe be what he had been born to be. Just once, before he got too old. Even if it cost him his life, it would be worth it. What was the point of being alive if you never got to be who you were meant to be? As Vasco's feisty grandmother used to say, "A short life is better than a life half-lived." Vasco couldn't help but feel he'd never even gotten a chance to start his life.

It was all waiting, waiting for that one moment when he could act and be real… when he could really and truly be alive. He'd felt it sometimes, in training or in tournaments. That special moment when time froze and everything fell into place. He knew he was meant for more. He would do whatever it took to reach that place. No intelligence report was going to tell him if he would get that chance.

The briefing officer finished his spiel, and the troops filed out. They were a quiet group. This, for most of them, was the last task before hibernation.

It was easy to tell who was slated for ship duty in Pod space. Those few luckless souls were the ones in ship's armor. Everyone else was on their way to the hibernation bays. Once they were put down and secured, the only people left on the ship would be in armor. That was when *Alexi* would finally fire up the main drive and maneuver to the Rumi tunnel.

Another twelve hours, and all but a skeleton Gyrene crew would be asleep. The ship's crew would all be up for the transit to the Pod jump-off point. Not a single sailor could stand the thought of being asleep for the jump. They could sleep after, in Pod space. But when the Pod field first went up and the drive charges went off?

That was the sailors' special courage. None of them had anything to do at that point. The calculations had all been done for the shot, and everything had been lined up and checked over and over. But when an array of shaped nuclear charges were pointed at your ship and triggered? You never noticed or saw anything from the Pod drive charge. Once the field went up, it was two years of vague greyness until the field went down at the pre-planned time.

If all was right, you'd wind up in the system you aimed for. Anything went wrong... didn't bear thinking about. But it was a thought that crept in anyway. The drive field went up, and you knew, just knew, that nuclear hell was smashing into you, squeezing you like a seed and squirting you out at superluminal speeds. If you knew enough to fear it was happening... you were safe. Safe to skip out the monotony of the remaining trip with hibernation—at least until it was your shift.

Gyrenes could count on being woken a few times for fitness and training rotations and extra classes. Mostly they slept though. Even a gigantic ship like a Tatar wasn't going to waste space on food when it didn't need to.

Vasco had elected to stay awake for the entire trip. He liked the time to himself. A small group of Gyrenes were required to be awake but had no real duties other than checking in with the ship's crew once in a while to see if they needed help, or walking the endless rows of vehicles and weapons. Most Gyrenes preferred to sleep.

The ship was busy. Crew was bustling about, making sure all the last-minute things were secured and safe for acceleration and no one was still wandering around out of armor. Vasco helped chivy the last straggling Gyrenes into the hibernation zone, then he decided he had enough time to work his way out to a viewing bay in the outer hull.

Vasco had been in the bay about an hour and was thinking about heading back into the inner hull before the acceleration warnings forced his hand. The outer hull was, in addition to mostly heat radiators, armor against impact and radiation. But you had to be on the other side of it to get that protection. Acceleration involved a great deal of radiation, and Vasco wasn't about to argue with regulations that limited his radiation exposure. He wasn't in too much of a rush though. These would be the last stars he'd see for two years, and in all likelihood, he would never see these stars again.

He heard footsteps coming up behind him and was surprised to see Neruda.

"Neruda! I thought you always opted for hibernation on these trips. Going to try to see what life is like in the dead zone this trip?"

"No, I'm happy to let you be the zombie, as always. I'm going to bed down with the crew. Joys of intelligence work, I've got to wait around for any last-minute information. I'll be up a few dozen times in any case, and up a few weeks before general wake up, getting things ready before the full crew is up and about."

"I hope they're paying you enough to extra work."

She snickered. "Yeah, it's not bad. But you know me, it's not the money. I hate not knowing what's going on, and I hate even more when someone else is making the decisions."

"I always figured you for the 'move up or move out' type. I have to admit, intelligence work does seem to be your thing. I'd rather have you working on that end than anyone else."

"That's because you like knowing who to strangle if things go wrong!"

"So don't let anything go wrong."

Neruda was silent, staring out at the stars. The last tenders could be seen moving back to the station, sparks and flickers of steel against the stars.

After a moment, Neruda spoke. "I need you to do me a favor. Walkure Sigma is going to be awake for the transit. Apparently she can't handle the hibernation drugs. She's effectively our first Laconian ambassador, so I can't lock her up for the trip. And for some reason, I really want to. I don't trust her. She's too damn good at answering questions without saying anything at all. I need you to keep an eye on her for me."

"I'm not much of a spy."

"I don't need a spy. I need... I need someone who can think on their feet. Someone who can figure out what the hell she's all about. I wouldn't put it past her to sabotage the ship. We know nothing about the Laconian and Sami relationship. She tells us they aren't interested in interfering with unification, but being on this ship with minimal crewing is a perfect opportunity for mischief. You're the only person I can trust to read her intentions.

"And hell, I think she likes you. That sabre bout was incredible. The whole ship's been talking about it. And she was almost smiling the rest of the day. I don't know what that was about, but I know you're the only asset I can figure out to use in this situation. Get to know her in the dead zone. Stay close, make sure I wake up in a whole ship, eh? I'll do my damnedest to return the favor when you're on the ground."

"Anything for a... on the ground? What do you mean on the ground? I'm billeted for training. I'm not going down the well until unification has started."

Neruda smiled a bit. "You think I don't know you? You think I don't know what you want? I know you're itching for one last chance at combat command. I know you want that one last check box filled. We wake up whole, I'll be grateful enough to let you cherry-pick the position you want."

"You're kidding…"

"Nope, already cleared it with the Timariot. He wants his fencing game improved by at least ten percent before he's willing to risk your limbs though. He's going to be taking up the last three months of your dead zone time, personally. He's having himself woken early just for that."

"I can get him ten percent better if he just learns to cover his line before lunging."

"Great, so spend the time you won't need going over rosters and picking out available troops. But make sure we get there in one piece. And if you can make a tiny effort to be a spy, I'd appreciate it."

"I'm not seducing her." Vasco said. Not that he'd had much interest in that sort of thing, but he did enjoy teasing Neruda sometimes.

"Ha! Good luck!" Neruda said with a snort. "If you manage that, make sure you do it someplace with camera coverage. I could make money off of that footage."

"A gentleman would never do such a thing."

"Uh huh. Seriously though, be careful. I did some research. Her rank? 'Walkure'? It's apparently an old spelling of 'Valkyrie.' It means 'chooser of the slain,' so watch your ass with her. There's more going on here than we know about."

Vasco wound up staring off into the stars right until the final acceleration alarm sounded, and he only barely made it back to the inner hull before the steady hum of the drive began.

Chapter Four: The Last

The giant ship disappeared from the universe with a cascade of camera-flash pops. At least that was what the multi-megaton drive charges looked like when they went off. A careful observer might have noted the pin-thin beams of the shaped charges stabbing into the ship at the very moment it vanished. Without the Pod drive, the *Alexi* would have been turned into radioactive scrap and plasma. With the Pod drive, the pocket of real space that held the *Alexi* vanished in a superluminal two-year trek to the star Anubis. And circling Anubis was Rumi.

Two years until Alexi would suddenly appear in the Anubis system. If all went right, she'd be right in the tunnel reception zone and her exact position would be locked into the tunnel computers. If, or when, she went home, she'd either go back on the same path and arrive where she'd started—after two years of more travel—or, if she went back on even a slightly different path, her crew would experience a two-year trip, but they'd come out of Pod space something like five thousand years after they left. At least that was what the last mission report on the subject had said.

As far as anyone knew, it always worked out. Only a few ships had gone missing, and it was easier to assume they'd been destroyed rather than become relativistic travelers to a far future.

Every Gyrene knew the risk though. Sometimes it seemed like it was only a rare person who signed up for a Long Drop and planned to go home after. But most did.

Vasco had never really had a home to go back to. He was grateful for what home he'd had, growing up. It was a better life than what he would have experienced growing up as a Creche citizen. Thanks to the Polity, Vasco had parents, adoptive siblings, relatives, and friends. But his past had never been hidden from him. He'd learned early to be as normal as he could be.

But it still felt sometimes that home was here, in the vast hollow spaces of a Tatar. Crammed full of equipment and services, but empty of life. Here he was lonely, but free to be himself. He had no need to hide his altered genes, his nearly alien roots.

The Tatar crew assigned to the Pod run were insular and clannish. The other Gyrenes who'd drawn the short straw of Pod space duty were a mixed lot. They would enjoy the extra pay and lack of duties, but they had to deal with their boredom.

It wasn't easy to be bored on a Tatar. Libraries of ebooks, games, movies, and shows were accessible in private nooks or in cafes in the Ring. There was a pub, open only during the Pod run. There were the gyms and classrooms. The Armory even had a zero-g shooting range with synthetic range drops. That was where Vasco was when he met Sigma. He'd slipped into his ship's armour earlier to get as close to the feel of his ground combat armour as he could, without bothering to dig it out of stores.

The range was automated and really showed the potential of the latest Tech. Vasco was crouched in his booth, tethered tightly in place. The heavy caliber sniper rifle he was shooting had a ferocious kickback, and that took some hefty management in zero-g. His armor had no problem distributing the kick, but the charge was enough to send him snapping back across the room. Safety tethers were mandatory.

Vasco took a chance and blinked. His eye had been glued to the scope for about twenty minutes. The range was projecting a mountain landscape, and Vasco had two targets to deal with. The range computer acted as spotter for him, but he had to move quickly. The first target was below him, the second on the difficult ridgeline, and he'd sweated for a bit trying to get the exact range. Both targets were sniper teams in excellent camouflage. It had taken him an hour to spot the high team, two to spot the lower team.

In that time, he'd lost two simulated trucks of the convoy he was trying to protect. But he had them now. Eighteen clicks for the lower target, then a rapid switch to sixty for the upper target. He'd have to be quick and accurate. He couldn't risk losing his track on the high team by moving after taking out the low team. He thought he could pull off the fast switch. It was time to find out.

He leaned back slightly, keying for a pause in the program. Realism was one thing, safety another. He snapped down his visor. The airtight seal was probably unnecessary—the range had a powerful vacuum system—but why take a chance of a speck of propellant drifting into your eye? He gave himself another moment to adjust his eyes, then he took his first shot.

He didn't even feel the substantial kick. The first target was down—the spotter. Vasco sucked in his rib a little, just enough to move the sight picture to the shooter. Another squeeze, and that target was down as well. He shifted up smoothly, moving his free hand to the scope and setting the right clicks in place. A brief flicker of glare... the spotter was looking right at him. Squeeze... miss. And to top it off, the nice buzzer in his visor let Vasco know he'd been hit.

Vasco sighed. Too many years out of practice. The skills faded fast. He would put in a few hours a day of straight target work and try the simulation again in a month. He had time to kill.

He snapped the stubby safety into place and waited a moment for the computer to tell him the air was particle free, then flipped up his visor. He was breaking down his rifle for cleaning when an entry requested beeped over the door. He cleared the entry, and the door opened to let Sigma into the range.

"Walkure Sigma! I haven't seen you since before we made Pod space. Been keeping busy?"

"I have. It's been quite pleasant having fewer people around. I've been catching up on my reading."

Vasco nodded. "Yeah, the libraries get more use with less people in Pod space than they do the whole rest of a drop."

"I gather that Gyrenes aren't big on learning from books."

"No, not really. They like to know how to do things—it's part of the job. But doing and studying are two different things. You don't have Gyrenes on Laconia?"

"Not Gyrenes, no. Is that a 20mm rifle?"

"This? Yup. I found a good selection of them in the armory. My old favorite. Fin-stabilized tungsten penetrators. It's a smoothbore rifle. Makes me feel like an old-fashioned musketeer."

"Is it muzzle-loading?"

"Uhhh, no, we aren't that..." Vasco looked up from his cleaning. Sigma had a raised eyebrow. A terrible suspicion sneaked over him. "Was that a joke?"

"Laconians do have a sense of humor, Centurion."

"Could have fooled me," he said, snorting in amusement.

"I apologize for my earlier stiffness. The Polity is very different from what we are used to on Laconia. I'm not sure how to deal with the different approach to life. My discomfort makes me more formal than I am used to being."

"I can understand that."

"May I try your rifle?"

Vasco was taken aback. She wore a military uniform but had implied she had little or no military training. They'd assumed the Laconians were peaceful. Maybe this would be his opportunity to find out more about them.

"I suppose," he said. "Have you shot before?"

"No. We don't have gunpowder weapons on Laconia."

"Ah. Well, this is probably the wrong weapon to start with. Why don't we go down to the armory and I can check you out a lighter weapon?"

"Why? I'm at least as strong as you, Centurion, and I can assure you my armor is more capable than yours. I'm more than able to stabilize such a weapon for firing and recoil."

Vasco wasn't sure, but her armor was certainly different. It was lighter and sleeker, but it lacked the bulbous joints and heavy external actuators. Now that he looked at it, he noticed a few other things as well. The plating seemed less for reinforcement and more for ballistic protection. That didn't make sense though. It was too thin to be of any ballistic use. For a scientifically advanced planet, they seemed to make some pretty poor ship's armor.

"Well... if you're sure. I suppose you could try out a few shots."

Vasco reassembled his weapon and explained the basic operation to Sigma. She grasped the principles quickly and asked good questions. He was starting to think that maybe she could handle the rifle.

When he instructed her to take a prone position, she balked. "Why do I need to lie down to shoot?"

"Well, first off, you use the ground to brace your elbows and get a good stable base for a shot. Secondly, your armor may be strong enough to handle the recoil, but sole magnets aren't strong enough to keep you grounded. You needed to be strapped in to shoot that rifle."

"My armor is far more advanced than yours. Here. Watch."

Before Vasco could say anything more, she snapped the big rifle up to her shoulder and cooked off a round downrange. She didn't even flinch. Vasco was stunned. He'd never seen anyone fire the big rifle like that. He thought maybe he could do it but had never tried. He didn't want to stand out.

He covered his astonishment by giving her a brisk lecture on range safety, but he gave in on her standing posture. "All right, let's try a few more shots. Don't worry about hitting the bull's-eye, just try to do the same thing each time, okay?"

"I can do that," she said, already squinting down the scope. Two more rapid shots ripped down range.

Vasco checked the monitor. Incredible. She hadn't hit the bull's-eye, but she'd managed a beautiful grouping. A near perfect triangle of big holes had been punched into the range clay.

"Are you sure you haven't shot before?" Vasco asked.

"Never. But it seemed pretty straightforward. I lock my body into position, memorize that position, and return to it with each squeeze of the trigger. Now that I have done that, I can modify my posture until I'm hitting the mark each time, correct?"

"Yeah, that's basically it. Are all Laconians like you?"

"No, a perfect human model was the goal of the Creche worlds, not the Laconian founders. We do train and live for physical excellence, though. Do you feel you are perfect?"

"No, I think they screwed up a bit when they made me." Vasco said with a smile.

She looked at him with a quizzical expression on her face.

"Perhaps the way you were raised was the problem," she said. "Maybe the Creche, if left alone, would have raised you to perfection."

Vasco nearly lost it. He had no idea he had so much anger inside him, but he felt as if he were a bubble of plasma about to burst. He took a huge breath, then spoke through clenched teeth. "The Creche were evil. And that is not a topic I care to discuss. Ever."

He snapped the rifle out of her hands and started the disassembly, forcing himself to calm down as best he could. She had a knack for getting under his skin, it seemed.

"Centurion, I apologize. We Laconians don't have the best sense of what is personal or private. Please forgive me."

Vasco took another deep breath. His hands were on the verge of shaking. He clenched them and released them and gave himself a shake. "Walkure Sigma, I don't care to discuss my past, especially a part of my past that isn't actually part of me. I have no memory of the Creche. I was too young to remember anything. I've always felt, and thought, I am Polity. It has only ever been other people who have told me different."

She looked at him calmly for a moment and didn't say anything. Vasco found himself looking into her eyes almost against his will, and he could sense her quiet analysis of him. "I see," she said. "I didn't understand that. I do now. Thank you for the shooting lesson. I enjoyed it." She turned to leave.

Vasco felt a slight qualm when he remembered Neruda's heartfelt request and swallowed some more of his anger. "Walkure, a question before you go."

"Yes?" she answered.

"Your shoulder patch. Is that a unit sign?"

"This?" she asked, looking down at her shoulder patch. It was an unusual patch, three interlocking triangles superimposed by a larger triangle with no bottom line. "It's the Laconian Sigil. It represents our founding philosophies. We are not what you think we are. We aren't really scientists—we're philosophers. The inner symbol is a Valknut. It's something we share with the Sami. One of our founders was a follower of the Havamal, a fairy tale of supposed sayings of the old Norse god Odin. Much of our social structure is built up from reconstructed Odinist beliefs. Laconia was originally founded by a society of reenactors.

"Our true growth did not happen until Lycurgus came among us, and that's the second symbol. It's from the Greek alphabet. It's a Lamba, the letter L. Lycurgus taught us the philosophies of Greece and shaped our society. This sigil reminds of many things. Our origins, our change, and the basics of what we are."

Vasco said, "You shoot pretty well for a philosopher."

"We are very good at being in the moment."

"I've learned some of the value of that in my fencing. Perhaps we could talk about it some time."

"Perhaps. It's a long voyage. Thank you for the lesson, Centurion."

The door closed behind her, and Vasco tried not to look at it as he cleaned the rifle.

Fascinating woman. Maybe getting to know her wouldn't be the worst thing.

Time passed, and eventually Vasco hunted up Neruda. She had been thawed out two days before, a requirement of her job being quarterly wake ups during jump. She'd been keeping herself busy sorting out wake-up training for the Gyrenes. She was dry running sims when Vasco caught up with her.

It was an odd sight. Neruda was tethered into place in the middle of the sim room, running in place. The walls had the slightest bounce as they played the scenario through in glowing vector lines. For the actual sim, they'd be replaced with a mix of computer-generated terrain and video footage. The room was meant for a squad at a time, and it seemed a bit hollow with just Neruda. She stopped running when she heard the click and crunch of Vasco's boots securing him to the wall.

"Vasco! Going to come join me, or do want to enjoy the surprises along with everyone else?"

"I think I can wait for your little treats. I'm sure I'll be spending enough time in sims before we're done."

"Probably not. I haven't booked your refresher training yet, but I've given you a full slate of close quarters combat training. I figured you'd want to pick your guys from the students you train."

"Not worried about breaking up existing units too much, are you?"

"Not really. The really broken-in teams are off-limits, and you won't see any of those guys. One or two troops missing from anywhere else won't upset anyone too much. I'll book your sim time just before we exit Pod space and give you time to break in your crew." Neruda unhooked herself from the retractable tethers and nodded to Vasco to secure the doors. When he did, Neruda spoke again. "How are things going with Sigma?"

"She's been avoiding me. We had a small chat. She kinda pushed some of my buttons."

"True love, eh? Well, no surprise. The time I've spent with her, she hasn't impressed me with her tact. How'd she get under your skin? That had to take some effort."

"Did you know she's a crack shot? I was in the range, getting my rifle work back up to snuff, and she fired a perfect group from an unsupported stance."

"Tell me you were doing counter-sniper with your .22…"

"No, I was using the big Twenty, the smooth bore."

Neruda look startled by that. "That's not possible. She must have pulled something on you."

"Nope. It was legit. She's a hell of a lot stronger than she looks."

Neruda took the news quietly, but she didn't look surprised. She nodded. "Figures. That makes a few things fit together a little better."

"Neruda... I need a favor."

"Whatever you need, Vasco."

"I... need to know about my birthworld."

"Oh, damn," Neruda said and looked away for a moment. She gave her head a quick nod. "Okay, I can do that. You sure you want to know?"

Vasco choked down the sudden flutters in his stomach. "Yeah. I think it's time. I need to know."

Neruda's intelligence station was a three-person pod under the bridge. The door was half normal height, an old-fashioned pressure bulkhead type, with a lever to engage the dogs and everything. Neruda slipped her legs in, holding on the overhead handles, and floated in. Vasco stuck his head in first.

The pod was roughly heart shaped and dim. Neruda's terminal was a saddle facing back toward the hatch, with small monitors all around. At knee level between the hatch and the saddle were the operators' tubs. Like the bridge tubs, they were designed to be a snug fit for the lower body, keeping the operator in place in zero-g. They only had a single monitor each.

Neruda motioned Vasco toward one of the tubs, and he floated down into it and fit himself in. The monitor came alive, but there was no prompt on it.

"Hold on a minute," Neruda said.

Vasco heard her tapping on a keyboard, and a few murmured commands.

"All right. Here it comes," she said. "I'm going to leave you alone. When you're done, just get up from the tub. The terminal will automatically shut down and scrub any info. You've got no outside lines, and I'm hoping you know better than to take notes. I can't turn off the security overrides, so don't do anything other than head for the hatch when you get up, or you'll wake up in the infirmary, sick to your stomach for a week. Last chance…"

"I'm good."

Vasco's stomach was already roiling. He wasn't sure he wanted to know a damn thing about his past or where he came from. If the Polity wanted that information hidden, it was for a damn good reason. He was pretty sure he'd be happier dying with this knowledge unknown… but there was no denying he felt a momentum building in him. It was, indeed, time.

Neruda drifted out the hatch without saying anything else and dogged it closed. Vasco was alone. The terminal had a single button on the screen for a prompt. Vasco stared at it for a moment, then abruptly stabbed it with his finger. Words filled the screen. Lots of information… folders, reports, summaries, contact reports, histories…

The Creche wasn't an accurate term. There were actually a number of Creche worlds. "Creche" applied to a small group of worlds that, before Unification, had separately adopted a unique practice of abandoning families. Children were raised in communal creches. The polity found the practice abhorrent. On most unified worlds, local customs were kept. As long as the Polity standard educational practice was universally applied to all children, and no religious, political, or cultural artifacts got in the way of that, customs were mostly allowed.

The creche system had been ruthlessly stamped out as dehumanizing, and Creche-classed worlds were forced into a more normal human model. It hadn't been easy and had required draconian measures. On one world, it had reached nightmare proportions. Alamansa. Vasco's homeworld. He hadn't even known the name until now.

Alamansa had gone a step farther than the other Creche worlds. Instead of just trying to create a balanced and universal society, Alamansa had adopted aggressive genetic engineering and selection. Humans still bred the old-fashioned way, but only at government direction. Babies were tweaked and selected after conception. Faulty fetuses were aborted, and all fetuses were modified to enhance whatever trends were seen as dominant in that child. As soon as the baby was born, it was placed in a creche that was designed to maximize its potential in its selected life task.

Humans became parts in a vast machine. More like insects than humans. The Polity insisted on change, Alamansa refused, and they went to war. The Polity had fought wars before. Real wars. Multi-system battles for life and death… but none since the Tatars. With the Tatars, they'd been able to overwhelm all opposition.

Alamansa had fought back hard. The first Tatar was destroyed by a battlefleet crewed by genetic soldiers of incredible ability. They'd struck back at the Polity, razing the next world up the line. It had taken a huge call up of fleets to turn the tide against the Alamansa. Every single Tatar available had been involved in the last effort at Unification. Millions of troops had died trying to take Alamansa. Millions of Polity troops.

At the end, the Polity realized the Alamansa would never surrender. The troops pulled back off the planet, back into the shattered remnants of Alamansa and Polity fleets. Alamansa was bombarded into a radioactive wasteland.

Against orders, a handful of infants had been retrieved and were later fostered out. They were all that was left of Alamansa.

There was a record of Vasco being rescued. Just a small note about how one unarmed woman had sundered the combat armor of a drop commando and seized his weapon, nearly wiping out almost a platoon… and killing almost all the children under her care. Vasco was the only survivor of that entire continent. They had no record of what his creche was. All the others had been bred to be teachers, artists, or laborers. Vasco was an unknown.

He was silent. The information hit him and moved through him. He read about the decision to bury all knowledge of Alamansa and understood it. The Polity wasn't built on love, but some tragedies were too much. It was a war no one had wanted, and it had ended in a way no one cared to remember. As far as Vasco knew, he was only Alamansan alive who even knew.

He read about the other children. The Polity hadn't bothered to track more than a few of them... Vasco's record was blank after noting that he had been fostered until he became a Gyrene. The few who had been tracked had mostly moved beyond their genetic programming and into different fields. A teacher-class had become a successful doctor. A dancer, a physicist. A laborer, a politician. Only one had stuck to her coding. Vasco was rather surprised to find his favorite singer was a fellow Alamansan.

Vasco leaned back, letting the knowledge sink in. He pulled off his ship's armor gauntlet, put his hand on the end of the tub's armrest—a simple square tube of metal, capped at the end. He gripped the welded metal end and squeezed. He squeezed as hard as he had ever squeezed... then stopped holding back.

The metal flowed under his hand, molding like putty and buckling. He felt a fast strength grow in him, along with a wild desire to tear apart the tub. Slowly, he eased back on the pressure and felt an immense pain in his hand. He turned his palm over. The fingertips were already swelling, the pads blackening with blood pouring into the crushed spaces. He balled his hand up tightly, wincing with the pain that was coming, and pushed out of the tub.

Neruda watched her friend come out of the pod. Vasco looked distant. She wasn't surprised by that—it was a lot of information to take in. She'd been exposed to the information when she started her intelligence training. It had been part of her general background education at intelligence academy, but it had hit her personally when she had realized her friend wasn't just a Creche baby, but an Alamansan survivor.

She thought about talking to Vasco, but one look at her friend's troubled brow told her otherwise. She'd known Vasco for a long time and knew that he handled problems best if left alone. There was a lot of alone on a Tatar in Pod space.

As Vasco drifted down the corridor, Neruda moved into the pod to secure it. She moved over to the tub Vasco had occupied and checked that the purge program had finished its run. Satisfied, she put her hand on the arm rest to push back... and noticed the deformed end.

It must have hit Vasco really hard, she thought, to overcome the feedback loop in a gauntlet that stopped ship's armor from doing that kind of damage. She decided she'd bring a bottle of something strong to Vasco's cabin tonight.

She never noticed how much smaller than gauntlet size the marks were.

Chapter Five: The Manifest

"My name is Centurion Vasco al Madina del Goya. I will be your Advanced Combatives instructor for the next six weeks."

A dozen students in two rows faced Vasco with uniform expressions of unease and discomfort. They'd arrived in class cocky, eager, and confident. The first lesson he'd taught them, and they didn't even know it yet, was never to expect anything in a fight.

"You've been woken from hibernation for the sole pleasure of taking my class. You earned this exquisite right by virtue of having earned black belts or the equivalent in your prior martial arts training."

He sneered as he said that. The sneer was an affection he used for this portion of class. It wasn't hard to affect it. He had rarely come across anyone in the times he'd taught this course who had the grace to arrive with any real skills of use. Probably for the better though. It kept him employed. And he did rather enjoy this job. Not only was it fun, but he could also actually see the improvement in his students.

Vasco also enjoyed knowing he was teaching skills that might save lives out in the field. But the sneer was important right now. He wanted to continue to make his students feel uncomfortable, off balance, and very, very vulnerable. They were used to feeling superior. He needed to peel that feeling from them before he could teach them his skills. Fortunately, he had an excellent tool for doing just that.

"Your previous training taught you patterns, reactions, expectations. Those will be what kills you out in the field. We need to strip you down to the bare essence of martial arts skill in order to rebuild you from scratch."

As he talked, he let his sneer pass through a leer before it became a smile. The students' discomfort would be cresting into something very like fear now. Being naked could do that. The whole class, male and female, were naked. So was Vasco.

"You may have noticed you are naked. You may have noticed your fellow Gyrenes are naked. Isn't this going to be an interesting class? You all come from different worlds with different traditions. You all have studied different arts. Traditions and arts are all civilized things. They have rules. Subconscious expectations of behavior. We are getting rid of all those rules and expectations."

And it would be easier for some than others. Most of the women seemed more embarrassed than worried, and almost all the men looked embarrassed and uptight. A couple of people of either sex seemed completely relaxed. There were still some worlds with much more relaxed approaches to nudity.

Everyone was fit of course. Gyrenes on a Long Drop, even the noobs, had no choice in that. Vasco wasn't the most fit, but the broad thickness of his muscles on his shorter frame made him look like a dwarven, rather than Greek, god. The fencing scars gave him an authority no uniform or medal could ever match.

"We start this class from scratch. You will learn to defend yourself with nothing. I will judge your progress. As you get better, you will earn back a piece of clothing. Every second person, step forward."

This was where it always got interesting. Vasco had worked out this first exercise a few different ways over the years. This one seemed to get the best results. He had harder versions for smaller groups.

This group was about to get their first exposure to what being advanced meant. As he had told them, everyone in the class had black belts or equivalents in whatever art they had. They were all experts. They were about to become beginners again.

"All right. Now I want you to turn around and face the person behind you. Each of you should be facing one person. Good. Take a moment and look at that person. Try to understand them, get to know them. In a few seconds, I will call out an action. At that time, you will both try to complete that action. Ready?"

Vasco paused to watch their reactions. Typical. Half the class was smirking and ogling their partners. That would end pretty quick...

"On my command... choke your partner unconscious. Go."

As usual, they had forgotten all their training when their uniforms were taken away. It was amazing how much humans shaped themselves around such little things. Amazing, but universal.

Mental anchors were what made people perform the way they did. Reference points were the first things people looked for. They had to know where down was before they could take a step. The more confidence a person needed, the more things they added to their behavior to become "down." In combat athletes, it often showed in ticks. Biting lips, clutching thumbs inside fists, clenching toes... all sorts of little things. An anchor to move from.

Vasco's success as a teacher, and his own style of martial art, depended on him being able to remove that anchor from the student and to stop them from reaching for new anchors. The goal was to have a perfectly fluid and adaptable martial artist. But first there were some other habits to take care of.

A good enough portion of the students was having the usual issue.

"Halt!" Vasco shouted.

The class froze. Most of them looked happy for the excuse

to stop and practically leapt away from their opponent. Mostly guys facing guys. Vasco shook his head. One correction at a time.

"All right, people. Let's get something out of the way first. You!" He pointed at a lanky fellow who was practically blushing from head to toe. His tiny Asian female partner looked furious. He'd been doing nothing but running from her. "What's your problem?"

"Sir? I can't... she's a woman!"

"I'm a woman all right, and I can kick your ass!" shouted his partner.

Vasco slapped his hands together. His callused hands cracked like hides of leather slapping together. Attention was focused solely on him again.

Always some idiot from some backwoods planet. It made Vasco's point easier to get across, but it was still a sore frustration that the Polity was pig-headedly lax about some worlds wasting half of their population's potential.

Vasco said, "Let me be clear about something. I'll quote from St. Moran. You can read his works later. The quote is this, partly: Woman are for fucking and cooking. Period."

The lanky fellow looked a little stunned. Most of the women in the class had their jaws hanging open, and at least one had blood in her eye.

"I don't teach women," Vasco continued. "Or men, or anyone between or outside the gender binary you learned about in kindergarten. If you think of yourself first as a man or a woman, then get the hell out of my class. I teach fighters. I teach warriors. I teach people, not genders. You understand me? There is no gender in this class. There is no race or planetary preference. No rank. Anything outside your skin needs to be treated with all the respect you show something that is capable of killing you."

He looked each student in the eye, making sure they were all paying attention. "By the end of this class, if you haven't learned that respect, they will be killing you."

"I feel like a teenager trapped in an adult body." Vasco

stepped ever so lightly off to the side as he spoke and flicked up his hand. Since his first bout with Sigma, and learning about his Creche potential, he'd been leaning into seeing what his limits were. It was a bit intoxicating.

Sigma's sword, parried just enough, slipped by his head without touching him. Sigma pulled the tip of her sword around to clear it of his guard and dropped the tip down to cut his leg. Vasco already had his dagger in position to block that attack. He pushed the blade a little forward and continued his light step by pulling his back foot around in a nice little turn. All he had to do was pull his sword hand down and deliver a cut to Sigma's midsection. She tried to parry it with her dagger, but her position was off. He laid the blade neatly against her belly and took a few steps back to get out of range.

The steps were the fastest part of the whole exchange. Their whole fight had been conducted at a snail's pace, slowing their natural speed down to a crawl.

Vasco had been thinking about his first bout with Sigma and decided he could probably beat her natural speed advantage with some practice. He had approached her and asked if she was willing to work with him on improving his fencing, and she'd agreed. At their first session of drilling together, Vasco had noticed an important point—Sigma was strong, fast, incredibly aggressive, and talented... but almost untrained. Capable, but not trained in the use of longer blades.

She'd only handled a long blade a few times before. Laconian training apparently focused almost entirely on unarmed combat and knife work. They had almost no sword training at all. Vasco wasn't entirely surprised. The Gyrene focus on the sabre was entirely an affection, an intentional throw back to their millennial-old origin as Marines. Outside of the world of Gyrenes, only a few worlds still practiced the ancient sword arts.

Vasco's homeworld—foster homeworld, really—was one of those planets. Madina was a world that prided itself on the trappings of aristocracy. Universal aristocracy though—the Polity frowned on any sort of hereditary power aside from that wealth alone provided. Vasco's adoptive father was a wealthy and well-placed man in the Polity. He'd inherited his family's wealth and estates, as well as their skill and love of swordplay.

Vasco had learned swordplay at his father's side. He'd had a sword in his hands before he could even properly hold it. He hadn't had a choice but to learn. His father's other children were grown and hadn't shown any skill with the blade. Malachi del Goya had sworn his name would only go to a champion fencer...

The weapon Vasco's father had forced him to master was not the Gyrene sabre, but the older and more elegant rapier. And it was the rapier he was teaching to Sigma. The sabre was well-suited to Sigma's natural talents, but Vasco was pleased to find she had a real affinity for rapier. It was also proving to be a real challenge for her to learn. The complex angles and footwork, combined with sophisticated timing, confounded her. Vasco felt a guilty pleasure in his technical mastery over her... while keeping no illusions about how she'd handle him in a real bout.

The slow work they were doing was the best way to sink the technical lessons into her. At full speed, she would rely on raw speed to land shot after shot on him. It was a fair, and realistic, outcome. But Vasco had learned many hard lessons in life and one of the hardest was that you could never depend on physical superiority. It was a useful thing, but injury, sickness, or age could steal it from you. Or you might run into a person with even more physical superiority. With improper training, you wouldn't know a person was better than you—you'd just be dead. Sharp swords don't respect a learning curve.

But skill, proper skill, was always an advantage. By any stretch of the imagination, Sigma was a master unarmed martial artist. And so was Vasco... which meant that watching her grapple with the unfamiliar weapon was a real pleasure. The pleasure wasn't in her discomfort, but in watching her adaptation. Every time she came across a technique she had trouble with, or when a trained instinct interfered with what was correct for the weapon in her hand, she had to modify what she knew into what would work. Slow work gave her time to observe, change, and reinforce that learning.

It also gave Vasco a chance to pick up some new ideas for his own swordplay. He was learning at least as much from her struggles and solutions as she was. He was also building a nice reconstruction of her home martial art by reverse engineering her reactions. Whatever art the Laconians taught was damn good. In fact, it was almost too good. And a moment later, his suspicions were confirmed.

Sigma had started in a high line attack on his outside. Vasco countered with a slight parry, turning it into a graze, a curving cut into her blade that pushed her blade aside and exposed her inner line to a lunging counterattack to her body. She sidestepped to counter, pulling her sword hand back to her hip to parry and leaving her blade at an almost vertical angle—just what Vasco had intended for her to do. He countered her parry by disengaging out, threatening the back of her hand with a thrust, and she pushed forward, extending her hand and cutting into his blade strongly with the true edge of her sword.

It was one of Vasco's favored attack sequences, taught to him by his father. All that work was intended to draw out the attack she had just thrown, to get her to strongly extend her arm and push aside his blade. From her point of view, it should look like the perfect defense. She had moved his blade completely aside with a cut, and was not only threatening him with her tip, but was in a perfect position for an easy hand extension thrust that would run him through.

The follow-up was the Alicorno attack. Many fencers would forget the rear hand, and this sequence brought the vulnerable weak of the blade close to Vasco's left hand. He would seize the blade, rotate his hips, and pull his sword hand back up to his ear... threatening her with a plunging matador thrust. That was the plan anyway. The minute his left hand reached forward, Sigma flicked her wrist over, turning the blade from one edge to another. It had the effect of not just freeing her blade from the trap, but threatening Vasco with a severe cut... to which he no longer had a defense. He knew that counter and knew where it came from.

"You've been lying to me." Vasco stepped back, out of her range, and crossed his sword over and held it by the blade in his off hand. The lesson was definitely over. "You've trained with a sword before, and not just a little. I know that technique. It's a master level technique. You've been holding back."

Sigma quirked an eyebrow up and regarded him coolly. "It's true. I have been holding back and holding back information from you. I've never trained with a rapier or sabre before, but I did tell you Laconia was founded by reenactors. We all learn to use a longsword. I am a master instructor in their use."

Vasco felt cheated. He'd been working with and enjoying the sessions, but now he felt as if he were being made a fool. She'd been pleased when he suggested they work on fencing together, and she had eagerly accepted all his suggestions and expressed quite an interest in rapier work. Perhaps he had been wrong to make the assumption he had, but she could have mentioned something. Truly, she could have displayed more skill. The technique she had used displayed an advanced understanding of line and measure with a sword, and she had deliberately not shown that understanding in any of their lessons so far. She had lied to him.

"I think we are done with these lessons," he said, turning his back on her. He walked over to his gear bag and cleaned his rapier.

"I held back from you, it is true, but you have held back from me since our first bout. How long have you held back from yourself?"

Her words cut into Vasco. There was more truth to her tone than her words. He'd felt shame over his Creche origins, and shame over how his differences highlighted those origins. He'd been hiding his strength and speed from everyone ever since he was old enough to know what it meant. He'd never actually tested himself. Ever. His training came with the life-long ache of knowing he could do better, of wanting to let himself explode and fly on steely wings, but instead having to plod, always plod, so he could be only just a little bit better than others. He had immaculate technique... but for him, full-speed fighting was always slow work. It always had been. It gave him exceptional skill, but he had always felt stilted and unchallenged.

Until Sigma. And even when fighting her, he hadn't been able to let himself go. The years of conditioning were too much. Maybe it had been long enough. Maybe this would be his last chance? He'd been holding back for his whole life, and the only thing that kept it possible for him was the belief, deep inside, that someday he'd have the chance to prove himself. Someday... but he'd already been through two Long Drops. Those came with more chances at combat than most soldiers ever saw. It was more than enough for too many of his friends and teammates, but somehow Vasco had never been tested. Somehow that day had never come. Maybe he had held back too much, and maybe that was why some of his friends were dead and he wasn't.

Maybe it was time to stop holding back. He picked his rapier back up and turned to face Sigma. She was still standing there, sword in hand. Waiting.

Four meters away.

He leapt the distance in one prodigious bound. His sword smashed against Sigma's. She managed the block only at the last second. He hit with such speed and fury that her blade was pushed almost against her face.

She flicked away. Almost faster than the eye could follow, she was gone.

Vasco was on her like a demon. Speed, supple speed, flowing out of him. Cuts and thrusts in unending waves.

Sigma moving like an angel, parrying and counterattacking.

Their feet moving in rhythms and counter rhythms, torsos and hands surging back and forth.

Vasco let himself go, felt himself truly open up. Everything slowed down around him, but he heard the air whistling past him, he felt the pull of momentum on his body and the force his muscles had to exert to pull him around. It was exhilarating. He saw Sigma was still faster than him—much faster—but he was truly the master of his world now. His skill was supreme, and without holding back his natural ability, there was nothing she could do.

And then she stopped holding back.

One massive sweeping cut, right at his face.

Her blade shattered against his, not even slowing. The jagged broken forte stopped in front of his pupil, faintly brushing an eyelash.

They froze for a moment, panting with exertion.

"It's not so bad to be better than everyone else." She pulled the broken blade away from his eye and tossed it across the room.

Vasco was almost relieved to see that it didn't land quite perfectly in his gear bag. He felt strangely calm. Peaceful.

Sigma crouched, picked up the broken blade from the floor, and examined the shattered end for a moment. She held it toward Vasco. "Excellent steel. A master made this. But it still broke. See the striations in the break? No crystallization. This was a perfect blade. It was made to fight with. It broke because stress built up in it. No blade lasts forever. No one ever lives forever. We all end. You tell me, Vasco al Madina del Goya al Creche... is it better to break from being used the way the way a sword was meant to be used, or to rust away over the centuries, hanging on a wall?"

She held the broken blade out toward him. He was still calm, as if he didn't exist. He felt... clean. His hand lifted of its own accord and took the broken end of the blade, and she walked out on him again.

He stood there for almost an hour, alone, until his thoughts came back to him like a weary dog, then he went and washed up.

Chapter Six: The Wise

Cave was tailoring an attack package. She'd asked Vasco if it was okay if she worked on it next to him and he agreed. After a year in Pod space, everybody was happy for a little company. Maintenance crews and the ship's crew had everything down to a predictable rhythm. The training schedule was six weeks of heavy teaching and three weeks down. It was twice as intense as normal for a Long Drop Pod training schedule. Vasco could have kept up with a heavier schedule, but even the most optimistic predictions always kept an eye toward extended time in system without resupply. The more time the troops slept, the less they consumed. Which meant that those with Pod duty were starting to feel the hollow emptiness of the ship. The busy schedule kept your mind off of it, but after a few cycles, you started to think around the empty times.

And working alone in a cubicle became a little much after a while. At first the alone time was nice… that much Vasco had remembered when he signed on for Pod. He had fond memories of long walks and lots of time to think in the giant lonely spaces of the ship. After only a few weeks on board, he remembered what he had forgotten… the long stretches of itchy boredom and slowly encroaching creepiness. He would even admit to an edge of fear that built up over time. It was the fear of living alone in a cabin in the winter woods. There were no wolves on the ship, but some things in the human genetic code would probably never go away.

Vasco took to reading in the larger library nooks. During the busy times, they were ignored, as people looked for privacy and sometimes intimacy. During the empty times, they tended to fill up more. No one really talked. They just took comfort in the presence of another human being. Vasco wasn't surprised Cave had come to work in this nook. It was only her first year in Pod—she wouldn't get the wanders for another few months yet. She was still taking comfort in the closeness of her duty station, letting it anchor her even if she wouldn't make use of it for another year... if then.

Cave let out another sigh, this one a bit louder than the last. Vasco could take a hint. Formality had a habit of disappearing in deep Pod space, but Cave was still hesitant to start a conversation with a superior. Vasco decided to let her off the hook.

"How goes the script?" he asked.

She raised her eyebrows and glanced at him, making a moue of her lips while she considered. "Well... not bad. You've done this before, haven't you?"

"Yeah," Vasco replied, "I had the same slot as you on my first drop. Why do you think Primus Always slotted me into your station? So you could keep an eye on me?" He smiled at her.

Vasco had been thinking a lot in the week since his last session with Sigma and was really in the mood to talk to someone normal. He was still okay to spend time on his own, but he was at the point where talking to an actual human being was something to savor... like a cup of coffee in the morning.

Each Tactical System Operator had their own customized attack package. Hacking was an art form, even in the midst of a battle, but battle offered no time for anything other than reflex. So a good operator accumulated a lengthy bag of tricks. Most were specific to known systems, but you always kept a scrap of exploits for theoretical situations. The attack package was a personalized menu that contained shortcuts to pockets of commands.

You might start with a command that listened for broadcast packets. Depending on the length of those packets, different scripts would be called up to determine headers and address protocols buried in the packet. Once those had been determined, scripts would be called up to search out the network or call up common exploits. Once a target had been found and identified, another set of scripts to try to penetrate. A whole series more to elevate privileges and root the enemy server... or make use of it in some other way. Vasco's last attack package had over 250,000 discrete scripts he'd collected or written and sorted into ten top level entries. It had taken him over ten years to polish it.

Cave had been in her position for less than a year, so she was probably feeling pretty overwhelmed. TacOps was a hell of a lot of responsibility. Battles, even wars, had been won on the skills of one side's hackers. The Creche war had been won by Polity hackers. Interstellar civilization lived and died on its computers, and the Creche did so more than most others. They had "bred" their citizens for physical attributes, depending on their computers to handle the more complex mental tasks. Vasco suspected that the Laconians shared the same weakness—breeding for the physical prowess and superhuman ability Sigma demonstrated and letting their Helots do the work of civilization. It was probably that flaw that the Polity would exploit when inevitable unification happened.

Cave smirked and nodded as she realized that she had actually been thinking of Vasco as someone she was supposed to babysit, and not the other way around. "I guess I was thinking that actually," she said. "Sorry, Centurion. It's just..."

"I know," Vasco said. "I've been there. You've got all the skill in the world burned into you and the universe to win. How can experience compare with that?"

"Yeah, something like that. At least I used to think that. But now that I'm doing the job, there's so much of it to do... and I guess I realized that if you've done this already, that means you've already been through all this. It took a bit for me to realize what that meant. So... can you help me?"

"Sure! I was hoping you'd ask. One thing I've learned over the years is that you can learn from everyone. I wanted to dig into your work, but I thought I'd give you a chance to offer before I tested your personal encryption skills."

"I think you'd find my skills are pretty good."

"I'm sure I'd find them at least as good as you found mine when you tried to hack my files last week."

Cave had the decency to look sheepish and wince. Vasco waggled his eyebrows at her. Hacking was almost as fun as fencing. He was looking forward to her realizing he'd been in her files since the first day.

"Pass it over," he said, motioning for her work slate.

She tossed it over, and he dug through her files, following her logic paths. She'd made some interesting changes in the last day or two.

"Where did you find a Sami dictionary?" he asked.

"It was in the library, buried in an ethnographic survey from almost a thousand years ago. I'm not sure it'll be of any use, but I figured it would give me a start."

It probably would. Brute force password hacking could be sped up significantly with a dictionary. Random combinations would eventually get you there, but at a huge time cost. Starting with known words could get you lucky. And with the right follow-up software, all you needed was a single entry point. One lazy user on a system might be the fulcrum for your pry bar.

And if you knew the encryption system the enemy was using, you could use the same encryption system on the dictionary and compare both sets of encrypted data. If you found a match, you found a word, and suddenly you opened up all the enemy's encrypted transmissions. If you were lucky.

Encryption was one of the more elaborate games in the world of warfare. Currently the hackers had a slight advantage over the codemakers... six thousand years of codebreaking had developed an excellent bag of tricks and some solid logic tools. Eventually the tables would turn again. The Pook moved on a whole different level, but that was a game for another day. Still, by digging up the Sami dictionary, Cave had probably shaved days off of their initial in-system reconnaissance work.

"It'll be a damn good start," Vasco said, "and we should be able to catch up with any language drift fairly quickly. I didn't even know they had their own language. It never showed up in the any of the recorded contacts during recent Helot sales."

Cave leaned back, sticking her ankles up on the nook's couch and crossing them. "Yeah, they speak Polity fair enough. I guess they learned it from someone. Makes sense if you're negotiating sales for someone else. Kinda makes you wonder though. All those years of being without unification and they still seem to have maintained some kind of contact."

"It happens. Just because a system is un-unified doesn't mean they are unknown or invisible. It just means for whatever reason, they aren't part of the Polity. Usually it's because they've lost contact with humanity over the years and kind of forgotten about the rest of us. Sometimes it's intentional. The Sami, in some ways, look like some of the religious systems that tried to keep separate to preserve their beliefs."

Cave looked disgusted. "How could anyone do that to their children? Warping their minds so young, hiding them from real knowledge... I've heard they don't teach them Polity history, or even pre-Polity history! No real rights or child protection, no proper insurance or health care. I just don't know how they can consider themselves civilized."

"I guess they see it differently, Cave."

Vasco was starting to wonder though. He'd spent his whole life fighting to bring the Polity way to humans. It did seem to be the right way. It was what he had been taught and come to believe was right. Humanity had splintered, and so many worlds had forgotten their own heritage. Worlds had devolved to feudalism and slavery, theocracies, and outright pirate worlds. There were no standards of education at all. Sure, some worlds had even better standards than the Polity, but always those worlds seemed to diverge from the human standard...away from how the Polity saw the norms of human behavior, at least. That mankind needed to be unified and cohesive was the core foundation and belief of the Polity. We all had to grow together. Too much growth over such a vastly spread diaspora inevitably led to splintering, and splintering led to cultures that lost their humanity.

The Polity's near-sacred mission was to bring its standards of education, technology, commerce, medicine, entertainment, and politics to every single human world. Once every world was at the same level, central updates—the Tech updates—would reach out in unified waves. Humanity would be one force, one consistent voice, the way its ancestors had meant it to be. To do anything less was to abandon the hopes and dreams of tens of thousands of years of human growth and civilization. All that amazing growth couldn't be given up.

And yet... Vasco had his doubts. A seed borne of his own differences, his own specialness, had grown in him. Was the Creche approach really so wrong? Maybe. But his long-denied abilities? Maybe they weren't evil. Maybe they weren't a source of shame. He had done good for the Polity, and he knew he was a good person. If the stock wasn't bad, then maybe the source wasn't all bad.

Vasco shook his head. Sigma must have rattled him good, or he was getting a little Pod-crazed already. "They see it differently, Cave, but don't worry. Our job is to help them see it the right way. And if they can't, we'll make sure they aren't around to wreck their kids as well."

"That's why I signed up," said Cave. "That and getting my veteran's land. I'm going to go for a city spot, maybe open a leather shop. It's my family business. I know everything there is to know."

"Leather?" Vasco laughed. "Do they even have cows on Rumi?"

"If they don't, I'll make even more money. Luxury goods! Importing is where the real money is!"

They spent a few hours daydreaming about business ventures before Neruda came by and took Vasco off for a talk.

"I gather you've been spending more time with our Laconian ice queen. Any reason for us to worry?" Neruda was looking through one of the interior ports, into the vacuum gap between the inner hull and the armor layer.

The viewing bay was one of the few spots on the ship built for sightseeing. Maintenance lights gave an impressive sense of scope. But Vasco didn't like to look out. The slowly rotating view just reminded him of his old problems with centrifugal living. It wasn't something he cared to remember. Sort of like not being able to eat a certain food after being sick shortly after eating it. Vasco was leaning on the wall, looking over Neruda's shoulder at a screen playing random bits of entertainment. He was happy to let his eyes unfocus toward it, and his thoughts drifted to match.

He spent a moment reviewing all his talks with Sigma. "No, no reason to worry. She hasn't really talked about the Sami at all. I don't think the Laconians really care. She doesn't seem to anyway."

"She's playing it close to the vest, I guess. Makes sense. They have to care. The Sami are their last buffer between them and the Polity. She's the first Laconian anyone has seen in over a thousand years at least, and we've bought dozens of Helots before this one. She's certainly helped get it integrated faster, but I can't help but wonder why now. It has to be for reconnaissance. Maybe the Laconians will propose unification before we send a Tatar… it's happened before."

Neruda was quiet for a moment. Vasco thought she was brooding and not really happy with her own conclusions. Vasco found he didn't have much opinion at all. He watched the moving images. The content never registered. Just shapes, shifting and moving. No sense to them at all.

"Do you remember Hawat?" Vasco said.

Neruda snorted gently and crossed her arms, looking out the port. Her silence was the only answer Vasco needed.

Hawat was a dry world. Heavy mineral production and radioactives. At one point, it had apparently had extensive salt oceans like Earth, but some horrific weapon had boiled them off and leveled most of the surface. Low, round mountains, thin atmosphere, and some giant freshwater lakes. A smattering of okay farmland. And rich, rich veins of heavy metals everywhere. It was a tough world no one wanted to live on, but it was too lucrative for humanity to pass up.

The Hawatians were a tough and ornery people. Violence was a way of life for them. A really ugly life. They had a strong theocracy and no regard for women as anything other than property. It was a world far overdue for unification.

The Hawatians were unpleasant people, but damn good fighters and even better strategists. The only reason they hadn't conquered the three other habitable planets in their system was because at some point in the past, the other worlds had managed to gain the upper hand in a war with the Hawatians and had wiped out their attack fleets, then held the orbital space. They locked the Hawatians into their own world and wouldn't let them up the well for any reason. They'd sued for peace and let a sort of economy develop. The system was in pretty good equilibrium when the Polity arrived to Unify.

The Polity had a lot of policies in place for initial Unification. Hawat was a hard case, and after some ugly initial contact, the Hawatians had tortured one of the Polity contact teams to death over the course of a day. Broadcast the whole thing live to the Tatar *Andromeda*. The Timariot hadn't stopped the broadcast. He'd actually had it rebroadcast throughout the entire ship... while they loaded up for a hot combat drop.

A Polity combat drop was about as no-nonsense as combat could be. The drop shuttles were two hundred meters long and loaded with troops. Tanks and armored personnel carriers were dropped from orbit in individual reentry packs. Banshee dirigibles ripped into the atmosphere as delta-winged black demons, cracking open into flat black ground support floaters.

When the shuttles were deep enough in the well to glide, the hammer fell. They chose the second largest Hawatian city and gave them a one-hour warning... then laid waste to it with kinetic impact weapons. Only from space could you see that the long ripping lines of silver fire tearing into the heart of the city were spokes. The Plate landed at the center of the spoke.

The Plate was a hell of a sight, dropping from the sky. They actually slowed it down with rockets. A piece of steel that size falling from orbit at orbital speed would have done more damage than even the Polity was willing to accept. As it was, when it hit at the center of the spokes, the city of one hundred thousand Hawatians became a memory. The shuttles and other toys landed at the edge of the newly sterilized zone.

The Gyrenes had a defensive perimeter up in under an hour, and an hour after that, they were on the move in full strength. They hit hard and fast, mopping up Hawatian forces. The Gyrenes moved at full speed in APCs, hitting everything they could and not stopping. If they hit any serious resistance, the Banshees provided overhead fire support until the tanks arrived. If the tanks and Banshees couldn't open the way, the mobile artillery would set down and fire away.

If they hit anything that could hold up to that, the High Guard Banshees would let loose with assisted kinetics from stratosphere height. And if that didn't do it, *Andromeda* had space-to-ground weapons to add to the mix. *Andromeda*'s weapons mix was a hellish brew of everything including bio and chemical warfare packages.

But the Hawatians didn't give them time for that. For a week straight, the Drop force smashed enemy after enemy. The Hawatians gave stiffer and stiffer resistance, but the Gyrenes just kept coming. And then the first surprise showed up.

The Hawatians had made the most of their mining world, and throughout centuries of warfare, they'd hid innovation from the other worlds in the system. Armies rose up out of the ground behind the Gyrenes, cutting off their logistics train. And in front of them, the ground gave way. The spearhead forces had been trapped neatly in a manmade cul-de-sac.

To Vasco, it had been madness. He'd spilled out of his Operations APC, sidearm in hand. He'd had his head buried in transmissions until their antenna had been shot off. He'd looked up from his console to discover they weren't moving and a glance through the block to the driver compartment had shown him why—some Hawatian sniper had taken out the driver. Vasco had been so focused on his task, he hadn't even noticed the other TacOps bailing out.

He'd stepped out of the APC, not knowing what to expect, and found a scene he would never have been able to anticipate. The howl of a Banshee's jet engines was the first sound he heard, and the sky was black with the shape of the vast dirigible. He looked up in time to see a flash of light as the Banshee's reactive armor blew off a shell from somewhere. An instant later, its phalanx guns ripped off in a spray of tracers, batting a missile or rocket somewhere out of the sky. It looked as if every gun port it had was firing. It couldn't have been more than five hundred meters up.

The air slapped against him, and he felt the dull rip of heavy rounds from the dirigible punching into the ground all around him. Everything slowed down. He found himself wondering why the stupid airship was shooting at friendlies and decided it was time for him to move. He turned toward the front of the APC, ready to charge into battle. Everything was still trickling by, and every motion felt perfect. This was his moment, his time. He'd fly into battle, invulnerable. He turned… and saw a bloody Neruda running at him, screaming.

He couldn't tell what Neruda was screaming. She seemed to be covered in a lot of blood, and her rifle was clutched in one hand. She ran right at Vasco, into him, and past him, dragging him along. Vasco barely kept his footing as Neruda hurled to the rear—just in time. The Banshee was letting loose with everything.

Vasco glanced up for the merest second and saw the airship fire almost all its rockets at once. Pulsing sheets of fire crashed into a wave of explosions somewhere in the distance. Vasco was picked up, pushed forward. Huge pressure hit him, enormous pain in his eardrums. He must have been screaming without knowing it or both eardrums would have ruptured when the overpressure hit him. The APC was venting fire straight up and out the open door. The Banshee had taken it out with an anti-tank round.

Neruda dragged Vasco a little farther until they ran into another group of Gyrenes, all firing wildly over Vasco's head as he was pulled down between them. The next few days were a blur. He later found out that they had been overrun and Neruda had called down fire on their position, thinking she was the last one left and surrounded by Hawatians. She'd saved Vasco's life.

It took them seven days of fighting to pull back to the landing zone. They lost two Banshees and would have lost everything if it hadn't been for a constant series of kinetic strikes. Some of them had to be called in so close, Vasco swore he'd never hear again. At least the engineers had been busy, having anticipated the withdrawal. It had taken them the last two weeks to winch the nearly hollow, engine-less shuttles up on the drive Plate and attach them to the giant central drive Piston, which had fallen with the tanks and ammo. But they were ready for launch.

Vasco waited, somewhat nervously, for his turn to board his shuttle. None of them had time to tape up before donning ship's armor. They'd survive to get back to orbit anyway.

He got a chance to see the last of the Banshees die. The crew abandoned out the rear in the small escape pods, stubby little pulse jet engines purring away. The top seams of the gas bags split with resounding crashes, and the airship slipped down with the residual airfoil effect left in their reentry shells. It slammed into the ground three kilometers away—about where the advancing Hawatian army was. Time was running out.

About twenty minutes later, the first enemy round hit the shuttle Vasco was in. Just in time for the Hawatians to learn that the Polity was a firm believer in Pyrrhic victories. The shuttles had been hoisted up and secured to the Piston, which was attached to the Plate. Those elements all combined to make a complete Orion lift ship. The first drive bomb, a shaped nuclear charge set off under the Plate, was a doozy and right at the design limit for the shuttle attachments. It gave the ship the kick it needed, boosting it up off the ground. Then the next bomb went off. If any of the attacking army had survived the first multi-megaton nuclear explosion, they hadn't survived the second, or the third, or the ones that followed.

A week later, a new landing zone had been carved for the Polity out of, this time, the biggest city on Hawat. They landed the complete ship with the Orion drive, which gave them more time to prepare and meet up with the reinforcements dropping out of the radiated zone. Hawat surrendered three days later.

Vasco wasn't sure why he had mentioned that now. The Sami were likely to be more compliant, and the Laconian unification was probably decades away. Assuming they could find out where Laconia even was. Vasco sighed. He had too much on his mind these days.

Neruda noticed. "You don't look yourself. What's on your mind? You've been holding something back."

Vasco considered for a moment. There were so many things he could say, things he wanted to talk about. Neruda was an old friend—Vasco's oldest, truthfully—but he still didn't think he could talk about his doubts or feelings with her. Not now, not with Neruda's position. Some things overruled friendship. But he had to tell her something and Vasco couldn't think of anything. There was nothing he could say about how he seemed to be changing. Nothing to be said, but maybe he could show her something.

"My Creche birth," he said, "you know how they specialized breeding of humans?"

"Yeah, it's my job to know that. What about it?"

Vasco didn't say anything—he slowly bent down to the floor and put both hands on the deck. They were on the farthest outside point of the Ring, where gravity was just a hair over normal. Vasco stretched his fingers out on the steel plating as if he could grip the smooth surface. He kicked a foot up and let his other foot flow up behind until he was in a perfect handstand. Neruda watched curiously.

Slowly, carefully, Vasco picked up one hand. The balance was fiendishly difficult, and only his enormous strength allowed him to counterbalance the rotational effect of the Ring. He managed to bring his hand up next to his leg and held a perfect single-handed handstand. Then he took a deep breath and arched his back, bent his right arm, and slowly, so very slowly and fighting for balance the whole way, lowered his chest to the floor, then back up again in a perfect one-hand handstand pushup. For a top-level gymnast practicing since birth, it would have been barely, barely possible, and only at the brief peak of their competitive career. For an untrained, sort of in shape man like Vasco? It should have been beyond possible.

Vasco did it three more times before he hopped back up and wiped off his hand.

Neruda looked at him, frowning. Finally she shook her head and said, "Let's go get a beer."

Chapter Seven: The One Who Encompasses All

The Pook model was posed on the table. Neruda was staring at it, turning it from side to side. She'd had the life-size three-dimensional model printed from a file stored in the ship's library. It was an odd-looking creature. The Pook were cat-sized and roughly feline, except for the large foreclaw that covered the back of each hand and extended forward. It almost gave them the appearance of a praying mantis. The exoskeleton armor they all wore added to that impression.

Under the foreclaw, the actual fingers curled. They looked tiny and fragile, almost flower like, under the big claw. The Pook could apparently extend their fingers quite far. They had agile hands and could do intricate work that would take a human a bevy of specialized tools.

Their armor was an example of that. Every Pook wore a set of hand-built power armor. Human ship's armor was strong stuff, but Pook armor was magic. Instead of batteries, they had tiny fusion generators. The Pook were usually only a meter tall at the most, but their armor made them as strong, and twice as fast, as a Gyrene in ship's armor. They usually carried a large assortment of weapons in addition to the ones built into the armor.

Add in an impressive sensor suite, and each Pook was almost a literal army unto itself. Humans still had no idea what the full capability of Pook armor was... or where the armor ended and the Pook began.

"One more time, Sigma," Neruda said. "I'm just not quite getting it."

Neruda had asked Sigma if she'd share some of what she knew about the Pook, and she'd agreed to answer what questions she could. In one of the Tatar's officer lounges, Vasco and some of the other Centurions had been invited along for the informal information session.

"Certainly, Primus Always. The armor is a mark of status to the Pook. The less armor a Pook wears, the higher their status. The Pook have an idealized genetic standard, and a Pook that is not up to the standard must wear armor to bring him up to that standard. It's how they overcome their perceived handicaps."

"So the top Pook is naked?" one of the Centurions asked.

"Yes. But neither I, nor any Laconian, has ever seen a Pook of the top rank. We don't believe any human ever has. The highest ranking Pook I have ever met was a captain of one of their ships, and she was helmetless."

"A bald cat," said Neruda.

"Indeed. A completely hairless cat is how I would describe the structure and appearance of a Pook face. With the marked difference that they are far more expressive than any cat I have ever seen."

"So how do they rise in rank? Do they lose armor as they go up in rank? Or achieve whatever it is a Pook achieves in life?" Neruda asked.

"A Pook can rise in station based on ability, but they maintain a reverence for genetic perfection. The armor an adult Pook wears is the armor they wear for life. It is never removed."

"But the Pook armor has built-in sensors and weapons, don't they?" Vasco asked. "Are you saying that the ideal Pook has these senses?"

"That we aren't sure of. Laconia maintains friendly and

frequent contact with the Pook, and they consider the issue of inherent abilities somewhat distasteful to talk about. Our best guess is that the sensors and weapons of Pook armor are analogs that match the result, if the not the specific method, of the more perfect Pook."

"Wait a minute," Vasco said. A sneaking suspicion grew in him. "Aren't computers and communicators part of their armor as well? Doesn't that mean…"

"That is correct, Centurion del Goya. We assume that some Pook have an innate ability to communicate over extreme distances."

"You mean they're telepathic." Neruda didn't look happy, but she didn't look surprised either. Vasco had the impression that this wasn't news to her, but confirmation.

Sigma was silent for a moment, but otherwise as expressionless as usual. "We think they have an ability to manipulate forces we neither understand nor are even aware of. But yes, we think that a Pook of high rank is capable of acting as an independent computer, communicating over long distances and causing significant damage outside the range of their own bodies. This would appear to be in line with the common human belief in psionics. Much like Pook superluminal travel, we don't understand the mechanism at all."

"What a lovely reminder." Vasco said. "Maybe in a million years we'll catch up with them. Something else occurs to me, Walkure Sigma. You've mentioned that they make each set of armor to match an ideal they see themselves as being short of meeting. Do they ever make armor to exceed that ideal? Are they capable of doing that, mentally or technologically?"

"They would never make armor for themselves to exceed that ideal. They are certainly capable of it, but to do so would go against their ethics. They don't regard failure as a bad thing. If an individual Pook must face a creature or sentient that is more capable than they are—and I have heard there are many such in the galaxy—they will do their absolute best. If they succeed, they will enjoy the personal glory. If they fail, it is accepted as what must be. In battles the Pook have fought against superior foes, and they have never tried to increase their individual abilities. They have simply striven to succeed with what they have been given and made for themselves. They are content to be what they are. Considering they are the dominant race in the galaxy, it appears to be an approach that works for them."

"Indeed." Said Vasco. "I can't see us imitating or even attempting to imitate the Pook approach, but us humans must be what we are, I suppose. Well. Thank you very much, Walkure Sigma. I think we all enjoyed this talk. Gentlemen, thanks for joining us. We make system fall in three weeks, so we'll have one more session in two days, when Timariot Smith has agreed to talk about proposed dirigible changes in the next Tech. Now, let's have a drink, shall we?"

Most of the gathered officers got up to examine the Pook model, and a few gathered around Sigma to ask her more questions.

Vasco hung around to be polite, but he found he didn't care much for company today. He drifted over to look at the model of the Pook and thought about his own origins. How would he fit in if humans used the Pook hierarchy? He had a lot more physical ability that anyone else he'd met, but there were people a lot smarter than him, a lot better looking, people who had accomplished more. He supposed it didn't really matter. As Sigma had said about the Pook, he would be content to be what he was. He'd strive for what success he could but wouldn't sweat the failure.

Vasco felt Sigma's approach a second before her hand touched his elbow. With her usual enigmatic half-smile, she walked him out of the lounge. Vasco was briefly amused by the envious smiles on a few of his fellow Centurions. Obviously they expected he was about to work on some deeper level of Polity-Laconian relationships.

Not that Vasco would have minded, but he didn't think that was what Sigma had in mind. Actually, it didn't seem like the sort of thing she ever had in mind. Vasco marshaled his thoughts before he started paying too much attention to Sigma's walk—then noticed they were heading toward her quarters.

She opened the door and motioned him in ahead of her. Her room was as spartan as he'd suspected it would. It was so neat and clean that it appeared unlived in. The only spot of near color was a long, narrow object wrapped in a piece of wool cloth, sitting on the simple bed. It was one of the smaller staterooms the *Alexi* offered and was probably meant for clerical help. It didn't seem appropriate for someone who was, in effect, an ambassador.

"I expected you'd have been assigned nicer quarters than these, Walkure. I feel like I should apologize..." Vasco said.

"I was assigned other quarters originally. I'm a Laconian. We neither need nor want luxury. I specifically asked for these quarters. They suit me better." She closed the door and looked at Vasco for a moment. "Centurion Vasco al Madina del Goya al Alamansa, you have a gift. You were born to a greater purpose. But that purpose can only be born in you of your own choice. You will find among the Sami a greater test for yourself than you can ever imagine. Rumi can be a forge that will change you forever, if you choose to make it so. There will come a day when you have to make a choice between who you are, who you wish to be, and who you might be. I can't help you with that choice, and the consequences of your choice will be yours and yours alone. There is no loss, no matter what you choose."

Vasco didn't know what to say, so he stood and waited.

She moved to the bundle on the bed and picked it up. "I've enjoyed our sessions together. I've appreciated the chance to see who you might be. When the time comes for you to make your choice, I would have a part of me be with you." She unwrapped the simple woolen cloth.

Buried inside was a sword. It was short, slightly curved, and simple, but Vasco's eye saw the work of a master bladesmith. It was a modern war sword. Compact enough to carry with modern arms, lengthy enough to do its job. The metal it was made of had an odd, almost golden sheen.

Sigma offered it to Vasco. "This sword is forged from

Pook armor steel. You'll find it almost impossible to break, and the edge will keep with only light maintenance. I thought this a suitable gift, since I broke your sword."

Vasco didn't really know what to say. Sigma's words had been delivered with more emotion than he'd ever heard from her, with a cadence that echoed inside him. There were implications to what she said that he knew he wasn't understanding. "Thank you, Walkure Sigma. I don't know what to say."

"It is a warrior's weapon. Be the right warrior to carry it, that is all I ask of you. My duties mean you won't see me again until the time of the choice comes. Maybe not even then. Be a warrior, Vasco. Be the warrior you were meant to be."

Neruda waited in the Timariot's office. Even in a vessel the size of the *Alexi*, it was an extravagant use of space. The office took up a sizable portion of the Ring, and a matching suite connected to the main bridge for use when under acceleration. Neruda had served directly under a few other Timariots, and none had spent so much shipboard space on their accommodations. Of course, none of them were as successful as the Timariot Emil Smith, and as such, didn't have his income either. Neruda had heard the crew discussing a rumor that during the planning phase, there had been talk about tailgating a battleship-sized vessel onto the *Alexi* for the Timariot's space-bound residence. Neruda knew it wasn't a rumor.

The office would have done a pre-space king proud. Rich wood was the main theme, traced with gold everywhere. The walls were mostly bookshelves, and the book selection was excellent. Neruda, with the Timariot's permission, had made good use of it during the voyage. She'd spent every spare moment perusing the ancient collection of pre-space paperback novels. Most were reproductions, but a few originals were scattered about. Sleek metal bars held the books in place—and had to be unlocked to read them—but Neruda found that only added to the specialness of the experience. She ran her fingers down the spines of some of her favorites. Some day she would retire and replicate this library.

Over the years, she'd amassed a careful mental list of all the best of the different Timariots' eccentricities. She planned to steal the best of their ideas for her own showcase of wealth. Wealth that would come in time—sooner, if her plans worked out.

Neruda turned as the Timariot entered the office. He was trailed by an ensign reading out readiness reports. The Timariot waved him off and sealed the office.

"I hate the wake up," he said. "I know it's not real sleep, but it feels like it to me. Only difference is the whole next week feels like Monday morning. All I want is to sit back with a cup of coffee and have a few minutes to myself, and instead I have to deal with all this crap. And getting woken up in zero-g is the worst. I hate that goddamn zero-g crap. Worst part of this business. Couldn't get my ass into the Ring fast enough. How's things, Neruda?"

"Good. We're on schedule to exit Pod space in a month, and everything is coming along fine. I'm happy with everyone's performance. All the special projects are coming along well..."

"How's our boy doing?"

"Right on cue. He's pushed for information on Alamansa and has been spending a lot of time with the Walkure. Everything seems to be moving right on plan. She's attempting to coerce him by appealing to his Creche origins, and he's starting to question Polity motives. He's not even aware he's doing it."

The Timariot chuckled and sat himself down in one a chair oversized enough to be clearly made just for him. "The best double agents are the ones who don't even know they're double agents!" he said. "Good job, Neruda. You still sure you're okay throwing your friend to the wolves like that? You were right about him being the perfect specimen."

Neruda managed not to grimace at this phrasing. Vasco was a friend, but once she'd learned the truth about his breeding, she'd realized he was the perfect pawn for her plans.

"He's a good soldier and a good man," she said, "but the Creche breeding can't be trusted. Maybe if we'd left him alone, it never would have been activated, but the opportunity was too good to pass up. I predicted a fifty-percent chance the Laconian would try to recruit him due to his genetics, and an eighty-percent chance he would turn traitor under the right stressors. The Laconian's still playing it low-key, but at least all we have to do now is keep an eye on Vasco during the unification. She's been far too difficult to track, but Vasco will be easy to follow."

The Timariot nodded in approval. "Good work," he said. "Now we'll make sure to put him in the worst of it on Rumi. A good grind ought to make him turn tail. Sure as hell those shifty damn Outlanders aren't gonna just roll over and assimilate, and that kind always puts up a dirty fight. Ought to do the trick just right, I think."

Neruda nodded along with the Timariot. It was a good time to do some digging of her own and confirm some of her own hunches. "That's the plan, Timariot," she said. "Although I'm still unclear on our long-term goals here. I understand we need to locate the Laconian home system, but I feel like this is about more than just completing Unification."

The Timariot was quite for a moment, and then heaved himself up out of his chair. He looked at Neruda, and then walked over to the nearest bookshelf. He ran his fingers over a few of the books and then nodded to himself.

"It's been above your pay grade," he said. "But the Unification of Humanity is almost done. And it was only ever meant to be the first step. Somehow or another, these Sami and Laconians have done gone put themselves in the way of our next goal—and provided us with the tool we need to obtain that goal as well. Think about it, girl. We have to reach beyond human space some time. And when we do, we'll deal with the little Pook bastards. The Helots are the perfect tool for keeping those snoopy little freaks out of our systems, and the Laconians aren't selling them to us fast enough or cheap enough."

Neruda felt her insides turn to ice as her hunch was confirmed. She kept her face relaxed and calm, though. "I see. So our long-range plan is war with the Pook?"

The Timariot shrugged. "Not a plan, girl. Just a precaution. You don't think we can trust 'em, do you? All that hacking, all that mystery—that's them trying to keep us in our place. Once we reach out past our borders, they'll be in our face. We're just making sure we can keep them out of our face, is all."

"So war for sure with the Sami? I'm pretty sure we would have no problem talking the city people into Unification. The Outlanders will be a problem, but I'm not concerned about a small group of illiterate savages."

"Yes. We give them no choice about the war. I figure some conduit exists for communication between them and the Laconians, and I want to send them a message. The Polity isn't fucking around. As soon as we see a target in Anubis, we waste it. I want a drop on the third-largest city with minimal warning. We're going in hell for leather. I don't want to give them time to think. Iron fist in the teeth, then we can show them the velvet glove after."

Chapter Eight: The Grateful

Vasco threw a hard cut at the Timariot's head. It was a simple cut delivered honestly. Had the Timariot not blocked... it wouldn't have split his head in half. Not with the training sabre.

It would have split his scalp nicely though. The Timariot probably would have enjoyed that, Vasco thought. It would have added to his image of himself as the manly conqueror type.

Vasco was not enjoying himself. You could, he had said many times, look into a person's soul when you fenced with them. He saw into Emil Smith's soul quite clearly.

The Timariot blocked the cut swiftly and brutally and threw a return cut at Vasco's head. Vasco took the cut lightly on his blade and whipped a cut back. He saw the evil gleam in the Timariot's eye. Some people were so simple.

Vasco knew the Timariot was an accomplished strategist, a great and proven warrior. He was starting to see why that was. A good Timariot could act decisively on the slightest instinct, right or wrong. In combat, it was often easier to correct a bad decision than to overcome the losses from a tardy decision. A swift and aggressive tactician could overwhelm a clever opponent almost every time. It was a style of combat that had won the Timariot not just battles and wars, but worlds.

And here, he was about to show Vasco the error of his

ways. The Timariot had detected what he thought was a flaw in Vasco's style—a weak parry—and he was doing exactly what Vasco expected him to do. The Timariot threw his follow-up cut with a surprising fury, attempting to catch Vasco off guard with a real attack instead of the steadily paced attack of a drill.

Vasco let the attack come in and met it even weaker than the last. His sabre was smashed down, and Vasco let it drop, helping it collapse by pushing his wrist up, straight over his own head. His sabre turned into a slide for the Timariot's blade, and the powerful cut slipped to Vasco's side. Had the Timariot not been an already accomplished fencer, he might have stumbled forward with the force of his cut.

As it was, the Timariot realized his mistake before it was too late, and he yanked his blade back as fast as he could to parry Vasco's already incoming attack. With his speed and strength, the Timariot just managed to block the return cut.

Or so he thought.

He froze in place, and Vasco would have laughed at the sight of the Timariot's eyes tracking upwards and crossing as he saw Vasco's sword resting on his skull—and the tiny trail of blood already dripping off of the Timariot's nose onto the carpet.

Vasco had timed his counter perfectly, expecting not only the cut but the response as well. He'd placed his sabre's blade just behind the Timariot's so that when the Timariot had pulled his sword back to parry, he'd actually pulled Vasco's sword into his own head. The only reason the cut wasn't severe was because Vasco had used a sizable portion of his own strength to hold back.

"Shall we try that again?" Vasco said. "Skill always wins, but it only comes with rigid practice. You need a more relaxed wrist and less turning of the body. Rely on the sword for defense."

Vasco considered explaining to the Timariot how Vasco had exploited his reaction, but he decided against it. The Timariot's ego was large enough that he wouldn't accept that he had made a flaw in his strong suit—tactics—and especially not from a mere fencer, no matter how well regarded. The best Vasco could do was to explain the flaw as a physical one. Something the Timariot could grasp.

Vasco preferred the Timariot with some flaws. Sometimes you had to leave a student with holes in their game. Nothing they would notice, or other fencers would notice, but the master always left a way for himself to be the winner if needed.

It seemed the Sami had elected to resist. The Alexi had come out of Pod space with no issue, unloaded her escort ships, and started in toward Anubis. For the first week, nothing. And then they had picked up three ships burning into them at full acceleration from Rumi orbit. They hadn't answered any hails, and it was clear they were on an intercept course, so the Timariot had ordered them destroyed.

The first salvo rippled soundlessly into the void. There was no flash, no explosion. The side of the Tatar *Alexi* was bumpy with weapon pods, blisters, and sensors, but the first salvo of kinetics came from permanent seams in the armor. Narrow bands ran the flank of the great ship, minuscule valleys in the otherwise solid armor. Ports opened and closed in less than a blink of an eye. All that could be seen of the kinetics—tens of thousands of millimeter-thick, thirty-centimeter-long rods—was incidental flickers of reflection. The railguns sent them out at such speed that it seemed like a faint sheet of frost knifing toward the enemy.

Against most ships, the hyperspeed kinetic whiskers were all that was needed. Any civilian ship would be utterly destroyed by the impact of even a portion of a single salvo.

Against a warship, armored with ice or radiator shielding like the *Alexi*, it was just a nuisance. Pook shields would nudge them aside.

The *Alexi* was a warship designed to fight unknown enemies. Humans were creative, and you never knew what they might have invented in a millennia of separation. Polity doctrine was to crush any opposition. Take the best they could dish out and annihilate them in return. So the whiskers were meant to clean space of any distractions, like missiles or fighters, before the real weapons came into play.

Vasco hated this part. It was too easy to imagine what was happening on the other side.

Best case (for the enemy anyway), they were alert, active, and well-defended. Even with the enormous closing rates, they would see their sensors light up with the incoming kinetics, and discern the individual nature of the weapons, not see them as just a dense cloud.

For the first salvo, the Polity always went with a vanilla shot. No fancy charges to attract or repel the rods to each other, no EM or active rods to lead the cloud in any sort of curving feints. No planetary EM field for them to fire the metal projectiles through to pick up an electrical load. The first shot was just a wall of steel.

Having recognized it, the enemy would have to think quickly of a way to stop it or maybe evade it. If they had planned ahead for this sort of attack, they might take the shot.

Each rod, at this speed, would hit with incredible force. Not quite at nuclear range—the railguns pumped them out at 9km/s, but the Alexi was just moving from a stand-still. If the Tatar *Alexi*'s captain had his way, they likely would have launched while hitting 50km/s or much, much more. At that speed, each rod would hit with the force of an anti-matter bomb.

But even that force, the *Alexi* could take. She was armored enough. The small ships of the enemy fleet? Probably not. At current acceleration, the impact would be about as much as a large artillery shell. At current spread, a round dozen or so of the thousands launched might hit each ship.

If they had good armor, they might be able to take it. No armor, they'd have to run or react.

Which was the point of the first salvo. See what the opponent did.

Mostly enemies did nothing but try to evade. Sometimes it worked. Mostly it didn't. And if it did, the follow-ups would finish them off handily.

Vasco focused morbidly on the imagined enemy commander realizing a rain of steel needles was about to hit. Trying to think on his feet, come up with a quick solution to save his ships... or would he give up and try to launch whatever weapons he had in a last-ditch deathclutch? Or would he smile at this primitive attack and start a series of preplanned counters?

A few minutes later, Vasco's imagination was piqued even more. The enemy ships flipped, turning tail to the incoming sleet. It looked as though they were going to try using their engines to act as a shield. Might even work...

Thermal flares blossomed from each of the three ships, as did radiation spikes. Big radiation spikes. The Helot AI that ran the *Alexi* instantly recognized what was going on and overlaid the ship images on the screen with rectangular halos and a finely dashed green line. The halo, Vasco knew from his mandatory astrophysics classes, was an estimate of remaining propulsion mass. The dashed green line was effective range.

"Fusion torch engines active in system," the Helot's voice announced.

The captain didn't even scowl. He nodded to himself and turned to the Timariot. "That explains their acceleration toward us. They intend to use their drives as defenses and want to keep some control of their measure from us. I'm going to assume, if the Helot concurs, that they have tuneable drives. Basically the entire ship will be a short-range fusion cannon."

"Concur," said the Helot.

The Timariot nodded, and the *Alexi*'s captain turned his attention back to the tracking plot. Tuneable drives meant the enemy was spraying space with open nozzles, effectively creating a shield by using engine exhaust to blast the whiskers into nothingness. Being able to open their nozzles meant they could also close their nozzles and channel the fusion exhaust into what was basically a fusion beam. A nasty, nasty weapon.

Sure enough, the small enemy fleet came to a halt. The whiskers were no threat to them anymore, and they were turning turtle—counting on the big guns of their engines to keep *Alexi* at bay. It was an excellent tactic. They were effectively marking a sphere of space as a kill zone. Enter that sphere, and you would take a blast of concentrated nuclear fire. No fun.

Worse, at its current momentum, *Alexi* was heading right into the center of that sphere. The enemy had suckered the Tatar good and solid, drawing the massive, lumbering ship into their trap. Or so they thought.

"Signals?" asked Captain Stern.

"Locked in, sir," answered the TacSys operator. The Tactical Sysadmin had been working feverishly at his job for hours, analyzing every byte of traffic between the enemy ships. His computers, and his team of operators, had no other job but hacking enemy systems. "No access yet, but we can spoof and flood."

"All right, start now. Keep up on attempting access." The captain turned back to the plot and traced a finger over the complex patterns. "Helot, let's cut this cord. I want a tangent here on the edge of their sphere. Give them a good five-second shot at us, and let's hit them with a body shot."

"Acknowledged," answered the Helot, then it broadcast to the ship, "All hands, main engine firing in thirty seconds. Combat maneuver in ten seconds, mark."

The Helot was the finest computer AI available and came at a staggering cost. One Helot cost as much as three Tatars, and they only had a life span of thirty years before they went senile. But when they ran, there was nothing like them. They had the unique ability to understand metaphor and reduce the most complex systems to a metaphor that was understandable and actionable by any human.

So the Helot understood the captain's order and translated it into action. The massive ship would skate the edge of the fusion drive sphere, presenting the broadside of the ship to the enemy in an irresistibly tasty target. It would look as if the *Alexi* had tried its best to escape, but it just wouldn't be good enough.

Signals would hammer the sensors and communications of the enemy enough that they would be scrambling to take coordinated advantage of the blunder. And hopefully they would be too busy to notice the body shot.

First off though, the surprise for the enemy. Combat maneuver drives fired—small fusion engines of their own—skewing the huge ship just enough. Vasco felt the centrifugal force temporarily giving him a bit of gravity... but nothing like what was coming.

Most ships aimed for an acceleration of one g, or about 10m/s to start. It was comfortable for the human crew. Under pressure, you could go up to three gs for a bit of time, but sustaining it was brutal on everyone. Combat crews could take a temporary bit of eight g acceleration.

The Polity had a strict rule for its crews. In hostile territory, all crew were in full ship's armor all the time. It was no fun. No one liked being locked head-to-toe in snug powered armor for days or months at a time. A lot of people couldn't take it... but enough could.

Enough that the Alexi could suddenly jump up to eight gs and maintain it.

Even with enforcing tape under the armor and all the other tricks built in, it still felt as if your face was tearing off, and your organs noticeably shifted inside you. You had to be in good shape to step on board a Tatar. Even so, eight gs was a killer.

Combat killed, even if not a single shot was fired.

The main drive lit up and slammed the *Alexi* on her great curving path out of the death trap the smaller ships had set up.

Everything was silent on the bridge. There was nothing to do. The Helot gave orders to whomever needed to be doing something, and everyone else watched. Or at least endured.

You never got used to slightly queasy, under-the-sea feeling of moving in powered armor under heavy acceleration. It felt like moving in slow motion while being battered by waves in a high surf. Most people tried not to move at all.

Acceleration was cut before they hit the edge of the enemy sphere—one more effort to keep the enemy focused on the *Alexi*'s apparent mistake. They would have one last moment of elation, thinking they had *Alexi* lined up for the perfect shot. One last moment of anticipation, fingers hovering over firing buttons.

If the body shot didn't work, *Alexi* would be brutalized. She was an enormous ship, but three small fusion beams were nothing to sneeze at.

Vasco tensed. He'd been assigned bridge tacops this rotation, so he had a front row seat. In another few seconds, he'd either be watching the enemy's scattered remains or not feeling another thing ever again.

Most of the bridge crew were feeling the tension but keeping busy enough to stop it from bothering them. The captain kept an iron face, and the Timariot looked too curious about what was going on to really notice how close he was to dying.

Vasco almost didn't care. Being seconds away from death was a matter of cold calculation to ships' crews, a roll of the dice, a chance they took once or twice every voyage. To a Gyrene, it was how you spent weeks at a time. It wasn't that Vasco didn't think about it, but more that you eventually got tired of holding your breath and waiting to die. Vasco was just a bit bored of it. After all, he hadn't died yet. He didn't have any reason to fear it yet.

"Enemy destroyed. Braking maneuvers beginning," announced the Helot.

And just like that, it was over. Three ships gone. No explosions, no music, no fanfare. Just three icons gone from the plot.

The showy maneuver and electronic attacks had been enough to keep the ships from noticing the three slugs *Alexi* launched out of the larger railgun turrets, with a pulse-drive assist timed to her emissions attacks. The slugs each carried a shaped nuclear charge.

Hell of a body blow.

Chapter Nine: The Independent

Vasco wandered the town, full of discontent. The first few months of the Drop had been the worst experience of his life, but that didn't feel like the real problem. Something else was bothering him.

He'd gone down with the first elements, and oddly enough, they'd had the easiest part of it. They'd been put down on the coast as a pacification and unification probe to one of the fishing cities. The coast-dwellers were an interesting bunch. They tended toward heavy, hard Arabic features and had a love of painfully hot spiced oils. They were friendly in person. Vasco's hands had gotten tougher from constant contact with rope-scarred hands. Everyone wanted to shake hands. But come nightfall, or being outnumbered on patrol out of town? The knives came out. And the bombs. And acids, and some creative uses of industrial chemicals and toxins prevalent in the sea life.

Most of his initial team had been lost. But he'd been safe. Again. It was his first time being a Centurion in a combat role, and so far, it wasn't all that different from being in a support role. He led, but not from the front.

Vasco's teams swept the cities. Easy patrols in the day… deadly at night. Hit-and-run tactics. There was never an enemy to face, but always a dead body by the end of the patrol. And always one of his. It had taken them the first two weeks to really work out a safe system for patrols. They'd stopped losing Gyrenes after the first week. The ones left were the smartest, the most paranoid, and the luckiest. The hardest to kill.

Still, they lost troops. Vasco was so busy trying to keep an eye on his various teams that he never wound up in any of the random spots where firefights broke out. He managed all the rookie mistakes. All the things he'd learned about and laughed at other Centurions for doing on their first combat roles, and he'd done them all himself.

He'd tried to run the combat element the way he ran the support elements. Methodical planning, overview, and control of everything. He'd micromanaged some Gyrenes into literal death, he was sure of that. Every time an organic situation developed, he had tried to impose some order on it. Tried to understand what was happening before acting. It wasn't a bad thing to do in electronic combat. Vasco was experienced enough in that to grasp the situation, understand, and react in milliseconds. He didn't have that experience in meat combat though, and what worked for him in support was failing him in skirmishes.

Still, he'd managed. And fast too.

The Gyrenes had expected crap when they got assigned to an op jock switching to arms. They could understand, if not approve, of the learning curve. They were pretty damn pleased when he'd figured out things faster than anyone anticipated, and he'd gotten an official note about that.

Not that Vasco planned on re-upping enough to warrant promotion this time around—he was still acting under the legally-binding whim of the Timariot—but the note would help when it came time to receive his allotment of the veterans' spoils.

It had been a rough start, but Vasco had learned, adapted, and excelled. It wouldn't save him from nightmares about nighttime screams and watching someone literally puke out a lung from corrosive gas attacks... but that still wasn't what was bothering him.

He should be pleased with his progress. He was on the

road to what he wanted: combat. The chance to prove himself. He hadn't been under fire and fought back yet, but he would. He felt it in his bones, as sure as the sun on his shoulders, as sure as the next breath. Combat was coming.

Still, Vasco was discontent. He couldn't stop thinking about his conversations with Sigma on the *Alexi*. He knew he was doing the right thing in life. He was chasing a dream he'd run from. A dream he'd buried in the back of his mind until he thought he was too old to chase it anymore. He'd reborn himself, rededicated himself, and he was doing the right thing. He knew that, felt it deep within himself.

And yet... something wasn't right.

He tossed it around his mind for a while as he wandered the streets, but nothing solidified. Just the slight nag. The feeling at the back of the stomach, like taking a wrong turn but not having noticed it yet or having left the house with your wallet on the desk and your brain mumbling about what you left behind.

He shook it off. He was in a lovely town, he had time to himself, and he was going to enjoy it. The seaside towns had been lovely, but up in the seaward edge of the plateau, things were different. The air felt different, and the people were different. The town he was in now, Akbar Left, was friendly and pacifistic. No opposition, no real care. They'd greeted the Polity soldiers and political officers with friendly interest, then politely done everything they could to separate them from their money.

It really was a lovely town. A rising valley with steep and interesting mountains on either side. The shops and houses all leaned toward an alpine look. It was spring locally, and one of the only times Akbar Left wasn't acting like a sponge for uplifting winds from the sea. Snowfall in winter was supposedly something to be seen, and summer was a mostly constant drizzle mixed with heavier rain and fog. Spring was a happy time for everyone.

The street Vasco was walking along was heavy with the smells of baking: butter, cinnamon, brown sugar caramelizing on the bottom of a pan somewhere. Vasco was determined to find every single variation of the product that produced that smell and eat it. He'd given himself the entire day to eat his way through the town and was only starting.

He'd just left a shop that had sold him something that was a mix between a croissant and a cinnamon bun. The tar-thick coffee was laced with some local spice that was almost cardamom, but with a strange blueberry aftertaste. He wasn't sure he liked it much, but as he was walking down the winding street—really, it was turning into a lane—the flavor kept changing in his mouth. It seemed to always hint at another flavor, then as soon as he recognized it, it changed to another. It brought a smile to his face. It may not have been a flavor he liked, but it was an experience he was enjoying.

He heard the noise first, a rhythmic *thump thump*, with a scuffing slide mixed in. It wasn't a sound he was familiar with, and he started to look for where it was coming from. He found a large shop, almost like a barn, with a big display window full of hats of all colors. Vasco couldn't think why a hat store would have such a noise coming from it, so on a whim, he decided to go in. Just before he opened the door, he noticed that the lintel had an insect carved into it. It looked like a fat praying mantis with a strangely featureless head. It looked oddly elegant.

Inside was a surprise. It was less a store than it was a workshop, and in the center of the large open space was an old man with burly shoulders and gnarled hands. The odd noise was coming from him as he slowly but steadily worked what looked like a piece of thick fabric over and over on a sturdy wooden table. The air smelled odd... it took Vasco a moment to clue in to an old memory from his childhood. A museum farm setup. Goats? Sheep? One of the animals, or a combination of the animals, had smelled like this.

Despite the odd odor, Vasco felt at ease. The shop somehow felt familiar to him, as if he were walking into a fencing studio. In the back of the animal smell was the old, never-fading scent of stale sweat. It was the most honest smell Vasco knew. It was the scent of effort, the scent of value earned. But the real feeling, the sense of being in a studio, came from the old man.

Looking at him more closely, Vasco saw that there was more to the man than a first impression left. He was a giant—many of the Sami were, but this man was something else.

His hands rolled with a steady rhythm, slapping over and over on the heavy, solid tabletop. Vasco saw now that the fabric in his hands was a thick mass of wool, wet and slightly sudsy. The man had huge knuckles and fingers like twisted oak branches. His forearms rippled in counterpoint to the drive of his hands, back and forth, lifting and shoving the wool in a rolling wave. His body swayed to the rhythm, and for all the man's apparent age, Vasco could think of nothing other than a young ox, snorting its way around a field and heaving a massive plow. His actions were quick and sure, and Vasco knew he was in the presence of a master. He recognized a skill that was on a level with his own. Only a true master could show such power, precision, and mindless confidence with such a simple action. Vasco was mesmerized. Never in his life had he met such skill that wasn't displayed in a combat art.

Instinctively, Vasco glanced around the shop, looking for the weapons he felt must be around. Nothing. Only hats... and all of the same kind, but in many colors. All the hats were simple, short cones with truncated tops. He'd seen the same kind in history books of ancient Turkey, from a time long before the Polity or even the New Ottoman Empire. He hadn't seen them on anyone in the town, yet obviously there was a market. He was puzzled.

As Vasco looked around, he became aware of another sound... a light, delicate "tok, tok" that came in time with the heavier thumping of the old man's task. Vasco looked back at the old man and finally noticed with a start the huge bug on the corner of the table. It was the same kind of creature as was carved in the lintel, and it was tapping a claw on the table in time with the old man.

With the realization, Vasco was overwhelmed with a sense of deja vu. His sense of reality seemed to twist around the edges, and he felt disconnected from the world, almost dizzy but still rooted in the spot, as if he had stepped sideways from himself.

"Are you a pilgrim, or just lost?" the old man asked without even looking up.

His voice was like a splash of cold water, snapping Vasco out of his fugue. Vasco found himself hesitating before answering. The old man's resonant voice seemed to carry a deeper meaning, and Vasco found himself wondering who the old man was and what he was doing in this shop. Something profound had just occurred, and Vasco was floating adrift mentally, completely in the moment.

"A bit of both, I guess."

"Hmm..." The old man hummed a little laugh. He still hadn't looked up, and the bug was still tapping in time with his actions. "Not a bad place to be, somewhere between the Fool and the Hanged Man. Want a hat anyway?"

"Uh. I'm sorry. I was just... walking by and came in. I'm just looking." Vasco's face was starting to burn a little. He felt, he realized, like he did the first time his father had brought him to train with a fencing master so many years ago.

Vasco had spent weeks peeking in the window, pouring over a flyer for classes his adoptive father had brought him. Weeks of anticipation and daydreaming about what magic things he would learn and the feats of derring-do he'd perform once he'd learned them. Weeks of build up, and yet when Vasco finally worked up the courage to walk in the door, he'd felt awkward, foolish, and senseless.

The master himself had asked Vasco what he wanted. He'd expected some sort of casual entrance—maybe he'd be able to slyly watch a class from the side or speak to a student. Faced with the fierce and recognizable profile of the master of the school, a man who had won tournament after tournament and actually killed a man in a duel? Vasco had nearly died of shame! Fortunately, the master was a grandfather and had a deep love of children and had won Vasco over almost immediately.

But now, Vasco was nine years old again and facing a different beast. And all that shame was coming back.

"Looking's fine," said the old man, looking at Vasco for

the first time, "and I see you have no room for a new hat anyway."

Vasco started, belatedly stopping himself from removing his Centurion cap. Curses! He felt like an awkward teenager. He was regretting walking into the store, yet strangely stuck. "No, I'm afraid I don't need a hat." He forced himself to say a little more. "I haven't seen anyone in town wear these hats. Who buys them?"

"Most everyone," the old man said, "but they don't really wear them all that often. They keep them at home. To remember."

"Remember?" Vasco asked.

The bug stopped its tapping and crawled off of the table. The old man didn't stop though. He kept on grinding the wool, for whatever purpose.

"To remember, O lost pilgrim. To remember to Listen. These are the hats of the Sufi teachers who came to Anubis and gave Rumi its name. We Sami don't follow their teachings so much anymore, but we come from those teachings, and we don't forget. Each day, it's good to remember, even for the failed, to listen. Sema, the Listening. Have you heard of that? Do they teach it to you across the stars? I see they don't, but I'm not surprised." He stopped his work and shook out his hands. Free of the mass of wool, they looked even more enormous. "Sometimes, O Lost Pilgrim, you need to stop and listen. You really don't need to do more than that to be a better person! Just sit still and listen for a while. You can listen for quiet, or you can try to truly Listen for the heartbeat of the world. Some even listen for the voice of God. Each man has to listen for himself, Pilgrim. You can never truly be lost if you can find a place to stop and listen." He gave his little humming laugh and pulled up the mess of wool.

Vasco saw that it had become a solid, thick sheet of fabric. Felt! Some small part of learning Vasco had read about somewhere cropped up into his mind. The old man had been felting wool by hand!

The old man took the sheet of felt over to a stand. He stood in front of it and draped the sheet over a block of wood that was the shape of the hats. Slowly, methodically, he pulled and stretched the felt sheet down over the form. In the course of a few minutes, it took on the shape of the form. The old man took a giant pair of shears and carefully snipped off the bottom. It was a nearly perfect hat.

"That's amazing!" said Vasco. "How long does it take you to do that?"

"Half a day. It takes a little more to finish the hat off just right, but I like to let them dry and sit for a day or two before I do the final touches."

"Half a day! But... why? Aren't there machines that can make thousands of hats in that time?"

"Of course! But it's not the way of the Sami. I'm an Outlander. We don't have any faith in things that are beyond the skill of our hands and the grasp of our memories. If I let a machine make my hats, then I might forget how to make them. I have to depend on the machine maker to fix his machine when it breaks. I have to have power and parts for the machine. And I have to have enough customers to justify the purchase cost and maintenance. I have to have a desire to do all that. It's so far removed from just making a hat.

"Why would I want any of that? This way I can make a hat for myself, and my friends, whenever I wish. They can make hats for themselves. It's hard work, but anyone can do it. People can buy my hats not because they need to, but because they appreciate the way I do the work and how well my hats turn out. I can make a hat anywhere. What good does a machine do me? A machine needs a culture and community. I need only myself. My community is the natural meeting of people like me. Machines destroy that by their very nature."

"But... you need machines and community for civilization!"

"I don't need civilization. I only need a hat. It's a shame you've got one already. I think this one would have fit you just perfectly."

Vasco laughed. "True! I suppose I might regret that someday, but it's still a good hat. I'm not ready to change it just yet."

"Nor should you. A man should be faithful to his hat. Now, if you'll excuse me, I'm going to get the next one started. The strudel house two blocks down will fill your belly. You'll enjoy it."

"Thank you, that does sound perfect…"

It wasn't until Vasco got to the strudel house and had his first bite of the delicious pastry that he realized he had never said anything about being hungry.

ACT TWO
TARIQAT – POTENTIALITY

Chapter Ten: The Powerful

Nils watched his breath form tiny clouds. One breath followed the other, and for brief moments, he created a miniature warm front, a wistful echo of the burgeoning storm coming over the mountain pass. He amused himself for a bit while he waited. He'd arrived at the meeting place late in the evening, and the others had trickled in over the course of the night. They'd need to sleep later than him.

Nils had always been an early riser. Today it had given him time to start a fire for everyone else and put some water on to boil. A cast-iron griddle was still almost hot from last night's coals, and he'd warmed a piece of flatbread and a little bacon on it. A warm breakfast on a cool morning, no rain… he could think of no better start to any day.

The others started to wake, and he kept his gaze wandering along the view to give them some privacy. He enjoyed the sound of a camp waking in the morning. The air always had a muted echoing quality to it. Quiet conversations amongst men and women trying not to wake others, the gentled clicks and scrapes of mugs and spoons. Coughs and other body noises.

When he was living with a woman, Nils had always enjoyed hearing her breathing change slightly just before waking. There was always that magic moment when you knew your partner was awake. It never came with any warning, and he'd never felt that he had observed the moment of waking... but you always knew. Even when nothing else changed, you knew when your bedmate was awake.

And a camp full of would-be warriors was no different. The first few noises, the first scattered souls rising, the first grumbled breakfasts and dressings... that wasn't really awake. Nor were the first few conversations or heartily shouted greetings over a mouthful of food. There was the gradual increase in noise and activity, but still the camp was essentially asleep. Nils closed his eyes, and let the sounds wash over him.

Eventually, without realizing it had happened, he knew everyone was awake. Maybe not as awake as they wanted to be or thought they should be, but awake enough that it was time to talk to them. He stood and stretched, savoring a last view of the cascading peaks of the outer plateau. He never tired of this view and the hidden stories in all the peaks. Today the mountains seemed to promise new stories to come. It was fitting. He turned to face the gathered people, and they all stopped to face him, waiting for what he had to say.

"The Polity," Nils said, "has come for us. We've planned for this moment for years. The time has almost arrived for us to fight back. Almost. We don't fight for ourselves, remember that. We fight for the vision of our founders, for the vision we all share. All that we have fought to learn, we fight now so that others may have the freedom to learn as well. Our way is not easy, but it is right. The Polity has no room in its soul for free thought. It only wants to teach, but it fears learning. They have put almost all of humanity under their heel in the name of right. Their version of right.

"They see only fear, out there in the dark spaces of the universe, and it's the same fear they see in their own hearts, in that dark space deep in their minds. They fear freedom. They fear what will happen if they have no structure, no simple ignorance. They want a hand to hold them at all times, and they have built a government to do what they think is right—to hold everyone's hand. They have no heart for the cold, so they seek to warm everyone.

"They have made a child out of humanity and refused to let it grow. They have removed all knowledge of what growth is. And this is what we fight. We fight to make life hard. We fight to bring the darkness to their eyes, to show them what lurks in their hearts and in the universe. We fight to show them what fear is, to show them there is no safety, no comfort... but there is life. Always life.

"We will shatter them. With the Laconians, we will break their fleets and crack their worlds and cast away the comforting grips of their wombs. We will shatter all they know and love and show them what they have been blind to see, what they have been blinded by in order to never see. We don't fight for ourselves. We fight so that all that is humanity might have a chance to truly live, to stop struggling every day, lost in the past or dreaming of the future, and instead see what is in front of their own eyes. Every moment the Polity lives, it steals the potential for life. It makes humanity into machines to drive its own engine. We will fight to shatter that."

He stopped and looked over them. They all watched him, intent, focused. There was no argument, no dissension, only complete support. They had worked years for this moment. They were as one in this.

"All we need to do now is wait. Let them come, let them press," Nils said. "When they have come as far as they can and have no more choice but to push on, when they have come too far to retreat, then it will be our time. This will be our last meeting here. From here, we move on to our caches and await word. The Hellmouth will be watched by the least number needed. All the Outlanders are moving. The Walkure has come and will show us more. It is not yet time to fight, but today the Polity begins to die."

As if to accent his words, the morning sky was ripped open with the rolling boom of a shuttle just visible overhead.

Sigma stepped lightly through the dark. She didn't try to be quiet or hide. She walked lightly and with purpose. It was the best way to be nondescript. It wasn't apparent that she was actively avoiding any surveillance, because her route had been carefully preplanned. It wasn't full dark yet. The sun had just gone down. Dusk was the perfect time for subtle movement. The human brain was most trusting, and most lax, at dusk, when the shift of light made the mind calmer than at any other time. No action of Sigma's was designed to interfere with that calm.

The Sami custom of walking after dinner helped. The streets were busy with strolling couples, families, and solitary wanderers. Street vendors walked around with light chest boards, offering tobacco or spicy dessert snacks, roasted nuts, or hot or cold Glög for those who imbibed. Sigma flowed in and out of the discrete groups. She moved sometimes quickly, sometimes slowly, and always from one group to another. She backtracked from time to time, just to see if anyone was following.

Finally, after purchasing a small pipe and a tiny supply of aromatic tobacco, she leaned against a wall. She fussed with the pipe, tamping the tobacco just so, and fumbling the scented wooden match she had purchased. She bent to pick it up... and disappeared.

She had ducked as a large, boisterous family paused in front of her, and Sigma spun into the alley. A few feet down was a low fence, partially open. Just enough for her to squeeze through, then another few minutes of winding through a maze of gardens, stoops, and tiny back-alley patios until she reached her destination.

It wasn't uncommon for Sami in the city to run small outdoor restaurants in their alleys. The winding roads sometimes made little openings where three or four houses shared a patio space big enough for maybe a table or three. Night had fallen, and this particular little restaurant was busy. Candles were everywhere—the tables, the walls, hanging from posts, in little pots all over the road. It was warm, beautiful, and mysterious.

A small crowd had gathered, and two young women were playing a song. One woman had a guitar, the other a small hand drum. The guitarist sang, and on the table in front of her, a Weta swayed along to the rhythm. Sigma paused to listen... this was where she was meant to be, but there was no rush. She had time to enjoy the performance.

By the time the second song was almost over, she'd watched everyone walking by and heading in and out of the houses. One house in particular was sending out servers with trays of spicy rolls, passing them out to everyone who walked by. Most people paid, but no money was asked. One server came up to Sigma, and after she had refused one roll, he offered her three. It was the signal she was waiting for. It meant she had two followers, but neither of them were near her now. She followed the server back into the house.

The kitchen was busy with a man and woman cooking at a frenetic pace. They both glanced at Sigma when she walked in, smiled, and went back to work. She walked past them into the house proper. She saw a dimly lit living room, stairs leading up, and a door in the front leading to the street. She went up the first six stairs to the small landing and pushed on the wall... which opened to reveal another set of stairs. After closing the concealed door behind her, Sigma followed the stairs down.

It was a short flight of stairs, then a short hallway led to another door, which opened to a larger room. Not so much a room as a convergence of entrances, exits, stairs, and a few walls. It was candlelit, but bright. A dozen men and women sat on chairs, patiently waiting. There was a small table next to each chair and a ceramic pot on each table.

Sigma walked to the serving table, as was expected of her, took the last remaining pot, and served herself a portion of the thick hearty stew simmering on a hot plate suspended over a nearly dead bed of coals. She took the last seat, between a young woman with jet-black hair and piercing green eyes and an older man with a tonsured haircut and giant forked beard. Everyone in the room was dressed as an Outlander, and the Ski'a stew was the meeting food.

As soon as Sigma sat, everyone ate. There was light conversation, but it was muted, only quiet words to neighboring eaters. Sigma's companions were mostly quiet, but the intense young woman seemed to be cracking jokes under her breath with the lady on her left. The stew was delicious, replete with flavors of rose, coriander, garlic, and other unique Sami flavors. The food was Sigma's favorite part of Sami culture. Only the Outlanders kept the traditional cuisine and rituals.

As the last to arrive, it was Sigma's duty to serve the traditional beer. She put down her pot once she had eaten a few mouthfuls and walked to the serving table. She made sure to walk through the middle of the circle, giving everyone a chance to surreptitiously observe her without being too obvious. She'd only met a few of them, so she thought it would be the polite thing to do.

The serving table had two giant clay pitchers, and she easily hoisted them both. She did pause for a moment… at just under twenty liters in size each, she wasn't sure the clay handles would support the pitcher's weight. She'd never seen the serving pitchers picked up by the handles before. Usually they were cradled in the arms and poured carefully. But it suited her purposes to give a show of strength, and this was as good a way as any. One pitcher in each hand, she easily pivoted, smiling at the stares that greeted her.

"What?" She laughed gently. "Surely you've heard what it means to be Walkure?" She raised an eyebrow at the Outlanders and didn't have to wait long for a response.

"We've heard, Walkure Sigma," said the young woman who had been sitting next to Sigma, "but it's another thing to see it. Did it hurt much?"

"Dying? Yes. I don't remember what happened afterward, much. There was much pain when I was reborn though. Mostly the pain of relearning to live. It's much easier now that we have the Sami techniques." Sigma moved around the circle, easily pouring beer as she spoke. "I suspect that if any Outlanders are ever chosen, they should find the process… enlightening."

The Outlanders nodded and smiled at her small joke.

The Walkure process required death, and the Outlanders' mental training required much focus on death. Momento Mori, the remembrance of death throughout the day, the constant awareness that each moment should ideally be lived as if it was the last. The Outlanders trained in the ability from early childhood, and each generation attained the ability just a little younger than the previous.

"We will be dying soon, won't we?" the woman asked. "Isn't that what you have come to tell us?"

"Yes," said Sigma. "You will be dying soon. Or submitting to the Polity and their social engineering. You can live and there will be little or no death, but you will be the last generation of Outlanders. I learned the fate of the Creche worlds. Gone, all of them. Only a handful of survivors left, and they don't even know their heritage. I managed to bring one here, but his worth is yet to be known. I learned too of the Sargossians. They followed their own ethos and yielded. They live, but their way is lost. No record remains of their teaching, and all the Great Symbols were destroyed. Schools and factories were built wherever they stood."

"This isn't news to us, Sigma," said the tonsured man, "and you don't need to convince us either. We know what will be lost. We've finished the hellbores, and you know we will fight. But the cost will be so high! Not just our lives, but the lives of the Polity as well. All that we are, is it worth so many lives? We are Sami. We are Outlanders. We know everything dies and is lost, but the balance of right matters to us. We are willing to die for our way, but killing for our way, killing so many… it's never wrong to be sure of our choice."

Sigma poured her own beer last, considering his words. She understood what he was saying. What gave them the right? Surely the way of the Polity was wrong. If she'd ever doubted that her time amongst the Polity, and her research of their history, had changed that. The Polity was a juggernaut of mediocrity, crushing all of humanity under its conformist heel.

"No," she said, "it's not worth killing them. The Polity is close enough to our version of evil that it deserves to die, but is it worth killing them all so you can preserve your way of life? No. In the end, they are still human. It's a horrible system that will crush the souls of trillions of humans for millennia and retard the growth of the human soul forever, but... it won't end humanity. As wrong as it is, there is still hope in it.

"But there is more to it than that. Legate Lycurgus saw this coming a thousand years ago, and he created the Laconians to fight it. We used you to make it come to this decision point. The Polity won't stop here, and it won't stop with Laconia either. Once it has all of humanity under its heel, the Polity will reach out to the rest of the universe. They will move Unification on to alien worlds and alien societies. Humanity will become the conquistadors of the universe. The New Ottoman Empire will reform out of the Polity, and they will bring war to the other races. They already plan to war on the Pook."

There was a rumble at that.

"That's mad! Surely they know the history of the Pook!" someone shouted.

"They know," she said. "They know, but they think they know better, and they think they have no choice. They will use Rumi as a staging base to conquer Laconia, and from there, they will take the Pook worlds, one after the other. They know the Pook will fight, but they believe the Helots will allow them to resist and win.

"And they will—for a while. But the Pook will eventually fight back for real, and the Pook way of war is final. The dead zone we came from will be a dead zone again. And that is why we will fight and die, why we will fight and kill. Lycurgus set us in motion to be the last warriors, to fight the last war humanity will ever have, and this is our time. We will fight the Polity. We will beat them here, and then we will conquer the Polity. Millions, billions will die, but it's the only way.

"We need to let the Polity drive us back until they know they have won. Once they have done that, they will send the order for the follow-up fleet that is waiting. Once that message has been sent, we can fight back. We push back the Polity until they need to recall their troops and use their mousetrap on us. That is the point where they will be most vulnerable. If we time our attacks right, we can maneuver the *Alexi* to be where we need her to be. With the *Alexi* in our mousetrap, we can prepare for the follow-up."

Chapter Eleven: The Knowing

Vasco's battle dress scraped on the ceramic wall and nearly made Vasco jump out of his skin. He was aware that the composite plates had a pretty good chance of saving his life against small arms fire, but sometimes he really wanted to go without them. At least in ship's armor, you had solid contact and rigidity. Battle dress was comfortable, hard-wearing fabric. The armor in pockets, or laced to the hard points, couldn't help but be somewhat obtrusive. Against Sami ceramic walls, the composite had an unfortunate tendency to make a scraping sound a lot like fingernails on a chalkboard. Bad enough, thought Vasco, but almost a little too much when you're this tense. His team of himself, Cave, Alberta, and Verne was in the overwatch position, covering teams One, Two, and Three while they slowly, and carefully, worked through the tough walls of the town.

Under other circumstances, the little town might have been quite pleasant. It was at the foot of a small, steep mountain, with low hills on the other side. It formed a pleasant little valley with a small lake at the north end of the town and a river running through the middle of it. The sky was tinged a bit purple. The weather was lovely, as it usually was on the plateau. The rest of Rumi tended toward cool, but the plateau was warm. Rumi's native plant life grew in shades of tan, red, and striking blues.

It brought to mind a desert world, but that was in colors only. The planet-wide tall grass ferns made the air rich with a delicate cinnamon-vanilla smell.

Vasco popped the tab on his collar. The brief ease of breath was welcome. "Weber, tag back a bit. Don't be too hasty."

Weber was the lead for team One, and he was being a little quick with his team when it was their turn to leapfrog. He wasn't giving team Three sufficient time to scan and secure before he moved his team into position. With three teams to watch his back, and two in direct support, he'd probably be okay. Vasco didn't want them taking any chances though. They were a little ahead of their support element because the big Banshee dirigible had been held up with a call for help from a convoy.

The whole push was getting a little ragged. Some elements were meeting little or no resistance, and others were getting caught up in annoying hit-and-run firefights.

Vasco thought their offensive was on the verge of getting a bit strung-out. If the Sami Outlanders were capable of mounting a serious offense, he'd be worried. But he wasn't. The Outlanders were just a scattered bunch of discontented farmers for one. For two, it wasn't his job to worry. His only concern was his unit, which somehow or another had wound up becoming the lead element. He'd received that cheery note as soon as they'd pulled into the little town—at the same time he was informed that a sizeable contingent of Outlanders had been reported as being in the same town. They'd already been dropped in the town by APCs that had promptly been pulled back to secure the route for follow-up forces. Vasco's small group was supposed to secure the town.

From the initial intelligence, it should have been an easy job. Now? Cool day or not, Vasco was sweating in his gear. So far so good though. No contact with the enemy. No contact at all. The locals seemed to have booked it when they heard the APCs coming. No surprise there.

They were as far from the big city as anyone in the Polity had been yet. Most of the smaller towns had either moved to the larger towns to negotiate a surrender as a unified body... or had run for the hills. The closer they got to the edge of the plateau, the more common that was.

They were getting close to Outlander territory.

So far the fighting had been sporadic, but that was bound to change. This town hadn't been deserted long either. A mill was still running some sort of process. Its constant shriek was right near their current position and was just loud enough to set them on edge.

Vasco watched the teams leapfrog position. It was just about time for his squad to move overwatch to the next position he had marked. Slow and steady progress.

Tan-and-black Gyrenes moved smoothly and easily through their rehearsed motions, covering each other and checking doors and alleys. They weren't being too thorough. The Outlanders had shown no desire for city fighting yet. Hit and run, hit and run. It was a good tactic, but eventually they would run out of room or resources and have to fight. The constant surveillance from orbit would eventually corral them.

Weber's point man went down.

"Sniper!" came over the com.

Everyone did exactly what they had been trained to do. Vasco's gut clenched up and everything went a little hollow for him. The point man had been between buildings with no easy way to see where the shot had come from. The buildings were all low, not a lot of windows, but lots of cracks and overhangs. A good sniper team could be just about anywhere.

Facing a sniper in an urban situation was one of the worst things Vasco could think of. A good sniper team could sit in the back of a room, protected from sight by shade. Or behind a derelict wall, a tiny crack serving to hide an opening just big enough for a bullet to pass through and a scope to see through. Or they could be in a pile of rubble. Really, anywhere—anywhere at all. Vasco's only hope was to catch a muzzle flash or systematically sweep the town until they found the hide.

They didn't have the resources for a full sweep, and everyone was waiting for Vasco to decide what to do.

Their overwatch position was their own little sniper hide. A rooftop on a single-story building, with enough cover to hide their movement. They were probably safe from an urban sniper.

The distant and muted crack of the sniper's weapon finally sounded, echoing off the surrounding hills. Vasco had been waiting, mentally counting. Dammit. The sniper was almost two kilometers off. Where was he shooting from? There were some shrubs on the outskirts of town, and Vasco saw them from his position. The shot could have come from there or…

Vasco rolled onto his back, tucked his knees up, and dropped his elbows onto his thighs, raising his scope to his eye. He'd brought his big twenty mil cannon for this run. He'd figured his Centurion's load was less than everyone else's, so he could pack his big gun. Plus, the terrain had struck him as sniper heaven. He'd been right about that but hadn't looked forward to being on the receiving end. In a minute, he'd switch to his binoculars and spot, and let his troops do the firing.

For the moment, Vasco's instincts took over. The shooter was on the mountain, far above them. Vasco let himself relax. He wasn't used to this position, but he'd put in the training and refreshed it in shipboard transit. Elbows on thighs, not on knees. No bone-to-bone contact, where your breathing would make the rifle wobble. Feet driving into the ground to provide a steady base for the heavy rifle. It wasn't a position you could hold for long, but Vasco didn't think he'd need long. He would either be right or dead.

He heard another crack as he was pulling his scope to his eye. He had no idea whether he'd lost another troop or not. He was being a terrible combat leader as well—reacting instead of giving orders. While he ran on his hunch, every Gyrene was waiting to hear him say something. He'd give them a moment or two yet though. They knew what to do for that long, and he had to go with his gut.

Everything had slowed down. Gyrenes were still dropping and shouting as Vasco sighted through his scope on the high ridge line above. Long shot. His fingers adjusted the scope almost on their own accord, and the usually muted clicks sounded like hammer blows in his ears. The slightly magenta sky made for a crisp and sharp outline against the exposed rock on the peak. Vasco started a slow scan on the ridge. The Sami Outlanders were supposed to be great shots and good hunters—but they'd only been fighting in a shooting war for a few weeks. They probably weren't used to being shot back at yet, which might mean...

For a second, the ridge silhouette changed. Just for the merest moment. Vasco squeezed the trigger without really processing what he saw, but he had time to think about it as the heavy charge smashed back into him. It was a good rifle, and the scope only wobbled a little sideways while the bulk of the rifle came straight back into him. Supine shots weren't anyone's favorite, and it was even worse when you'd accidentally put your shoulder in a braced position. Vasco's strength would let him get away with only a slight bruise... but he wasn't going to move yet. He'd fired just below the rounded movement. In retrospect, he realized it was the top of a head, and he confirmed it a moment later when he saw broken bits fly up in the air from his shot. Binoculars. He'd hit the spotter. He still couldn't see the shooter.

"Alberta! Sniper on the ridge, follow my impact and get the location!"

Alberta shouted something in reply, and Vasco let fly another shot in the same area. He was aiming for where he thought a sniper might be, but there was no way to tell for sure. If Alberta could see his rounds impacting, he'd be able to use his laser range finder to spot and mark the location. Whatever they had due for overhead support should be able to land some covering fire. Artillery was always the best way to deal with a sniper.

Vasco heard another rifle firing and saw someone else's fire landing in the same area. Excellent, he thought. Nothing like good troops. Confident his team was taking over suppressing the sniper, he turned to see what was going on with the other teams.

Looked good so far. They'd moved to deeper cover but were still taking fire. More than one sniper team was working them over. They weren't hitting Vasco's teams, but they'd locked them down good. Vasco's unit couldn't move while under fire, and the Banshee wouldn't be around for a while yet. This wasn't good. They were caught in sniper crossfire coming from high ground. Vasco glanced up at the mountain and the hills on the other side of the little town. With the lake at the only open end, they were caught in a killing pocket. This wasn't a hit-and-run attack. They'd walked into a solid trap and were going to pay for it.

Vasco keyed open his com on unit broadcast. "All teams, prepare for incoming. Find a hidey-hole, folks. They're only pinning us down so they know where we are."

He didn't even have time to finish his broadcast before the first explosions. Things got noisy for a bit. This really sucked. The only thing worse than being pinned by snipers in an urban environment was being pinned while taking artillery fire. There was no way they were going to take this for long. Vasco switched his com to open Polity broadcast. Maybe someone was in the area...

"Polity support, this is Centurion del Goya. I'm pinned down by sniper fire at forward position 1224 by 316, taking artillery fire. Any support elements available, over?"

Response was immediate, much to Vasco's relief. "Del Goya, this is Tech Morgana. Banshee Seven is inbound close fire ETA one five minutes. You are in MRL range extreme range now. Can we support, over?"

Banshee Seven was much closer than Vasco had expected. They must be redlining the jets to push the big dirigible that fast.

"Banshee Seven, hold one," Vasco said. He pulled out his tablet, configured as always to show his current location and map as a default.

An idea had occurred to him. The town was a kill pocket, but the Outlanders were clever. They'd wipe him out, but they weren't willing to die for the privilege just yet. They'd have an escape route. On the map, the town was inside a pocket made of the small mountain and the two hills, but on the other side of those three obstacles was only a narrow valley before the first rise of lowland mountains that made up the main ridge at the end of the plateau. That valley had only had one exit point heading to the plateau—a dry riverbed. Tall hills ringed the far side of the valley. Not as tall as the small mountain, but tall enough. Vasco had a plan, but first he needed to stay alive.

"Banshee Seven, I need MRL smoke rounds on the town ASAP, then I have a few other requests, over."

"Roger Centurion, Banshee has MRL away."

Vasco switched his com to his local units to give the heads-up about incoming "friendly" fire, then switched back to the dirigible. The long-range rockets would be arriving on a ballistic arc in less than a minute and should give enough dense smoke cover to allow his Gyrenes to move to better shelter. It wouldn't get them out of the trap, but that wasn't part of the plan anymore.

"Banshee Seven, can you come around from position 1250 by 316? We may be able to block off the escape route."

He'd suggested that the dirigible swing a little wide on her way to support him, and instead come in along the Outlanders' escape route. It meant his team was now the bait in a bigger trap and would have to be under fire for longer. But if they could survive it, they'd have a chance of wiping out the entire attacking force, plus their artillery. Vasco hated to even think it, but that was probably worth the lives of some of his troops. It was worth his life, he knew. The sooner they got any artillery out of Outlander hands, the sooner this war would be over.

It would be even better if they could flush the Outlanders into trying to escape first. Ideally, they could have the Banshee catch the Outlanders in the open before they made the riverbed. A Banshee was a hundred meters of floating support weaponry. The Outlanders wouldn't have a chance against that. The problem was Vasco didn't know what unit resources from higher up he currently had accessible to drive away the bad guys... and without extra resources, he probably wouldn't live long enough to even be bait for the trap.

He looked over the tablet map, scrolling through the list of area resources. There didn't seem to be much in the area. The APCs had been routed back at the first contact report but were still ten minutes away at top speed. Still, he could probably get them to change route slightly. With careful timing, they'd be able to move up the forks behind the flanking hills and stop any Outlander stragglers from getting out the other way.

The MRL rounds arrived while Vasco was still looking for resources. The rockets had burned out their motors earlier and were coasting in—at the speed of a bullet. They made a most impressive series of cracking booms as they landed, casing the perimeter of the town. Dense red smoke poured up and out. Time to move.

"All teams, move to cover!" Vasco called over coms.

They should have enough time to move to better positions. The smoke wouldn't help with the incoming artillery, but it would slow down the snipers. And since the snipers were what was holding them in place, they could find a hide. Most likely once the incoming rounds landed, the attackers would pack up and run. They'd done their damage and didn't need to risk staying around and getting caught, unless they were greedy for a few more kills.

The incoming artillery wasn't letting up yet. That worried Vasco. He hadn't recognized the sound of the rounds coming in, but they seemed pretty big. He'd assumed someone had humped up big mortars into prepared positions. Now he had to reconsider. If they weren't pulling back, that meant they still felt safe. So either the Outlanders had a bigger force than he thought and the support was coming into a trap, or it was almost as bad and the Outlanders had some serious artillery that was ranging in from farther out.

He zoomed out the map's magnification, thinking. He wasn't even aware of the ground shaking under him, the air rattling with concussions and the sharp cracks of gunfire. All around him was chaos. Debris spattered around him as his team screamed at him to move under cover with everyone else.

A small red indicator dot caught his attention. An orbiting observation platform was passing over, just hitting the horizon. He'd have two, maybe three minutes of orbital coverage. Maybe thirty seconds of overhead. They weren't due coverage in this area for another hour, but someone had made the call and burned some reaction mass for them. Now he had to make use of his new guardian angel.

He keyed up Tech Morgana on the Banshee again. "Banshee Six, Centurion del Goya requests priority access from Overwatch platform. Surveillance and arty suppression, over."

"Roger, del Goya, hold one."

Vasco didn't even have to wait five seconds. Overwatch was on the ball and monitoring coms already. There were days when Vasco was truly glad to have the Polity on his side.

"Del Goya, Overwatch three confirms. Incoming. Splash in one minute. Surveillance feed online now, authenticate to receive."

Sure enough, Vasco saw the incoming stream icon pulsing. He tapped it and entered his authentication code, and his map was overlain with live imagery. He saw his teams in infrared, bright clusters of bursting artillery ringing the town... odd. The Outlanders seemed to only be landing the odd round inside the town. They must have been expecting Vasco's team to try to break out.

He even saw the streaks of incoming artillery as they burned through the air. Tracing those lines back, he could easily see his fears confirmed. A small cluster of artillery pieces were firing from the next valley over. The Sami had better equipment than they were supposed to have.

But the worst thing was the mountaintop and hilltops. There were no signs of snipers, spotters, or any support troops at all. Nothing. No footprints or residual heat marks. That was impossible. They'd been receiving sniper fire moments ago. Even if the snipers were dead, he should have seen cooling bodies. If they had left already, he would have seen heat remnants. There should be something... and then, just before the filters kicked in to mute the surging heat flare from the incoming kinetic, he saw it.

A single, thin red line. A rifle barrel, hot from firing. Attached to nothing. He couldn't make out any more details because the incoming kinetic made daylight feel dark for a moment. Unlike landing bombardments, the Overwatch support fire was as brutal as the Polity could make it. The tungsten kinetic energy weapon was fired down as fast as Polity science could make it go.

Vasco's exposed skin felt the slightest tingle of heat as the weapon ripped through the atmosphere, creating a plasma sheathe that pumped out radiation. It hit with multi-megaton force, completely obliterating the entire valley the artillery was in. A moment later, the sound hit—a great cracking roar that shook everyone. It was overkill for a single artillery position, overkill to support one four-team unit, but it was the Polity way. Vasco wasn't complaining.

The live feed flicked off as Overwatch moved toward the horizon. There was no more sniper fire, and Vasco heard the APCs rolling past the town and into the side valleys. In another few minutes, the Banshee should show up from the other side, trapping the Outlanders as they made a run for it.

Vasco and his teams would hold tight for a little while longer. No sense in being the first to move and the first to learn a sniper had decided to stay put and bag one more Gyrene. No one was in a rush. Vasco let himself relax, but just a little. He wouldn't fully relax for some time yet.

He was thirsty, but he didn't feel like drinking yet. He was still buzzing, still fragmented. His thoughts were all over, now that there was nothing to focus his amped thoughts on.

Alberta was prodding him for some reason. Vasco looked at the stocky redhead to see why he was picking at him. Ah. He'd pulled up Vasco's pantleg, where a thumb-sized strip of flesh was missing from his shin. Alberta was swabbing at it with a first aid cleaning patch. There was a red mess on the ground and a shiny, jagged piece of steel in the middle of it.

Vasco glanced at his wound just before Alberta pressed the sealing patch on it. He had the briefest glimpse of bright pink skin and bright white patches that looked all foamy, welling with pinpricks of blood that rapidly pooled to fill the wound... then all covered up. Nice and neat in a little brown square.

No pain at all. Vasco hadn't even felt the piece of shrapnel hit him. It struck him suddenly as a little unfair. He'd carry that scar on his leg for the rest of his life. When he was an old man, he'd look down and see that scar. Didn't even feel it. What kind of story was that gonna be? He laughed at himself.

Alberta looked at him. He'd been talking the whole time, but Vasco had tuned it out. "—least he doesn't have any cooties! I think I got all the bits out, but you'll need a real medic to check that out, Centurion!" Alberta was grinning like an idiot and shaking his head.

Suddenly what Alberta had said hit Vasco and he looked over at Verne. Verne was a big, thick man, tough as nails. He was the mule of the unit. He'd carry anything, never complain, never stop. Tough as nails.

Cave was patching Verne's back. The shrapnel that had hit Vasco's shin had ripped through Verne's back —doing almost no damage. It had shredded his shirt and left little nicks across the width of his shoulder blades. It looked as if a couple of kittens had swiped Verne. It probably stung more than it hurt… but Verne had passed right out.

Alberta had tried to make sure there were no bits of Verne stuck in Vasco's leg. Vasco gave in to the urge to stand and pace. The APCs were letting loose on the hillside now with their guns. No sniper was going to be picking targets through that hail of depleted uranium. His legs felt weak. The pacing was at least making the shaking go away.

Vasco's hands were gripping his rifle, and he felt tired. He really didn't want anything more in the world than a beer. A cold, frothy beer. Or maybe a shot of whisky. Make that a glass… hell, he thought, a bottle would be nice right now. He just wanted to shut off his brain for a moment—or longer. His clothes felt itchy. Maybe he could find a place to take a shower, get these filthy clothes off, and get clean in some hot water, drink that bottle of whisky in the hot pouring shower, and stop thinking about the broken bits of binocular spinning off in the air. Had the guy been looking through them? Were they on his chest? Had Vasco shot him in the head or the body? Not that it mattered... a twenty-millimeter round wasn't going to leave much of anything at all. Vasco shivered a little as he thought about that impact.

Why had that stupid son of bitch been there? Why had he been shooting at them? Damn him anyway! Vasco wanted to kill him all over again. Wanted to squeeze that trigger again, feel that single perfect shot all over again. No, he wanted to hit the man over and over with the rifle. Teach that bastard to shoot at him and his troops! He'd showed him what happened when he did that.

Jesus, it could have been Vasco dying. That sniper could have shot him. It could have been his head or chest, his rifle scope spinning up in the air...

Vasco fought back the urge to shiver. He was sure it would turn into a convulsion, and he didn't feel as if he'd be able to stop that if it started.

This was supposed to be easy. He'd never shot anyone before. In the back of his mind, he'd always thought it was less personal to kill someone with a rifle than right up in their face with a sword or knife. Maybe even less honorable at some archaic level. It wasn't the sort of thing he'd say out loud, but it was one of his secret thoughts. He admitted to himself that he'd always felt a little superior about his fencing training with that thought— as though he was some sort of higher killer.

But now that the momentary elation over killing had passed... Vasco still felt the singular moment of utter joy that had passed through him when he'd squeezed the trigger. It was a moment of absolute, time-slowing perfection. One of those incredibly rare moments when everything came together just right, and in this case, it was made even better by the briefest appearance of a savage killing beast inside him that was let out of its civilized cage for a tenth of a second. But with that moment in the past, a sick oily nausea threatened to creep up the back of his throat. Killing was killing, Vasco realized—sadly, belatedly. It was just as personal through a scope as it was at the end of a blade.

He had the sick feeling he'd be thinking of those spinning, broken binoculars and nothing else for the next few days. His tablet chirped and Vasco glanced down—duty was calling. The Banshee was making contact with the ambushers. He heard the heavy firing of its ground-support guns churning away in the distance.

New orders had arrived. Hold in place for the main force to catch up... and write a full engagement report. He shook his head. Paperwork. Debriefing would probably be later tonight or tomorrow, then right back to the spearhead. At least they'd get a few hours downtime, maybe some solid sleep.

Vasco dropped back down, glancing at his tablet to note the time. He was too numb to be really shocked that only twenty minutes had passed since they'd entered the town. It felt like... he'd swear to the end of his life that it had been a four-hour battle. He was too tired to argue with his own brain.

He put down the tablet and popped the magazine out of his rifle. Time to reload. He pulled up on the tab on his farthest ammo pouch and dug out a shell, then slotted it into the magazine. He snorted when he realized there was still room in the magazine. He picked up his rifle, carefully checking to see if there was still a round in the receiver... no, all clear. He must have fired two rounds out of the five-round magazine. Amazing.

It had really seemed to be only one perfect shot. He had no recollection of firing another shot. *Damn, I must have been really wired on adrenaline.* He slotted another shell into the magazine. It was still ready for more. He loaded one more. Then another.

He'd fired a total of four shots and only recalled firing once. He shook his head. No doubt about it, he was a real veteran now. Now he just had to survive. He'd had enough fighting. No more. He'd been damn stupid to want this. But they still had kilometers to go and Outlanders to fight.

Chapter Twelve: The Victorious

Weber bought it three hours later.

They'd stopped at the next checkpoint, their last as point rotation. They were meant to hold the position for an hour until everyone caught up, then tail end the column for the next week. After that, a month doing support on a Banshee—the closest they would get to leave for three months yet. They'd stopped under the cover of a passing Banshee, which had swept the area with infrared and visuals and pronounced it clean. Nothing in the area, nothing on the last satellite pass. Not even a herd of goats.

They pulled under the hovering zeppelin and made their preparations to hold. Snapped off the extra armor on the side of the vehicle, trucked out the sandbags, and dug in. They weren't meant to hold off any kind of enemy force, just sit tight and observe, report back if there was any activity at all, so they needed just enough cover to give them time to pack up and run if they had too.

Vasco had his binoculars out. Low hills, scrub... nothing of note. They were still in the big valley leading to the edge of the plateau. Still over a week away from the beginning of the giant mountain ranges that sloped gradually down to the ocean. The mountain ranges were home to the Outlanders and where they expected to meet the most resistance. They had expected from the start to have a nasty guerilla fight with the Outlanders. They lived in the mountains and were fanatically religious about self-sufficiency and independence.

The Polity planners had expected the Outlanders to be a tough nut to crack, which was why the Drop had more than the usual complement of special forces and mountain troops. The Outlanders were supposed to be tough but simple. Which left the big question in Vasco's mind of where the artillery his team had encountered came from.

The Outlanders supposedly had no industrial infrastructure and no contacts off-planet. Hell, they were supposed to be opposed to getting support of any kind from anyone! Which in no way, shape, or form explained what the hell they had been doing nailing Vasco's position with accurate time-on-target artillery fire. Making, transporting, training, and supplying artillery should have been impossible for Outlanders, and no one else on the planet should have had the will or the means to fight. Something damn fishy was up. Something didn't make sense.

Weber grunted. He was looking through his scope—probably looking for game. On point, they'd had nothing but iron rations to eat and no time to prep anything else. Weber had been going on for the last few days about how he was going to bag something meaty to dress and eat when it was their turn to tail. Vasco turned to see what Weber was looking at, but he couldn't see anything. Weber's rifle was pointed between two low hills about two kilometers away.

"What's up, Weber? See some dinner?" Vasco wasn't as angry as his tone implied. Weber was a good troop, and Vasco knew he wouldn't be seriously planning on doing any hunting until they were completely secure. But he figured it didn't hurt to get the point across. Reinforcement was never a bad thing.

"Nope. I don't think so…" Weber turned to Vasco, taking off his helmet and giving his scalp a vigorous scratch. "This area is supposed to be secure, right?"

"Yeah," said Vasco, "it's been swept. Mighta missed something though. What do you see?"

"Dunno. Nothing really. It's just over here—" Weber turned to pick up his rifle and there was a wet punching sound and the now-familiar ripping noise of high-speed lead.

Vasco had the sudden, mad urge to grab the bits of Weber's head and shout at him for being such an idiot as to let his head explode like that. For the merest moment, Vasco reacted as if Weber's exploding skull was a glass of water slipping off a shelf and if Vasco was swift enough, he could catch it and stop disaster from happening.

Then Vasco froze. Just froze. He was stuck for a moment with indecision—whether to jump forward and try to help Weber or just... Vasco was squeamish for a heartbeat. He had time to think about how he didn't want to touch Weber's blood and brains, a brief moment of fear of getting dirty or catching some disease, followed by a weird relief of realizing it was too damn late anyway. And only then the realization that it was enemy fire.

"Sniper!" Vasco yelled, diving under the barrier Weber should have been hiding under. The barrier that Vasco's conversation had pulled Weber up and away from...

The Banshee stayed and swept the area again while Vasco and the rest of his team hunkered down. Two more hours of searching and nothing was found, and finally the Banshee let loose on the probable firing area with a full barrage. The entire push was held up for a day while search-and-destroy teams moved in, but they never found a trace of the sniper.

It was three in the morning, and Vasco was still up. His eyes felt swollen and packed with sand. He was so tired he kept hallucinating strange little creatures in the corner of his vision—little white men in overalls, running about. But he couldn't sleep. Every time he closed his eyes, he saw Weber getting up and turning to talk to him. Vasco thought of a million things he should have done differently. He should have crouched down with Weber at his post and gotten a report. He should have kicked Weber's feet out from under him and saved his life. He should have been leaning over Weber and taken the shot himself. He should have yelled at Weber for taking off his helmet. He should have been a stricter Centurion and kept his troops more disciplined so Weber would have never acted the way he had.

Vasco spent the entire night detailing, painstakingly, every single thing he could have and should have done to keep Weber alive. He got sick to his stomach twice when he thought about the morning... and how he'd have to give orders again. His mind cheerfully gave him images of someone dying every time Vasco opened his mouth. He knew what was going on, and he knew he had to stop his brain from playing out its sick fantasies. He knew he should get help... but instead, he sat up, looking at the stars and shivering.

Nils watched the Banshee prowl through the air. The big black delta was an ominous shape against the sky. Perhaps if it had been a jet, Nils thought, it would be less impressive. The slow steady approach tended to give one more of an appreciation, more of an anticipation, of its effect and power. Somewhat like a Tatar but on a smaller scale, the Banshee achieved much of its effect by presence alone. It was obviously designed for that purpose. A giant floating flat black diamond with howling engines? Subtle. Certainly not designed for maximum military efficiency.

Nils supposed it was cheaper to transport and maintain a flotilla of Banshees as opposed to the equivalent firepower weight in helicopters or fighters. There were so many better solutions though. Off hand, he could think of an even dozen better ways to conquer a planet. In time, he was sure he'd be calling on all of those techniques. Even a behemoth like the Polity would eventually have to innovate when pushed hard enough. And they'd be pushing the Polity hard enough soon.

But not just yet. For now, Nils was content to let them have the upper hand. It was costing the Outlanders, but it was well within the predicted loss rates. Sacrifices had to be made for the greater good, and what better way to spend one's life than for the good of all?

They were going to be cutting it close though. Perhaps,

Nils thought, they could have the mills and lathes turn out turbine parts... or perhaps a pulse jet engine? The Banshees were ground support and only had limited air-to-air defense. If the Sami launched a few dozen fighters, they could knock out most of the Banshees before anyone knew what hit them.

He chewed over the problem for a while, playing with different scenarios. Eventually, he put the issue aside. The Banshees should cease to be a problem once their communication abilities were taken out. They would still be formidable fighting platforms, but they were limited by Polity doctrine. All the Sami had to do was attack the doctrine. Easy enough to do, but the cost would be high. It was already high, but it would get worse.

He turned as he heard footsteps coming up the rise behind him. It was a messenger. Nils was about to greet him but stopped. The boy's face was tight—bad news. Best to let him get it out. The boy was an Outlander, but the way came at its own pace to everyone. One had to be patient.

"Nils Sayiidison, I'm afraid I have bad news. The Polity forces reacted much stronger than we expected. They used kinetic strikes. We lost the supply depot and all its troops. Badr Nilsson was killed in the blast. I'm sorry. The surviving Outlanders have moved on to the fallback position and were relieved."

Good news then. Nils said, "Thank you. Was there any news of how my son died?"

"The last report we had was that he was in the supply depot to straighten out a problem with food storage. The supply depot had the misfortune of being directly under the kinetic strike."

"Ah, I see. Thank you then."

The messenger nodded and left with a confused look on his face.

Nils wanted to laugh. The poor boy was new to the way and probably didn't yet have the training to understand the grin on Nils's face when Nils had heard his son had died. Nils's grin grew wider, and he did chuckle as tears coursed down his cheeks.

Badr was a bright boy. He'd been a wonderful child, but an absolute terror. Nils had spent so many nights holding his son.

As a babe, Badr never seemed to fall asleep unless Nils held him, rocking and crooning to him for hours. It had felt like years that Nils only ever slept with a baby cradled in his arms, Badr's tiny head against his chest. He could still feel it now as if it had been yesterday. It felt as though it had been yesterday.

Nils let his memories run free for a moment. Badr's marriage. His first tooth lost. Angry words when he was in his teens. Pride when Badr had argued about correct thinking with his father and had proven his point with courage and excellent memory. So many memories.

Nils smiled again. He'd have a hole in his heart forever, but now his son's life was complete. Nils could celebrate that life for what it was and have all the joy of having known Badr for all that he could. He was truly blessed to have had such a son who lived such a complete life. Nils looked out again, watching the Banshee through his tears, and marveling at how wonderful life was.

It never occurred to him to wish that things could have been different. He turned his thoughts to tomorrow. He would grieve for his son. The pain and loss would hit him at moments for weeks—years, truly. But he would deal with each bit of pain by remembering his happiness and by accepting the pain and letting it flow over and past him.

But for now, Nils had a war to plan. In some ways, his son's death was the trigger he had been looking for. The Polity had met some resistance and crushed it. Surely they must be committed by now. Another week, and the Polity scouts would touch the edge of the plateau. The plan was all laid out and awaited only that trigger. Once the Polity hit that point, Outlander strike units positioned across the entire circumference of the plateau would activate. The scouts would be rolled up, then the lead elements, then they would roll up the Polity.

There was no single plan past the initiation of action. Every leader carried a complete set of battle plans in his head, triggered by whatever circumstances each commander came across. All the plans had the same end goal, and each subordinate down to the last trooper had the same plans, plus their own specific orders, memorized. The Outlanders were not in any fashion warriors, or even soldiers, but they did not have to be. They only had to be strong where the Polity was weak. They had no soldiers, no training, no weapons, but they had generations of training in memory and logic—and the gift of the Weta. They knew how to listen.

The kilometers flew by. Vasco lost track of how many hours he'd spent watching the landscape. Moving from point to point on the map. It looked easy enough on the map. The satellites the *Alexi* had put up for surveillance covered the distance in minutes. Vasco had started by plotting their travel on his pad but had given up after the first day. From space, it was just a blink.

Vasco tended not to travel much when he was down the well. He liked to find a nice place to live—a good city—and settle down. Walk, catch public transit or taxi or whatever was in the area. His childhood was haunted with an unspoken desire for an unknown home and a community, and it had left him always trying to stay put.

When not down the well, travel was in kilometers per second on the slow side—never kilometers per hour. He knew the difference of perspective, but he couldn't help looking at the pad map and predicting travel times. He was getting sick of the constant anticipation of looking at the next checkpoint and figuring out how many hours of travel time, then watching that travel time tick slowly by on the map.

It didn't help that Vasco had taken to obsessively watching the surveillance satellite footage. He was constantly trying to monitor what was ahead of them. The problem was the most up-to-date footage came from the satellites with the lowest resolution. The best resolution came from scopes on *Alexi*, but they were only updated on a weekly basis. The hourly updates came from a fast satellite, and the resolution made their progress look like the slowest crawl in the world.

It had taken a week from Weber's death for Vasco to relax and watch the scenery fly by. The last two days, he'd watched the landscape change from the roughly arid plateau's scrubby low hills to the steep valleys and peaks of the lowland mountain ranges. The air was growing damper, cooler, and the color of the vegetation was changing, as was its density.

Strange images and sights met Vasco's gaze, and he thought about what the old hat maker had said. Vasco found himself trying to listen to the scenery as they drove past. A stray sheep. An abandoned, collapsed barn. An ancient burned-out husk of a tree. Dotted caves on a cliff across a river. Everything seemed to whisper a story, and he found himself wondering at the forgotten tales.

And wondering what his own tale would be. Weber's tale was done, wrapped and written. Vasco didn't really know anything about it. He knew who the soldier was, but he didn't know what kind of child Weber had been, what he'd dreamed about being as an old man, or who he'd loved as a teenager.

Vasco remembered his own loves, the ones gained and lost and never realized. How would those, he wondered, figure in the tale of his life? Would anyone ever know those heartbreaks that were so important to him? Would those stories ever be told? Would anyone ever know?

He looked at the other soldiers with him, all intent on their work. They didn't look like people with loves lost or tragic thoughts lurking in the back of their skulls... just hard workers. People focused on their tasks, lost in their jobs. They looked for all the world as if nothing existed inside their heads but the job in front of them.

Vasco felt a little lonely. His only job at the moment was to be in charge, and there was nothing for him to do at the moment. He'd already finished all his make-work and made enough to keep everyone else busy. It occurred to him for a moment to wonder what he looked like to everyone else. Was he as taciturn-looking, as focused as they seemed to him? Or were his turbulent thoughts as transparent to them as they felt to him?

Vasco shook his head to clear it. Too much deep thinking. He was really off his game. This Long Drop wasn't going according to the book, and it was getting to him. For some reason, these

Sami weren't exactly getting the program. They didn't yet seem to realize they'd lost. That wasn't too unusual. Most Unifications started like that. Once you'd lost the high ground, the battle was over. With no space domination, no planet could hope to hold off from the unlimited resources and overwatch that space dominance gave.

It was usual for a society to have a collective reaction of rage, and sporadic fire fights would break out. The really hardcore types, like the Hawatians, would organize and try for one last solid push. But once that push was crushed, the spirit for fighting went right out of a society, then the Polity social scientists would get to work.

But the Sami? They hadn't even really bothered to fight for space. Just the three ships, and not even a peep about them on ground side. No real organized army, but a constant series of skirmishes and incidents. Things stayed quiet once an area was pacified, but the word didn't seem to spread. It was almost as if each individual Sami needed to be slapped before they got the message. At least the Outlander Sami seemed that way. The Plateau Sami were more reasonable and got the message as a group almost right away. There had been some grumbling, but nothing major.

The Outlanders were just as bad as, if not worse than, the fisherfolk. It was looking to turn into a protracted guerrilla war, which was just stupid. There was no way that could be won, not against a space-dominant society like the Polity.

Vasco could understand if the Outlanders fought a solid guerilla war—he'd faced those before—but this was different. It was strangely low key, but vicious and precise. It was like fighting a boxer who was not only a power puncher, but also had surgical precision—except that you were supposed to be playing badminton.

Either way, it should be over soon. They'd pushed the Outlanders right to the edge of the plateau, and there was nowhere left for them to go but the mountains, and the mountains were empty. Sure, the Outlanders lived there, but everything they'd been told about them was that they lived lives of austerity. There were no resources in the mountain. The Outlanders would be finished at that point. They'd be cut off from the plateau resources, and pure attrition would kill them as a fighting force within weeks. It was almost over.

Vasco pulled up his pad and obsessed over his map again.

The last week had flown by. It had been swift, with much to do, but Nils still found himself amused by his twinges of impatience. There was risk… things could still be lost. It wasn't likely, but nothing was guaranteed. They were cutting it to a fine edge. They had one weapon to knock out the *Alexi* and only one shot with it. From the beginning, they had planned not to fight the Timariot, but rather the Helot computer that ran the Polity ship.

It was a gamble that the Polity would rely on the advanced AI to plan the invasion. It was a good gamble—the Helot was the perfect machine to coordinate and plan something as huge as the invasion of a world. The well-honed teams on *Alexi* would be used to doing everything themselves and would have experience, but they would be unlikely to pass up the chance to use the novelty of such an advanced piece of equipment. And the Helot would be proving itself, time and time again.

Which was what the Outlander plan depended on. Humans were complex and given to unpredictable bouts of insight and intuition. The Helot was unmatched at reducing complex systems down to actionable metaphor, but it relied on using known information. The sensors of the *Alexi* and the associated web of satellites she'd launched made it difficult for the Outlanders to hide their actions from the Helot, but they didn't plan to hide at all. The plan was to use misdirection.

The Helot took in new data, compared it with existing and archival data, and produced a constantly updated prediction of tactical and strategic outcomes. It was very, very accurate. The Outlander method was to salt the observed behavior in order to tailor the predictions. It was an ambitious and complex plan, and only the Outlander mental training allowed them to even consider such a strategy, but it seemed to be working.

The Polity was pushing the Outlanders off the plateau. They had gradually hit the Polity with surprising attacks, which should push the prediction algorithms one way. The Outlander failures and casualties would push the predictions another way. If one were to imagine the predictions of the Helot as a straight line pointing the path to victory, the losses would drag it one direction, the victories in another. The Outlander strategy was to make that line point precisely where they wanted it.

Combined with the geography of their world, the careful structure and placement of attacks, they should be able to maneuver the *Alexi* into falling into one precise orbit that would lead her right into the Outlander trap—right into Nils's Hellmouth. It was almost time. The varied Polity spearhead forces were almost at their trigger points and as coordinated had been hoped for.

Nils reflected on the latest reports from the scouts. The Polity forces had been aggressive, driving strong and only stopping when they ran into recognizable military engagement. They had passed the dummy cylinders routinely and never stopped to examine them. They had minimal interest in intelligence, only in fast assault… but then, that was what they had been led to believe was the correct thing to do. Soon they'd find out how wrong that belief was. The lead elements would be cut off, communication disrupted, and the Outlanders would finally be able to fight back. It wouldn't be easy for them—the Sami weren't soldiers like the Laconians—but they would perform to the best of their ability. It would suffice.

The only thing that seemed even slightly off wasn't a tactical concern. The scout watching the strike force closing in on Nils's position had gotten a good look at the force. The commander was an older hatchet-faced, dark-skinned man. Nils had no doubt it was the Alamansan the Walkure had told them about. Nils wondered what the fates had in mind for them. It seemed that they would meet, and Nils felt himself looking forward to it.

The Alamansans had had such potential. As a younger man, Nils had studied them, disappointed with how they had drifted away from their potential but were enamored with the lofty goals of the original colony. They had intended to create a Roman-style utopia, with genetic coding to help everyone grow to their best potential. It should have been a world of happy people, but as usual, the desire for power amongst a few had eventually corrupted the entire system. It seemed only the Sami and Laconians had escaped that fate. The Laconians via their extreme austerity, and the Sami by a quirk of local zoology.

Nils thought it likely he would meet the Alamansan if the fellow survived the surprise the Sami had in store for them. It would be interesting to compare the remnant breeding of the Alamansan with the mental training of the Sami. Perhaps something of value would be found there. If he survived—which, Nils thought, wasn't likely.

Chapter Thirteen: The Light

The lead elements of the push to drive the Sami off the Plateau just suddenly stopped reporting back. Neither Vasco nor anyone else had heard reports of any kind of conflict, booby traps or anything else...just one moment, the forward elements were going about their business, the next, silence.

Vasco found out shortly why the lead elements had disappeared. It was the damn metal cylinders like the one in the back of a cart ahead of him. The cylinders were all over the place—they'd been seeing them since they started to press out on the plateau. No one had bothered to find out what they were. Everyone had assumed they were containers for water, or fuel, or something else no one cared about. One or two were seen every day, in every village or town. Banded metal drums about two meters long and a meter in diameter. And new... all new. Hiding in plain sight, the whole time. In retrospect, they should have paid more attention.

Vasco's team had just received a com that their meet-up element was offline. They were supposed to catch up with them in eight hours of steady road time, then leapfrog them to take over the lead for the next twenty-four hours. But the units weren't reporting in, and all their connected hardware and software was showing as offline.

Vasco had just noticed something worse on his pad when

he found out what the cylinders were for. He'd called up the current specs on his element's vehicles and personnel and should have seen the icons for the neighboring element on the right… but it wasn't there. He zoomed out farther, seeing his element and the related spokes, but no lead elements at all. He zoomed out to overview the entire plateau. The leads of all the spokes were gone. The entire front line had gone offline. He saw one element in his tier, on a nearly opposite spoke, disappear. Just like that, its icon was gone. He was about to com up to the closest relay to *Alexi* when the cylinder in the nearby cart exploded.

It didn't explode much, as things went. Just a really big bang. A puff of dust. The cylinder ruptured, bursting more than exploding. There was a flash, but not even a firecracker compared to what something that size could have burst into had it been filled with explosives. It wasn't full of explosives though. It was something worse for the Polity.

Vasco was looking at his pad when the cylinder blew. He glanced up to see what had made the noise, flicked his eyes back down to his pad when he saw no huge blast… and froze. The pad was dead. So was his radio. The vehicle stuttered to a stop.

It was an EMP bomb. The illiterate, low-tech Sami Outlanders had seeded the attack route with EMP bombs, killing all communication. Every bit of electronic gear they had was fried. Unit communication was gone. Reporting and backup was gone. They were on their own with no surveillance and no intelligence. Vasco's gut went cold and empty.

He didn't remember if he screamed to everyone to bail or if someone else did, but for a moment, it looked as if the entire vehicle's personnel load had developed the power to fly. It looked as if two troopers had managed to levitate out of one window at the same time.

Most of them made it out before the Sami blew up the vehicle. Vasco clutched his ears and screamed to try to relieve the awful overpressure of the close-range explosion. He felt as if his whole body were being crushed under a tank.

Vasco didn't remember firing, but he knew he must have,

as he saw the distinctive shape of Outlander cloaks moving from building to building, swarming in on their position and firing. He knew he must have fired because his pistol was clicking emptily in his hand as he pointed at an Outlander. He couldn't hear anything—just the muted, blank roar of his ears and the occasional "crack" of a rifle sounding as if it was a kilometer away. He turned to look back at the vehicle, thinking to shout some instructions to his troops, but there was no one there. He was alone.

The Sami came steadily, if not professionally. No rush, but no pausing. Just a smooth tactical leapfrog from point to point. Vasco looked to his right and left and saw more of the same. Behind him was only the burning vehicle. He couldn't make a break for it without exposing himself to fire. No hope.

Vasco crouched, turned, and decided to risk looking over the top of the low wall he had somehow found himself hiding behind. He looked right into the face of an oncoming Outlander. They'd moved faster than he thought.

He pulled the Pook sword from its hanging scabbard without even thinking about it. It felt good in his hand, like a solid knife with a bit more reach. Not the sabre he would have preferred, but he'd never have carried something that bulky with him. He had time to think about how right it felt as he vaulted the wall into the enemy. He had luck on his side. They hadn't expected someone so close, which gave him almost a full second to move freely.

He vaulted the barrier with a smooth leap, cutting down with a backhand cut across his foe. He felt the contact, the thick slap of impact, and the blade kept moving. He didn't look to see what he'd done. His eye was already on the next target. Three steps away, the point man. They had been closing in on the wrecked vehicle, coming into a loose wedge once they'd cleared the buildings. It was a good formation for sweeping and driving, with lots of coverage for each other. Not so good for close contact though.

Vasco aimed for the point man with a deep low drive. It was a wrestling move. He dropped his level, almost picking up his feet to let gravity drop him as fast as possible. The point man was just swiveling his gun up to where Vasco was, but Vasco was already under his line of fire. By the time the point noticed it, Vasco had hit him low, driving his right shoulder into the man's belly and grabbing him around the waist with his left arm.

Vasco drove his sword all the way through the Outlander's thigh, then stood, easily hoisting the man up and over him. He let go and slammed into the next man in line, rolling up one side of the wedge. The solid impact of the man's body didn't even slow Vasco. He drove his shoulder into the center of the man's chest as hard as he could. The enemy actually ricocheted off of Vasco and into the man behind him. Vasco took the quarter of a second that gave him to extend his sword in a perfect lunge, aiming at the next man's eye. It would have hit had he been using his rapier or even his training sabre. With the shorter blade, he found himself looking down the spine of the blade as it pointed like a ruler into the man's eyes.

The Outlander, a young man, scruffy haired with a wisp of a beard just starting to show, stared right back into Vasco's eyes. And just like that, Vasco was frozen in place. The man's eyes showed complete knowledge of his impending death. Knowledge… and acceptance. There was a calm, peaceful awareness in the boy's eyes, and it struck Vasco to the core. Never in his life had he felt the calm that he recognized in the Outlander. It was the oneness, the ideal moment of a warrior's life. Vasco had heard of it—every martial artist had heard of it and trained for it—and some barely sprouted young man was showing its face to Vasco.

Vasco didn't even hear the voices around him. He didn't feel the sword being taken from his hands, or his hands being bound. He didn't even really notice the hood being put over his head. Only those eyes, and the sure knowledge that Vasco had lost. His moment had come, the perfect moment of combat… and he'd been bettered by a boy who stood there and accepted his own death.

Vasco had no answer for that, and he had no idea why he

had frozen. He felt broken and lost. All was lost. Somehow, the illiterate primitives of this world had done more than acquired artillery and sophisticated EMP weapons from somewhere. In his moment of wonder, Vasco noticed not just the incredible mind of the boy he'd nearly killed, but also the smooth coordination of the Outlanders.

Too smooth. It was the coordination of solid communication equipment and tactical oversight. All of which should have been impossible in the aftermath of the EMP weapon. Something far over his ken was happening, and in his grief and self-doubt, Vasco had no choice but to let himself be drawn along with it. He didn't even care enough to hope it would end well.

The sun was well up. The heat hadn't started to sink in yet. Vasco was starting to wonder if it ever would. He'd never been this high up before. He'd slept poorly during the night. The cold was one of the reasons, but not the only one.

The Sami were obviously in a rush to get moving with what was left of the morning. They weren't using campfires really, just small fires big enough to get teapots going. Some of them seemed to be getting a kind soup cooking as well. Vasco figured it was breakfast. It didn't seem to be universal. Some of the Sami were eating pieces of jerky. Others had cheese or some kind of filled bun. It made his stomach hurt to watch. They'd either feed him or not. He didn't have much choice in the matter.

He took a small break from observing his captors to check out the scenery. They were pretty high up in the mountains. From above, it must have looked like a tiny goat trail. If it looked like anything at all. An impressive overhang neatly hid the entire party.

The valley below wasn't visible from where Vasco sat. He could see the peak across the valley though. It was a sheer, smooth face of blue granite rising to a razor edge. Peeking over the top of that ridge was the rest of the range. Wispy clouds were visible off into the horizon. Vasco hadn't realized how high the plateau was. The elevation numbers didn't reflect the reality he was seeing now.

A world looked small from space. It didn't look much bigger from a spaceport, or the inside of a pub, or especially in the middle of a firefight. It struck Vasco that the best way to grasp the size of a world was to be snugged into an alcove on the top side of a high-elevation plateau. If it wasn't for the soft, busy noises of the party all around him, he might have felt all alone. He still did. The vastness sank into him.

"Gyrene, breakfast," said a voice to his side. It was one of the Sami. A little older than the rest, with a distinct Arabic cast to his looks.

The Sami were a pretty racially diverse people, but the Arab and Nordic strains seemed to be winning out over time. Hook-nosed blond giants were not uncommon.

The food on offer was a small bun crammed with meat and cheese, and a little tin cup of tea. The tea was a little suspicious looking. There was an oily sheen on it.

Vasco's face must have shown some concern, because the Sami smiled and spoke. "Goat, smoked, with some sour cherry glaze for flavor. The cheese is salted. You might find the flavor a little different than you are used to. The tea has butter and sugar added to it. We have a long day ahead of us. You will need the calories. Try it. If you don't like it, we can find something else for you."

"Thank you." Vasco took the offered food and the Sami left before Vasco could say anything else.

He sipped the tea. He'd had worse. It was hot, and it tasted like energy. The meat in the bun was surprisingly good, but the cheese was almost painfully salty. He ate it all.

With breakfast taken care of, he reviewed his situation. He'd been on at least one vehicle last night. He'd woken briefly after being dumped on slightly corrugated metal. Shortly after, there had been engine sounds, and bouncing had started before he fell back asleep. He didn't recall more than one vehicle trip though.

Maybe two or three hours in the vehicle. Rough roads, likely. Vasco vaguely recalled some bumping and the roaring of gravel. Some patches of asphalt hum. Maybe fifty klicks an hour?

He'd woken with a slight pressure in his bladder the first time. The second time, he'd woken with a painfully full bladder. Fortunately, that was when they started to walk. A guard had let him piss before the small patrol moved on.

The night march had dragged on forever. Probably twenty kilometers. Maybe less, maybe more. A lot was downhill, but it was rough terrain. So he was probably two hundred kilometers away from where his patrol had been wiped out. He wasn't thinking very well, he realized. Something had broken a little in him, seeing the calm face of that Outlander, and he wasn't back to himself yet. He decided to just go with it a little more.

He was probably off the plateau now and far into the outlands. He could track the sun for direction during the day, but he didn't think he'd be able to do that in the steep valley. Rough walls meant he'd been in shade most of the day. If they even traveled during the day. No one was really sure yet how the Sami Outlanders managed to get up to the plateau. Somehow they'd managed to evade satellite visual and thermal imaging.

If it was night travel, he'd be able to determine direction pretty quickly. The first thing he'd done after the Long Drop was to stay up long enough to find the local Polaris. A few hours' work. He sighted in a couple of notable stars. An hour later, he checked them again. He knew his latitude. Some Gyrenes didn't. They didn't care about anything but finding the nearest pub or whorehouse. Vasco had been in enough bad scrapes on different worlds to know the value of being able to figure out where you were.

Once he had his star positions plotted, he picked out a rough area of the sky for north. Three likely stars sat in that area. Vasco had put himself on night watch, where he had nothing better to do than watch those stars all night. By the end of the night, he'd settled on the local north star equivalent. He'd also named a few constellations to make night navigation quicker.

He could have used existing star charts to speed up the process. He could have also relied on his compass or his pocket aide. But he found value in the process more than the result.

Mastering the process meant he could repeat it at will. Mastering the process meant he didn't have to depend on anyone else. He smiled as he realized the words of the hat maker were still resonating in him.

And surely none of the Sami would be so kind as to point him the way home. Another day and night, and he'd know where he was. He'd know exactly where he was if he could rig up something to use for a sextant. And if he could find a little privacy to use it. If he managed to escape first, it would be easier. One problem at a time.

In truth, Vasco was just keeping his mind occupied. This crew, like most Sami, looked pretty damn competent. His only chance of escape would likely be a random occurrence. The most likely outcome was that he was going where they wanted him to go. Which meant he had best prepare for that. Start up conversations and try to make a friend. Gather what intelligence he could. And see who he could get on his side. In this sort of situation, you needed every advantage you could get.

The Sami were looking a little busier. Most of them had finished breakfast and were smoothly packing. They didn't seem to have much more than a small kit bag each. It was almost a purse, a little grey thing the size of a hardcover book. They had that, their weapons, and the clothes on their backs.

Vasco had to be missing something. If he wasn't misreading the signs, they looked to be about to take him on a long trip. He wasn't sure how they planned to do that with no food or other equipment. There had to be something he wasn't seeing.

Then two rocks at either end of the recessed overhang moved. That made the situation a lot clearer. The two lumpy boulders at either end were the watch. Motley grey wool cloaks blended perfectly into the stone of the mountainside. Even the long rifles and scopes they carried were covered in wool strips. Perfect camouflage.

Hell, Vasco thought, that would even explain why they hadn't shown up on thermals. Insulation was insulation. A felted hat or cloak would stop thermal emission the same way it kept the cold from creeping in. And the camouflage was good enough from his viewpoint. It would be invisible from a satellite or any of the Polity ships. One mystery solved.

Now that he knew what to look for, the alcove looked quite different. The lumpy boulders on the back wall were more big grey cloaks. Sure enough, the Sami were pulling them up and passing them around. Under the cloaks were backpacks. They all looked stuffed. The alcove wasn't a random resting stop. It was a cache.

If the mountains were full of caches like this, it was no wonder the Polity wasn't stopping the flow of Sami Outlanders onto the plateau. There wasn't any secret logistics supplier. The Sami were just amazingly self-sufficient. There was even a water catch basin concealed behind the slightest curve of wall.

Vasco was being left alone for the moment, but not unobserved. He thought about making a break for the trail. As soon as he had the thought, the Sami reacted. It was nothing obvious. They just all suddenly found a task to do at the front of the cave. Probably one of them was assigned to watch him. Picking up on body cues would be easy enough, and subtle hand signals could have gotten everyone reacting. Still, the group response was a bit unsettling.

Vasco let go of any thought of making a quick escape. At least until a better opportunity arose. They hadn't bothered to re-tie him once he'd awoken. Obviously. they had a reason to be confident. Now didn't seem the time to find out where that confidence came from.

The Sami were passing out the backpacks and cloaks. It wasn't an urgent action, but it was sure and practiced. Vasco stood and stretched. He hurt everywhere. Every muscle seemed stiff. No injuries were apparent though, and the pain was in the muscles, not the joints. He should be fine for a day's walking. It wasn't as if he had a choice. Maybe they had some horses tucked in the cave somewhere.

The muted chatter of the troop stopped. Everyone was looking at the entrance of the alcove. At the corner of the opening, walking down the trail, was a Weta. Vasco shivered a little at the sight of the bug. The cat-sized insects were his least favorite part of Rumi.

He'd heard that the Outlanders worshiped the insects. Even the Sami on the plateau treated them with respect. Like stray cats. They'd leave food for them. Most houses had a little water basin at ground level and kept it topped up no matter the weather. At least the little horrors never went into a house. Vasco had never seen one this close, except at the hat shop.

This one was clicking its way across the path until it suddenly stopped. It lifted its torso, looking like a centaur. The Weta brought its clawed forearms together and bowed its head. Vasco had heard that they did this. All across the world, every single Weta would be doing the same thing at the same time. Six times a day, they froze in place. Six times—three in the day, three at night—they "prayed."

Each Sami clasped their hands and bent their heads in an imitation of the Weta. The alcove was silent for a moment. At the opening, the little insect swayed ever so slightly. For a moment, Vasco thought he heard it humming a deep, low, and oddly soothing song. The Sami were stiff and upright like grey statues instead of men. The Weta seemed the only living thing in the place. It gave the whole thing the air of a priest orating to a cathedral of ghosts.

And then it stopped. The Weta dropped down and continued on its path. The Sami went about their business, ignoring the bug now that the sermon was over.

One of the older Sami, a giant man with thick wrists and a heavy braid rolling all the way down his back, was looking intensely at Vasco. Vasco felt an unaccustomed moment of doubt—almost fear. There was an air about this Sami that spoke of ancient battles on ice, fur capes, and battle-axes.

"You heard it," he said to Vasco.

"I... don't know." Vasco thought he had imagined it.

The giant wasn't questioning him though. He'd turned back to packing.

Vasco felt dizzy. Something had happened. Damned if he knew what. He really wanted to sit down all of a sudden.

A Sami held one of the cloaks out toward Vasco. "Take this."

Vasco took it and the man walked away. A taciturn group. It wouldn't be easy to make allies. Maybe the giant, but Vasco felt uncomfortable even thinking about approaching the big man.

The cloak was thick, but not as heavy as it looked. The hood and shoulders were felted like Melton wool. The bulk of the cloak was a looser, loftier weave. It was an odd-feeling garment. Its purpose was pretty clear to Vasco though. The loose weave would trap enough body warmth to be useful while allowing the wearer to stick twigs and leaves through it. It was an effective gillie suit. The cloak fit easily on his shoulders. The air was chilly if not icy cold, and the warmth on his shoulders was surprisingly pleasant.

One by one, the Sami filtered out of the alcove. The path was narrow and winding. The drop to the valley below was farther than Vasco cared to think about.

Vasco waited for one of the Sami to escort him and felt an odd trepidation when he realized that no one was paying attention to him. He stood awkwardly. The alcove emptied. He had the embarrassed sense of being the last one standing at the wall at a high school dance.

Vasco shook his head. He was a prisoner. It was his duty to try to escape at every chance. Perhaps this was that chance.

Then he froze in place. The giant blond Sami was looking at him—almost through him. Vasco was trapped by the man's eyes and riveted when he saw the Weta climb up the giant's shoulder and join in staring at Vasco.

Vasco felt as though he was pinned on an exam table. All the Sami were gone now. It was just him and the giant. And the Weta. The part of Vasco's brain that wasn't immobilized weighed the odds. The giant was big and for sure had solid muscles. Vasco's Creche world genetics were probably enough to balance out the strength equation. The giant's eyes were too aware for him to be a slow man.

Vasco figured he could take him. Take him... but Vasco would be too broken afterward to make the walk home. He hadn't felt such confidence in an opponent's skill since the Walkure. As if he had a choice in the matter, he waited.

Finally the giant spoke. "The Weta aren't telepathic."

As soon as the man spoke, Vasco's strange paralysis vanished. He realized he'd been holding his breath. He should have run... but despite his training, he was curious. He took a slow, steady breath and waited.

The Sami continued. "If we could find a way to blind them, deafen them, kill all their senses, they would still be smarter than any human ever born. They're the geniuses of the galaxy. They have incredibly sophisticated senses. They take in so much information constantly that it's not possible for them to be truly sentient the way we think of it. They are completely one with their environment. They aren't even aware they are sentient. No sense of self, just a moving loci of viewpoint.

"As best we can tell, that is why they pray. Their awareness is so deep, they feel a rhythm we don't. The Pook tell us that six times a day, our planet—maybe our solar system—completes some sort of deep cycle. The Pook don't know what it is. No one knows but the Weta.

"We don't pray with them. We just listen. Sema, the listening. Maybe it's God, maybe it isn't. The Sami listen, hoping we can hear what the Weta hear. Sometimes we do hear. We hear what you heard. Do you know what a Sami is?"

Vasco started to answer, but then he heard the depth of the question. Like a ripple appearing on a still pond, the trick was to see the rock. Or the fish under the surface. Something was happening to Vasco. He felt on the verge of something giant, as if a huge wall was pushing against his mind, or as if his thoughts were riding on a giant bubble about to pop. He just stared.

"The Weta aren't telepathic," the giant said, "but they are aware of everything. Things we cannot perceive. I am Nils Sayyidison. I'm a Speaker, Gyrene. I can read the Weta. I see the subtle signs in them as their perception changes. As far as you are concerned, it means I am telepathic. And I know you heard."

Silence drifted and ebbed.

"A Sami is one who listens. You heard the Weta. You are one of us."

Nils turned and walked out of the alcove. The Weta swiveled its smooth featureless head toward Vasco until they walked out of sight.

Vasco watched Jakob staring at the sky. There was a wide universe up there, and it struck Vasco as sad that a smart young man like Jakob was so ignorant of it. Jakob was one of the younger Outlanders, and he'd taken to chatting up Vasco. The Sami were bright people, but there was a world of knowledge out there. The emphasis the Outlanders placed on self-sufficiency and independence was one thing. Lack of knowledge was another.

"Jakob," Vasco said, "what do you know about the stars?"

"Everything I need to. I know when they rise, when they set, what season it is when they are in which position in the sky. I know the names of all the calendar stars and the days they first rise. I know that because that star there—that red one, see it?—because it is just over the horizon now, I know that it is time to prune back my roses. What do you know about stars?"

"I know that that red star is red because it is old, and it's much larger than Anubis. I know that I can look up its specifications in the star catalogue and tell you what planets orbit it, whether anyone lives on those planets, and what the star's fate will be. It might go supernova and turn into a black hole or a white dwarf, or maybe a quasar. I don't know for sure, but I know where to find the information."

"Sure, you know how to read, so you can find that stored information. But what good does that do you out here, where there are no pads and no network for you to access your information? Or if you aren't allowed to have access to that information?"

Vasco bit back his instant response. He hadn't really thought about that at all. "Well," he said, "I can't see anyone in the Polity stopping me from knowing that information. We only block information that is dangerous. And one of the first things the Polity will do here is set up a satellite broadcast network. We're already doing that now. Pads will be available to everyone for a modest price, and everyone can have access to all the information that is out there."

Jakob laughed. "Vasco, I know what you're trying to say. Your ways aren't unknown to us. I think it might be easier for us to talk if you understand a bit more about the Sami, the Outlander, way. If you'd like, I can teach you some of our memory ways."

Vasco grinned back at him. It was hard not to respond to Jakob's enthusiasm. "Sure, I've got time. I have to admit I am a bit curious. I've heard of people who can memorize things. It seems like a useful skill."

"Useful skill! It's like walking. It's the background of your life. It's a constant action. You Polity people are like children who have never learned to walk, trying to tell everyone how great crawling is! Let me show you." Jakob stood and pulled Vasco up with him. "Look at the stars. See that bright one there? Sharp and blue, like the point of a knife? Think of it as the end of a cut. Now follow the path of the cut up to that darker red one. It's faint, but its color makes it stand out, yes? That marks where the knife cut. Now move across the sky to those two stars that twinkle brightly, like a pair of eyes. There is a story there, do you see it?"

Vasco did. The stars described an arc across a quarter of the sky, and it was easy for him to visualize a line moving from one set of stars to the next.

"Now make a story," Jakob continued. "Something graphic and bold, unpleasant... something that will stick in your memory. We call that set of stars 'The Lover' and see the eyes as belonging to an angry woman who has discovered her lover has cheated on her, and she's gutting him with a knife."

"Gah! That's a lovely image! You guys really know how to take the romance out of the stars!"

Jakob smiled indulgently. "It's important that the image

stick in the mind. Strong emotional images fasten in the mind better. Now, look at those stars. I want you to face the eyes, then physically step until you face the cut, then step again until you face the knife."

Vasco did as he was directed, staring for a moment at the "eyes" and seeing them as an angry woman. It was easy enough—he'd angered a few in his time. Actually, that twinkle reminded him of Elise. Not a happy memory.

He stepped to the left, looking at the red star, and he remembered how heartbroken Elise had been, how his words had been like a red wound to her. Vasco felt a little nauseated as he remembered, and he turned quickly to look at the knife. He remembered the clean cut, the next time he'd seen her—with his former best friend. He shook himself, trying to shed the memories of his adolescent years. He'd been a foolish young man…

"I see you have a story!" said Jakob. "Good. Three points. Four points, if you count the left and right eye separately. Now you have four points of reference in your head. Those will be your storage areas. Let's try a little experiment."

Jakob reached into his gear and pulled out a small deck of cards. Vasco had seen the Outlanders with them before. They looked like playing cards, but they didn't play games with them. They laid them out in patterns and stared at them and moved them from pattern to pattern constantly. It made no sense to Vasco.

Jakob laid out four sets of four cards in a square on the ground, adjusting the lantern so they were easily visible. "Okay, look at the cards. I want you to memorize the order. Take a moment."

Vasco looked over the cards. It seemed easy enough. The figures and images on the cards were graphic and obvious. He noticed that one of them was a young woman cutting at a man with a knife, in almost the same pattern as the stars. Interesting. "Okay, I think I've memorized it."

Jakob picked up the cards and shuffled them, then laid them out again. "Now put them back in the original order."

It took a little bit, but Vasco got it done. It was harder than he'd thought it would be.

"Not bad!" said Jakob. "Not bad at all. Now we'll do it a little differently. This time, for each group of four cards, I want you to think of the image you placed in your mind with each star. Look at the cards, look at the star, think of the image, and mentally place those four cards into that image. Move from one star to the next until you have all sixteen images memorized in the four stars."

Vasco did as directed. He saw the logic to it, and the exercise did make memorizing the images much easier. Even with a new series of sixteen images, he memorized the sequence perfectly, and quicker than he had the first time.

But Jakob wasn't done. Once he'd seen that Vasco had figured out sixteen, he made Vasco memorize two sets of sixteen images, then three. To Vasco's surprise, he could do it without too much trouble.

"Well done!" Jakob said. "So now you see a little bit of the art of memory. Four stars in the sky, and you can memorize a sequence of random images. Now look and see how many stars are in the sky. As children, we Outlanders learn to memorize the positions of thirty-six of those stars, and we memorize one complete sequence of the card deck for each star. And each card has an image which we can carry many memories in. That's just what we learn as children. That knowledge allows each Sami to carry as much information as we want in our heads, for as long as we find it useful, and recall it when we need to with no need of pads or information access. All we need is our teachers and our resourcefulness. That's why I know the red star is a member of the asymptotic giant branch and has not yet undergone its first helium flash. It's not a carbon star either. I've carried the memory of the complete Hertzsprung-Russel diagram and its implications in my head since I was six. But don't worry, I'm sure you can look up what that means if you ever get your pad connection working again."

Timariot Smith stood on the bridge, arms clasped behind his back. At least, as much as he could manage in his customized armor. He'd hooked his index fingers together. It wasn't comfortable, but impressions mattered. It was important that he project the right air of command. *Power emanates from the top down, and every action my people perform is a direct consequence of the power I project.*

The bridge was busy, but relatively quiet. There was no need for a captain's chair on the bridge designed for zero-g. He had a command platform he stood in, low railings concealing the shock-absorbing structures that would activate in battle. For now though, he had his own pulpit to preach his orders to the masses. Or an Olympus to watch over them from.

He found the flow of lights and multiple displays soothing. The cup-shaped bridge was crammed full of workpods, the command platform inserted in the middle like an electrode in a crucible. Emil had a series of small touch screens arrayed around him, from which he could access and message every individual workpod. He didn't use that function much though. All the information he needed, everything relevant to him, was displayed on the curving rectangular screen that ran through the middle of the pods. The Helot kept a constant stream of information flowing on, studying the Timariot's eye motions to anticipate his interests and guide him toward information if necessary.

That flow of information was what he was there for. It was time for his daily report from the computer. Emil was silent, commanding the Helot with eyes alone. The flow of troops to ground, Gyrene battle reports, territories in Polity possession, Psyops predictions of populace reactions, a complete report of orbital, system, and space command. Timeline predictions for new territory acquisitions, predicted resistance, Gyrene and equipment losses.

The next two years of warfare and conquest were all laid out on neat charts. Next to it, he laid the complete roster of the *Alexi*. The Helot extrapolated from that, producing a month-by-month projection of relative power against resistance, compensating for several worst-case scenarios. In the end, complete conquest in one year. Unification in three years.

The last figure almost made the Timariot raise an eyebrow. Unification of sixty percent of the population usually was quicker. Not much so, but every time he'd seen that figure in his previous Timariots and in all his studies, it hadn't varied from the standard year. Tough people, the Sami. Tough, but malleable like all the others. They'd come to heel eventually. They always did.

Satisfied, the Timariot nodded. The Helot dumped the whole package into a presentation and dropped that into the memory banks of the Pod courier. The Helot could have launched the drone itself, but this was a moment of ritual and a moment of personal success for the Timariot. Eight times before, he had sent this message, this electronic cry back across space that another lost child had been found and returned to the fold. Eight times before, the Polity had gathered its industrial might and sent a follow-through fleet to fully integrate the prodigal child.

This time, the ninth time, it would be different. The courier would go out, but no fleet of succor would follow. The follow-up would be different. No less than five Tatars would come, and a hundred fleet colliers. Almost a thousand war ships. Almost five percent of the military might of the Polity would come to roost at Anubis. Anubis would become the launch pad for humanity's new expansion. From Anubis to Laconia, wherever it was. From here would be built the new Tatars, the new battleships, equipped with Helots to start a war with the Pook and all other races. Here, at Anubis, mankind would begin its true conqueror heritage and take its first steps to win the universe.

The Timariot slipped off the override switch and entered his key. He paused slightly before stroking the Wall command. Every monitor on the ship froze, every system paused and shunted into the background, putting the Timariot's face across every screen on board.

"Mark." Said the Timariot. "Anubis Timariot has completed phase one. Beachhead is complete. Mark."

He paused briefly, savoring the history of the moment. "Launch."

And with that, they were committed. The Pod courier would trace back their path, squirt its data to a waiting ship that would move to the next system. A short week in Pod space. The Beachhead fleet waited and would launch the moment the ship arrived.

It was up to the Timariot now. The Anubis system had to be pacified by the time the fleet arrived. Had the message not been sent, a warfleet would have followed, a dozen more Tatar's to crush whatever had defeated the *Alexi*. The beachhead fleet wasn't configured for conquest, but for construction. All its mass was committed to materials...the ships themselves would be stripped for raw materials. Anubis would become the forward firebase of humanity, an impregnable stronghold. All that was required was for *Alexi* to hold fast and pacify as much of Rumi as possible.

The timetable allowed for ten years of construction at Anubis before the next stage. The Timariot had two years to conquer and Unify Rumi, and when the fleet arrived, the Sami would be trained into first a workforce, then a fighting force. The Sami would build the fleet and firebase, then man it on its conquest.

Rumi's days of being a distant backwater were over.

Chapter Fourteen: The Giver of Forms

The circle of Outlander Sami sat in silence. It was a companionable silence, for all that they were having a disagreement. Even in the middle of a strong conflict of opinion, Nils found much to appreciate in his fellows. He'd learned long ago to accept that most people had some aspect of their personality that rubbed him the wrong way, but if he ignored that one thing, he could accept the rest of their emotional makeup in a much more friendly way. Right now, they were being quite bigoted and small-minded, and Nils was very much opposed to that point of view. He found it ugly, and so limiting as to seriously smack of ignorance.

But he knew his fellows much better than that. They were not ignorant or really bigoted. They were just having a moment where they found it difficult to adapt to new circumstances. In other circumstances, the Alamansan would be a novel guest, and they would all be eager to share his company and learn about his background and philosophies. But since he was amongst them in the guise of a prisoner of war, they felt different.

The way of Rumi was not an easy one. No true philosophy was. It was easy for Sami, especially Outlanders, to feel that they had an inherited right to an enlightened view of things, that their natural philosophy had been ingrained into them along with their mother's milk and needed no more maintenance than birthright.

Which, Nils thought, was so much hogwash. Personally, he had a hard time imagining how anyone could think maintaining a consistent philosophy in life was anything other than a result of constant effort, learning, and practice. Much like pushups, you had to continue to practice to gain results. It wasn't enough to do a single pushup, think you had mastered the action, and expect strong muscles for the rest of your life. Apparently Nils was alone in thinking this. At least this conversation made him feel he was. He sighed and resigned himself to explaining to his fellow Outlanders how to think, as well as how to feel. It wouldn't be the first time, nor the last.

"The Alamansan," Nils said, interrupting a diatribe about crushing enemies, "has given his parole. This means we have taken his word that he will cause us no harm, nor try to escape, until we release him from the conditions of his parole. So yes, he is free to walk among us and learn our ways."

"Nils," interrupted one of them, "we can't do this. He's an enemy! He has killed our people, and everything he learns will just go back to his kind and bring more death on us. Why are we going to let him learn this? You can't think it will bring any kind of peace. The Polity has no interest in peace!"

Nils replied, "No, I don't think it will bring any kind of peace. But he's a person. He woke up this morning just like us, hungry and cold, thinking about what to eat and how badly he had to piss. Just like us, he probably wondered what kind of assholes and problems he would have to deal with, and he decided, just as we did, that he would do his best to get through the day anyway. Maybe he even took a moment to think that everyone he met might feel the same way and decided to try to keep that in mind for the day.

"And even if he didn't, we should. We Outlanders should keep that in mind more than anyone. We all wake up and think the same and try to do our best in the day. No one who isn't sick in the head wakes up and thinks ill. This Alamansan is a good man. I've spoken to him. He isn't sick in the head. He's a reasonable person, and it behooves us to be reasonable people as well. He's just a man, not the embodiment of the Polity in person. Let us treat him like a man.

"If nothing else, we owe it to the Alamansans. This is one of the last of their sons. All that is left of their legacy is what is in this man's genes. Nothing is left of their teachings or ways of life, so let our way of life be a gift unto them."

"But how can you be sure of him? We trust you, Speaker Nils, but enlighten us. We have natural concerns about this prisoner walking free amongst us, days after killing us in war. How do you know he means no malice to us?"

"You have all the same resources I do. You are all Outlanders. Listen. You have the ability yourselves. The Weta spoke to him. Listen now, for yourselves."

The discord was forgotten when the Outlanders Listened. They stopped their worrying, stilled their minds, and emptied themselves. It was not an easy thing to do, to Listen, but they were the leaders amongst their communities because they had the most ability. So they opened themselves to what could be heard. There were no words, no images, nothing a mind not truly receptive could describe or understand… but there was something to Listen to.

And they heard.

As was their way, they sat for moments longer in companionable silence. To argue and talk was human, but in the Listening, the Sami became something other than human.

Chapter Fifteen: The One Who Causes Contraction

Neruda floated into the space bridge, careful to catch the hatch just right with her fingers. The powered ship's armor had a knack for throwing you for a loop if you ever got casual about using it. Some poor ensign had done that a few days ago. She'd looked up as she came through the hatch and tried to use the door to stop her momentum. It was a classic gravity move, and she'd paid for it by whipsawing through the bridge. No damage had been done. A Gyrene was always standing by in the bridge, and this one had managed to intercept the ensign and almost make it look as if it was an intentional action, but the Timariot had noticed. It had not gone well for anybody.

Freefall was not popular with everybody. The Gyrenes trained for it and the ship's crew did too, but the Timariot hated it. He'd ordered the Ring to stay in operation while they orbited Rumi. It wasn't exactly against regulations. Rumi had no space-force left and no orbit-capable weapons, so the threat level was low. But the amount of time the Timariot spent in the Ring encouraged officers and crew who wanted to curry favor to spend more time in the Ring. That meant most of the crew wasn't as comfortable with their freefall actions as they should be after so long in space.

Which was why Neruda was being extra careful. The time she hadn't spent in the Ring, she'd been buried deep in the intelligence workpods. If it hadn't been for her ship's armor exercise routines, she'd probably be in seriously ill health by now. As it was, she wasn't in the best shape.

It had been worth it though. With the help of the Helot, she'd turned over more than a thousand years of records. Tied in with shipboard telemetry and some sophisticated spy gear, she'd discovered something amazing.

The space bridge was an amazing sight, and she took a moment to enjoy it. It wasn't commonly used on a Tatar ship, but you couldn't tell that from the look of it. The bridge was laid out like a giant, flat, princess-cut diamond. She saw the soaring length of the *Alexi*, the deep black of space, and the vast orange and blue curve of Rumi. The top of the diamond was all black currently, the polarizers only letting through the smooth white outline of the star Anubis. The rest of the walls were transparent, except for the thick support girders and the packed workstations. It was a beautiful place to work, but it was still a working bridge.

Timariot Smith had the powered workpods attached to the wings of the space bridge instead of in a more usual pattern. It gave him a better view, and he was taking advantage of it. He was tethered in front of a set of windows that gave him an uninterrupted view of Rumi. Neruda figured he was probably planning where to put his palace. He wouldn't like Neruda's news, but there was no help for it.

Neruda floated noiselessly through the bridge space. She'd given herself just the right kick and swing to drift slowly toward the window the Timariot was at, and she waited until the last moment to catch the grab bar. She rotated down in perfect position, her feet clicking satisfyingly as they locked to the deck.

The Timariot glanced at her out of the corner of his eye. It was all the acknowledgement the Timariot would give her today. Things on Rumi had gone bad. Not so bad yet, but bad enough to make the Timariot testy with everyone—especially his

Intelligence Primus, who should have been ahead of the curve on what was happening and not left the Timariot floundering and reacting instead of decisively attacking.

Neruda decided to dive right in with her findings. "I don't know where the Laconians are, but I know what they are."

The Timariot didn't react for a moment, staring at the planet below them. Then he snorted, softly, and spoke without moving his eyes at all. "And I care why?"

"The Laconian on our ship was a nanoborg."

The Timariot turned, eyebrows raised. "The hell, girl... those are myths. They aren't real."

"Over fifteen hundred years ago, a New Ottoman Empire senator was exiled for research into the nanoborg process and for advocating its use. He disappeared, and the records were sealed. I've accessed them. He was actually on the verge of creating a successful nanoborg, but the process brutally killed every test subject. I managed to surreptitiously get some scans of the Walkure, and some anomalies showed up. Didn't think much of it until I got to work with the Helot and realized that she had internal maskings covering up more substantial changes. On a hunch, I opened the nanoborg files, and much of what she had matched the prototypes. That senator disappeared and must have found his way to Laconia. The Laconians aren't peaceful scientists at all. The Walkure isn't just a walking weapon—she's a walking strike tank!"

The Timariot snorted in a thoughtful way and kept looking out the window. Neruda let him think. The Timariot often came across as a bluff, arrogant, and thoughtless man, but Neruda knew better. There was a brain working under all that old-boy bluster. A brain that was churning away, weighing options and deciding. Neruda could do few things worse than interrupt him right now. The implications of the information were staggering, and Neruda had to use a lot of self-control not to go overboard with suppositions and fantasies. The Polity had dealt with genetically modified races before, and cybernetically modified ones as well. Human ingenuity was boundless without the constraints of

Tech and Unity applied.

"Do we know where she is?" the Timariot asked.

Neruda said, "No, she hasn't been seen since her drop. I put tails on her, but she lost them almost immediately."

"No point in looking harder, I'm guessing. Not at this point. You think she's behind this Sami resistance we are seeing? Behind the technological surprises?"

"I can't see any other way. We haven't been able to get a good read on the ground forces opposing us, and it was only luck that we caught the signature of the first EMP attacks. That sort of sophistication is completely beyond the Outlanders or even the Sami. The idea, the know-how, must have come from the Laconian. They've got the science background for sure, but how much of that translates to military knowledge... I don't know. In any case, the manufacturing of all these devices has to have happened somewhere, and that can't be all Sigma. There's more going on here than I can really get a handle on."

It was a painful admission, but a necessary one. It was also good policy with the Timariot to make sure your weaknesses were mentioned by you first, not by the Timariot. That had been an early and painfully learned lesson for Neruda.

He nodded. "Well. I don't think it matters too much. Not at the moment. They've hit back harder than we thought, but it's nothing I haven't dealt with before. They might push us to Orion, but they've got nothing left past that. Hell, I might even encourage our boys to pull back a little faster. I think we'll break these Outlanders easy. Are you sure of the Helot?"

"I've had our ops section run a thorough code review. It's clean. I even had them do as much of a hardware exam as we could. Everything looks above board, and I don't see any concern there."

"All right. Keep this nanoborg thing quiet for now. I think the rest of this little war is about to wrap up. I want you to pack up your Rumi work, pass it off to someone else. I think you need to start working on plans for the Laconia leg of this operation." The Timariot glanced at Neruda and held her gaze for a moment, then he was staring back at Rumi.

Neruda took that as the dismissal it was and kicked herself off with a quick glance over her shoulder to make sure the way was clear.

She had her work cut out for her planning the attack on Laconia. Her first instinct was to send some capture teams down to Rumi to look for the Laconian—it would be nice to get a few more samples from her and start to tailor some biological weapons. Neruda wasn't even considering a conventional attack on Laconia. Once they found Laconia, it would be a pure orbital kill mission. If they really had cracked the nanoborg code, sending in a ground mission wouldn't be worth anyone's while. They needed the Helots for the next step, but between the existing samples and whatever they could recover from the remnants of Laconian salvage, they should be able to pick up production in time.

And if she worked her plans just right, she'd be the Timariot to lead that mission…

ACT THREE
ARIF – KNOWLEDGE

Chapter Sixteen: The Living

Vasco took one step after another. The Outlander Sami were obviously on their way somewhere, but it was getting past strange that they kept dragging him along. He'd expected to be dropped off at some sort of prisoner facility at some point. At first, he'd thought he'd be shot somewhere, probably after being interrogated. Now he knew that such things were completely out of Sami character. They had no interest in the Polity at all. They asked about how he felt, about his experiences, but never about military plans or capabilities. He didn't know what to make of the interrogation, if that's what it was.

Vasco was past his numbness and bored. Somewhere out there, his troop was maybe still fighting. He didn't want to think of them as dead. Cave had to be still alive. He hadn't seen Tessa since that first inbound flight, but he knew she was part of the ground force. She was out there somewhere too. He should be with them. He had to find a way out of this.

And just like that, Nils was suddenly beside him. "Vasco, what do you think of the Sami, of us Outlanders?"

"You're good people. Solid. Not as backward as you seem. Just different. Not like any other people I've ever met," he said.

Nils didn't reply, and they kept walking for a while.

After a bit, Vasco found that he was talking again. "I don't know why you're fighting. The universe is vast, and you're all wise. Surely you can see the value in all of humanity coming together in a unified collective. Your children might lose some uniqueness, but in return they will inherit the stars as part of a united humanity. Equal opportunity for all. They'll be able to live where they want, do what they want, get rich or learn from our vast libraries. You aren't giving up anything. It's just more opportunity. Why are you fighting that? Because of some stupid sense of independence? Do you really feel like you're that much better than the rest of us?"

At that, Nils stopped walking. He let out a deep sigh and looked around. For a moment, Vasco thought Nils would do his damn wise sage silent thing again, but he finally spoke.

"Humanity has always had a dream of being perfect. We make stories up about heroes. We dream about fantastic kingdoms and people who are more special. A breed apart. Kingdoms and nations of ideal humans, of perfect breeding.

"We aren't that. We knew of the Creche worlds and shared much with them before the Polity came along. We know you are of the Creche worlds, those who bred humans to be more special and unique than all others, yet I find nothing in you that shines of perfection. Exception, for sure, but not perfection. The Sami are not supermen, Vasco. We are not better. Neither is the Polity, or the Laconians. But we are different. We are unique. It is the way of life to move to variety, to uniqueness. We evolve, we change, and the universe changes with us. The Polity seeks to crush that. They seek to end the uniqueness of life and stamp us like a machine until we are all the same. We don't want to fight. We are just a force of life. The Polity is a force of stagnation and thus death. We fight like all living things do for one more breath against the crush of drowning. There was never any choice.

"The question is why are you fighting, Vasco? Why are you set so firmly on crushing all difference out of the universe?"

Vasco had no answer. He knew in his heart Nils was right, had known that all along. He'd grown up with the shame of his upbringing, but some part of him, it seemed, had always railed against that cruel lie. A deeply buried part. He'd signed up for his first Long Drop to prove he was so much better than what he'd feared others would think of him if they'd known. He'd crushed other worlds as his had been crushed to prove he was worthy of being seen as the same, to show that he was not, in any way, unique.

He was suddenly sick. And lost. For a moment, Vasco thought of chucking it all, of joining the Sami. But he could not. Right or wrong, he had sworn his oaths, and duty was in the deepest part of his soul.

He would sell his soul, but he would never betray his sworn duty. After all else, that was what made him what he was.

Nils was looking into Vasco's eyes, and he must have seen the conflict. He held up a hand, and the column halted. Nils gestured to two of the older and more taciturn Outlanders.

"Vasco is leaving us. Escort him back to his people, to where they are heading. Release him back into his duty. We will not keep him from them anymore. He must choose his own way now." He grabbed Vasco by his shoulders and leaned in. "Vasco, I release you from your parole. Return to your troops. Obey your duty. But remember this, oh warrior, remember what I tell you. The difference between a warrior and a soldier is that a soldier fights for the love of their people, love of their leader and fellow soldiers. A warrior fights for the love of the universe and for the love of all people, everywhere.

"Go, and see if you can find out which you really are."

It was a week of walking to get out of the mountains, and a week and a half through the plains. A week of winding through farms, then villages and finally towns… and no sign of the Polity anywhere, aside from wrecked vehicles. With each kilometer, Vasco's heart sank deeper as he saw how badly they had been beaten. Never had he heard of the Polity being beaten so thoroughly on the ground, and he knew what that meant. The Orion option was next. And after that, the biologics or worse. Rumi and all the Sami on its surface were going to experience true hell.

And as he thought that, Vasco and his escorts rose up out of the river bed they'd been following and his guides disappeared. Ahead, Vasco saw a city, the peak of an Orion launcher jutting above the buildings and one shuttle already tethered in place. Then he heard the gunfire and saw the APCs and knew he was back amongst his people.

In a few days, he would be riding a pillar of atomic fire into orbit, leaving behind the ashes of tens of thousands of Sami.

Chapter Seventeen: The One Who Gives Life

Nils looked out across the mountain ranges. This view from the edge of the plateau had always been his favorite. In daylight, the rolling mountain peaks stretched out and away like a view from the roof of the world. His favorites had always been the cluster of two-score ragged spiked peaks. Majestic and eery, a dark-blue hued ore was the main component of the rippled crust that had formed them. Some Sami called them "The Mountains of Madness" and others, like Nils, saw something else in them. Nils and those like him called them "the Hellmouth." From the first time the Weta had woken him that night so long ago, until he'd left to fight the unlearned, his life had been spent in those mountains.

Thousands of Sami had labored under those peaks, and the reason for it was now rising above the horizon. Nils had chosen this point of view because he would never see the Hellmouth again. If he wasn't careful, he would never see anything ever again. It was a risky place to be, but he felt the risk worthy. The sight would be a few seconds of wonder. A moment, but what a moment.

On the horizon, a faint spark was just becoming apparent. The night sky was clear, and all the stars showed up sharply. Breathtakingly clear. Nils absorbed the view with complete pleasure. If it was to be his last sight, it was most worthy. He knew he'd find it almost impossible to pull himself away in time. His last view of the Hellmouth outlined with stars. The constellation Hafiz was just touching its foot to the earth, like a man dancing in perfect ecstasy on a single point. And from that point, the faint spark blazed, impossibly bright, and grew and raced across the sky. *Alexi* was a burning point of fire racing up from the horizon.

Nils was captivated. The Polity was his enemy, but there was no denying the beauty of such a vast and powerful thing as the *Alexi*. It was a marvel what humans could create. He felt a tear trickle down his cheek. It was awful. It was majestic. It was an archangel come from across the stars to dominate them, and to destroy it, they'd have to shake the world.

The Sami had no books and did not read. But they understood memory in a more profound way than any human culture before them. Every Sami carried a library of knowledge in his head. Their ability to share that knowledge with each other had broadened and deepened in the last five hundred years. They had an intuitive grasp of each other's thoughts that neither they nor the Laconians could understand.

And they had used that ability to the utmost in the Hellmouth. Orbital calculations. Mass of a Tatar. Nuclear force, industrial smelting, orbital ballistics. The Laconian had arrived with the final information needed—the structural layout and allotment of the *Alexi*. Now they knew where to aim, and the final shaping and tamping had been done while the Outlanders had bought time with fierce fighting.

Nils let vision linger for one final moment. *Alexi* was a burning spear almost overhead. He turned and dived into the shelter that had been constructed for him.

As the Hellmouth opened and vomited a pillar of hellfire into the sky.

Each of the peaks had been drilled out to form a bore. Each bore had been reinforced, and the base of each had been plugged with a metal slug. The chamber beneath the slug was a crude but effective nuclear shaped charge. The Sami had reversed the Polity's Orion drive principles and the Hellmouth range had been turned into a battery of nuclear-charged cannons.

As the *Alexi* passed overhead, each peak in the Hellmouth range had blown itself to bits, accelerating the massive plugs of steel far beyond orbital speed—all the way up to intercept speed. Twenty-four kinetic bullets ripped through *Alexi*, carried by titanic beams of radioactivity. Only her vast size saved her. Her size, and careful planning by the Sami. They wanted her to go home. Home, but no farther.

The Tatar design was a spaceship surrounded by an armored warship. The Sami blew away the armor, taking away most of the *Alexi*'s weaponry with it. The Pod drive was intact. Almost nothing else was. Her armor worked well, but massive solid slugs moving at high speed was the ship's worst case. With the armor gone, *Alexi* had also lost her ability to shed heat rapidly. Her fusion reactors automatically dropped output. She had no power left for her remaining weapons. And little crew.

The sleet of radiation that followed the projectiles did the most damage. The metal slugs were pushed by columns of plasma. The damaged armor couldn't do its job anymore, so lethal doses of radiation killed the outer layers of the *Alexi*. Electrical arcs shorted out huge banks of electronics on the ship and killed even more of the crew. The Ring died. One fusion plant shut down, venting its plasma into space. Sensors and computers were lost, except for the Helot's hardened connections. Fragments of impact ripped through the entire ship.

No one would be hibernating on the way home. Those who made the trip back would be crippled from the two-year trip in zero gravity, with no functioning Ring to keep them in shape. At least with the crew deaths, there would be enough food for everyone. With strict rationing. *Alexi*, and her mission, were effectively dead. All that was left was a lifeboat for the survivors.

Survivors who still had to get off of Rumi.

Walkure Sigma watched the Orion liftship. It was, she thought, impressive in its way. The Polity had stormed its way across all of human space in under five hundred years. There had never been a more efficient or powerful empire in all of human history. The liftship was a relatively crude solution to a complex problem. It was also a relatively elegant solution to multiple problems. It had one purpose—to lift the human element of an expeditionary force off of a planet as fast as possible. It was a lifeboat in reverse.

All its other strategic uses were a result of policies of use more than design. The Orion had worked time and time again. As had the Polity's policy of Unification. The Polity had never had a reason to think its approach was wrong. It may have had its own internal quibbles about morality, but the doctrine of the greater good always won out in the end. And it had worked. Over more than a thousand conquests, it had worked.

But now it was Hrist's turn to show them another truth. Hrist was her real name. Sigma was her number—Six. She was number six of only twelve women who had survived the Walkure process. She'd been rebuilt one cell at a time and fitted with carefully modified Pook armor and weaponry.

It was time to show the Polity the error of its ways. Sigma stood on the corner of the last bit of shattered rooftop of the building she was on, thirty meters in the sky. Below her, the orderly loading of the shuttles was proceeding rapidly. They'd be done in forty minutes, no more. She needed to stop them from launching and killing everyone in the city. The Outlanders would be in firing range in fifty minutes. The perimeter of the launch ship was being guarded by the forlorn hope, the last to board—one hundred special forces soldiers in drop armor. Each of them in their armor was almost as strong as Vasco, though not quite as fast. But they were completely bulletproof and armed. Sigma jumped.

The motion caught the eye of the first Drop Commando and drew his focus to the impossible sight of a woman floating, wreathed in purple glow. Her arms were outstretched, and her hair writhed and snapped in the flux. She had the face of an angel—until she smiled.

The Drop soldiers had access to the most cutting-edge weaponry—at least one Tech ahead of everyone else, if not more. The Commando raised his rifle, a Gaussian accelerator, and fired. The apparition continued to smile as the hypersonic slivers burst against her shield or bounced off to rip into the sky. The Pook energy source in her spine had the side effect of being an anti-gravity device, and with that ability to warp physics, shielding was trivial.

She spread her fingers, and electrical arcs jumped from finger to finger. Her hand reached out to beckon the commando. He paused in his firing, confused and a little frightened. She called him to her with her gesture, like an angel of death. The powerful lightning bolt she sent slammed him off his feet, rending his armor and killing him instantly.

Every commando in line of sight opened fire on Sigma. Even with the shield, enough energy would have an effect on her. She was more than the technology though. Laconia was a hard school, and they only turned out warriors.

She reversed the AG field and dropped thirty meters in a tenth of a second. Every combat veteran waiting to load dropped to the ground at the *crack* of her impact, as loud as an artillery round going off. The commandos reacted as fast as a human could, teams forming and charging in for close contact. Those who didn't react as fast spread out to form a perimeter, half of those covering an arc over the backs of the others.

It took them a third of a second to react and move, and another third to coalesce in groups. They were best selected and trained soldiers in the Polity, the best of thousands of worlds. In less than a second, they would have moved from shock to a concentrated attack pattern with backup in place. It wasn't fast enough.

Humans reacted in a third of a second. Sigma's rewired nervous system reacted in a tenth. Her internal battle computer reacted in nanoseconds. In the time it took for the first soldier to start moving forward, she was already out of her crater. She used her AG shield in combination with her particle accelerator to launch herself into the closest target.

Vasco sat at his console in the nose of his shuttle, riveted. He was finally seeing what "Walkure" meant, as Neruda had warned him about so long ago. Sigma was an angel of death, a Viking war goddess come to life. She was tearing apart armored drop commandos with her hands, ripping apart armor and weapons with what appeared to be particle beams.

Through the outside monitor, Vasco could almost see Sigma's expression. He thought he must be imagining the serenity. He didn't think even a Sami Outlander would be that serene while dealing out that much death. Nothing seemed to touch her. Vasco was sure he'd seen her take a direct hit from an anti-tank round, and it had only slowed her for a moment. It must have done something—the lightning flickered just a little less—but it wouldn't save the commandos. One hundred to one, and she was going to kill them all.

Cave was swearing, and Vasco turned as she leapt out of her seat and tore at the wiring under the fire control console. Made sense. The Orion had only one weapon, mounted on the very top of the Piston. It was a light anti-ship laser, tasked to the TacOps station to make use of its computer power. It only had enough power for a few shots, but if anything could get through that shield of Sigma's, the laser might be it. The problem was the safety interlocks. They served to stop a foolish operator from depressing the laser enough to shoot off the nose of one of the shuttles by accident. Cave was willing to inflict that amount of damage to the shuttle intentionally in order to get a shot at Sigma. One of the advantages of the Orion was crude power—even missing a nose cone, they'd make it to orbit. They'd have no hope if Sigma killed off the drop commandos though.

Hell, even if Sigma didn't kill them all off, she was still winning. The drop commandos were their last line of defense. They expected to die or be left behind to protect the Orion. With them gone, there was nothing to stop the Outlanders from setting up their firing positions and damaging the Orion too much to launch.

Vasco looked at the last projection they'd gotten from *Alexi*. Forty-five minutes until the Outlanders got close enough to fire. Loading was happening pretty quickly. Order had gone out the window, and everyone was trying to get on to the Orion as fast as possible. They still kept discipline—there was no other way to get on quickly—but they were giving new meaning to "expedite."

Vasco looked from the projection to Cave. She'd have the rewiring done in a minute, maybe two. If it worked, she'd be able to stop Sigma from damaging the Orion. But it wouldn't be in time to save the commandos, and without them, there was no stopping the Outlanders. There was no way to win. The *Alexi* was crippled and would be able to provide no more support. Their only hope was to launch and catch the last possible ride home.

Cave was working like a madwoman, and Vasco was caught for a moment watching her. Her hands moved just so, a little wisp of hair sneaking out around her ship's armor face seal. He'd never noticed how slim her waist was. He was struck for a moment, imagining Cave in different circumstances.

Cave not in armor, but in comfy clothes in a kitchen somewhere. Laughing and talking, leaning over the counter and smiling. Holding a drink and gesturing while a child ran up to her leg and pulled on her pants, wanting to be picked up. Cave in love. Cave with a family, a husband. Cave growing old and watching grandchildren growing. Cave living a life, being human. Or Cave dying in the next few minutes and none of that ever coming to be.

Vasco was frozen. He knew now why he had not killed the Outlander in the ambush. He knew why he'd resisted signing up again after his previous drop. He loved his fellow Gyrenes, and their company was where he truly felt happiest. He wasn't a coward, but he'd held back in previous drops and found ways to make sure he was never tested. Not because of cowardice. It was love. It was hope. He'd always felt the weight of the moments to come, the promise of the life he just saw Cave live in his mind. He'd felt the promise in his heart of future joys, future love and enlightenment. He'd always known that life would be full for him;

he would always have some happiness and it was his sacred duty to enjoy those moments. Nothing had ever seemed worth sacrificing for, balanced against that hope of the future. It was a future promised to him, and he had always believed it was coming to him in due time.

For a moment, he weighed that future in his mind and in his heart. He tasted the bittersweet love of it, then he let it go. Life was precious, and wonderful, and it was worth all the weight of his future to try to ensure that Cave could have her future. It wasn't who she was as a friend or a fellow Gyrene. In this moment, it was enough for Vasco that she was a human being. A singular human being, in this time and place, who needed to live. Nothing else mattered.

Vasco felt his belief in the Polity fade and disappear within him. It's goals were not his anymore. He felt no loyalty anymore. The mission had died for him when he learned the truth of the Sami. Perhaps, in some way, it had died for him even earlier, with Sigma in Pod space. It didn't matter.

The mission was wrong. Unification was wrong. He had more sympathy with the Sami than the Polity now. There had to be a better way. If he could go back to the Polity, he would never again support its policies. He'd even do what he could to stop them, to change them.

But none of that mattered right now. What mattered was that he finally knew what he had to do. It was finally time to act, finally time to live. For once, for the last time, and for the first time. He unstrapped himself from his console, spun about as he stood, and opened the escape hatch for the compartment.

Cave slammed the last relay home and forced herself to take one last glance over her hasty rewiring. She wasn't going to get a second chance. She didn't think she'd really had time to take this last look, but she had to. The software interlock could have been routed around, but there was no time. And that insane woman was going to kill them all if this didn't work. Cave had spent endless hours learning every last cable and bit of wiring in every station she was meant to be in. Mostly, it was so she could make battle repairs, but sometimes it was so she could customize and hack things to work a little better, a little faster. You couldn't make a lot of changes to a terminal when two other shifts were working in the same place, but she'd often found the other techs were willing to work with her changes.

As long as she made no Tech changes, it was all good. So she had learned, studied, and thought about how to change things on the fly. She'd never imagined having to do what she was about to do, but there was no other way. She was almost amazed at how fast her mind was working and how she'd made the connections. The software interlock was all that stopped the laser from depressing. The hardware would allow it, since there were circumstances where the Orion might be in space with less than the full complement of drop shuttles attached. The shuttle's umbilicals sent the signal that engaged the interlock, and the port that the umbilical connected to had a secondary terminal cap that acted as a secondary safety. Without the electromagnetic signal "echo" from the cap, the interlock was still active.

Cave had ripped out a sensor cable and the parts from a dedicated decryption circuit to fake a terminator and send the "no shuttle" echo. She'd disabled the damaged leads, and she should be able to override and control the laser now.

She jumped up, put herself back in her seat, and typed furiously. Access the laser control system, authorize her local station. Overlay the aiming site to her display. Energize. Authorize firing rights to local station. Emergency power override. Override safety key lock, reset to typepad key from joystick safety.

Sweat dripped onto her keyboard from the tip of her nose. The overlay switched from green to red. She was live. She swiveled the crosshairs down… and they slid past the safety line. She was on manual. There were no automatics for an anti-ship weapon that had coding for a human target! She skewed the crosshairs and the camera around, trying to pin down the whirling demon that was rending the commandos into tissue.

Sigma pulled back from her destruction for the merest moment. The Orion's laser was starting to track on her. Good. Someone on board had some sense. The anti-ship laser might be powerful enough to blow through her shield and her reinforced skin. If the operator managed to hit her more than once, she might even be killed. She smiled at the thought. It wasn't likely, but it was possible. Ah well. She was about done. The few commandos left were starting to understand what they were facing and pulling back to form a perimeter to protect the last crew charging into the Orion.

Fair enough. She'd done her duty. The Outlanders would be in position soon enough. She could take the chance and play a little tag with the laser. She crouched, looking up at the laser… any second… now! She leapt aside, but not quite fast enough. The laser grazed her. The shield took the energy, absorbed most of it, but the remaining energy was almost all kinetic. It hit her like a mule kick in the side, spinning her completely around, but she managed to keep her feet.

She smiled at the Orion. She was pleased to note that the laser had shot a neat fist-width hole right through the nose of one of the shuttles. The shuttle had probably absorbed enough energy before the beam reached her to limit the damage. Someone on board that Orion was a real killer! She wondered if it was Vasco, but she hoped not. If he was truly the warrior she hoped he was, he would have chosen a more active approach.

She'd expected him to come out and challenge her, but maybe that was too much. Maybe… her eye caught movement heading away from the shuttle. It was a figure in full ship's armor, completely covered, but it could only be Vasco. No one else would move that fast. And he was heading for the Outlanders. Sigma understood. He was going after the real threat, giving up his chance to return home and probably giving up his life. She would have been pleased had he chosen to come fight her. It would have been glorious. She certainly would have killed him, but it would have still served her purpose. But this… maybe a true hero was what Laconia really needed. It was time. She was done.

She spread her arms and turned the AG field back on, rising into the air.

Cave was stunned. She'd fired at the Laconian witch, but the damn woman had pirouetted out of the laser like some incredible bull fighter! That was impossible! And now she was lifting up in the air, arms spread, the air shimmering around her like a halo. She was beautiful and terrifying. She was looking right at Cave, right through the monitor. Cave felt numb and frozen. It was as if the witch were hypnotizing her... but Sigma drifted right up into the center of the crosshairs and didn't even flinch or notice as Cave fired.

Vasco dropped down to a three-point squat, cringing at the impact. Ship's armor was meant to take massive gs and allow a Gyrene to move normally under a steady eight gs of acceleration. But dropping fifty meters was never going to be easy. The massive *thwak* he made on landing mostly masked the sounds of things breaking in the armor, and only the tight underwrap stopped his right knee from ripping itself to pieces. The concrete under him had shattered into dust and gravel. It didn't give a lot of traction for his next leap.

Which was just in time. He slipped but managed to bounce up as three rockets hit the spot he had landed in. At least one of them had the sharper bang of an armor-piercer, but the remaining had enough HE to boost him a little farther forward than he had intended.

Vasco slammed into the side of a building. He had a moment to try to scrabble for any kind of handhold, but there was nothing. He slipped and bounced the ten meters to the ground and landed flat on his ass, and no amount of g-force protection could stop your diaphragm from bitching about that. It was like taking a punch to gut. A punch that came down your throat. The pain was agonizing. He froze for a moment, overwhelmed by what felt like the worst heartburn ever. He spasmodically swallowed. It was like gulping down his own guts, but he felt a little better.

He hoped they'd be able to fix him up later. Something was for sure broken. No time to deal with it though. He felt crosshairs on his neck, but with no electronic communication left, his only hope was to run until something better appeared—better than the five-rocket-armed militia that just appeared.

No time to think, Vasco arched back from the ground, bridging up on his hand and kicking off from the wall in a cartwheel round-off that would have made an eleven-year-old gymnast proud. Two rockets ripped through the space he had been in before exploding farther down the street. He dodged and looked up to see what they were aiming at him next. Nothing. They were cursing and fumbling for backup weapons. The other rocket launchers must have been empty.

Ship's armor was tough, but sidearms with penetrator rounds would still kill him. The only weapon Vasco had was his knife. He didn't remember pulling it, but he wasn't surprised it was in his hand. Not surprised at all, and not thinking anymore.

It was thirty meters to the enemy. It was possible to reach and kill a man ten meters away. In the time it took that man to draw his gun, aim, and fire, you could charge and gut him. Vasco had three times that distance to cover, and five times the manpower to deal with. In his favor, they hadn't properly patrol-strapped their sidearms and were fumbling to recover them from around their backs. It was dark, and they couldn't see as well as he could. And in addition to his ship's armor enhanced muscle, Vasco's own natural muscle gave him impossible speed. His mind was in full combat mode. Survival was surrender; it was berserker, shield-biter time. In the time the ragged battle computer that was all that was operating of his brain calculated that, he'd covered almost twenty meters.

The militia saw only a spattered black demon screaming at them from the depths of hell, coming at them faster than their rockets could fly.

He almost made it to them before they could react. Almost. All five of the militia opened fire with full magazines of penetrator ammo. And behind them, charging around the corner, were another twenty.

Vasco leapt over the first bullet. It wasn't planned or even reaction. It was anticipation. The fastest enemy had let his rifle drift up, almost in line with Vasco. A slight tightening of the shoulders hinted at a trigger about to be pulled. Years of fencing instinct taught Vasco where the aiming point was. So he leapt. It was the quickest possible response. With his muscles and the ship's armor, he was two meters up when the first round of the burst went through the space where his chest would have been. Nothing human could have reacted fast enough to correct that aim.

The soldier was aware that Vasco had moved and was sickly fascinated with Vasco's hyperkinetic fluidity. The Sami's muscles strained to their utmost, every ounce of his being struggling to raise his weapon to track the black monstrosity.

Vasco tore his head off.

In the time he'd leapt up two meters, Vasco had cannoned the rest of the distance between him and the first group. His right foot planted into the chest of the soldier, and Vasco grabbed his head. He meant to slow his momentum and pull the soldier to the ground in a spinning throw that would place Vasco in a better position to deal with the rest. It was his first lesson in how frail a normal human was when faced with Vasco's enhanced muscles, backed by ship's armor. Vasco's momentum slowed and he spun, but the soldier's head came off in his hands. Vasco landed on his feet, facing the back of the remaining four soldiers desperately trying to turn around and face the demon.

With his left hand on the ground for a pivot point, Vasco hit the backs of the knees of the farthest soldier. He arced his legs like a scythe and took both soldiers off their feet at once. He pulled the legs and feet of the first soldier with him, spinning in place on the ground and corkscrewing himself on top of the unfortunate man. Vasco felt his enemy's legs snapping and breaking in his hands as Vasco twisted the man like a pretzel. He grabbed the Sami's rifle with his left hand and twisted his body up to face the remaining two soldiers.

Vasco didn't even notice the hammer blows of rounds on his armor. He didn't hear his stolen weapon firing, didn't hear himself screaming. He emptied the entire magazine on the two, dragging the weapon in an arc that put the last two rounds into the skull of the last soldier. He turned to face the larger group.

They were frozen in absolute terror. Five dead men in less than two seconds. A head spinning across the ground toward them, a slick trail of blood spiraling out from it. An impossibly fast black metallic blur that had flown through the air, hit the ground with a spray of sparks and a banshee howl, stood up to two full magazines of automatic fire, and was now facing them and screaming in rage. It was a demon right out of the darkest pits of humanity's imagination. A demon of racial memory, left over from countless battlefields, and the sight of a man gone beyond all human limits in killing rage. A demon that was part man, part black metal death. A shattered demon, with its right forearm blown off, and half of its jaw missing, shot clean off when its helm and armor had shattered under the weapons' fire.

The Sami were locked in that place, caught perfectly between the desire to run and never stop, and the desire to kill the thing that would surely rend their backs and eat their souls if they turned.

Vasco didn't think at all. His mind was long gone. He was more a demon than even his enemies knew.

He moved.

They fired.

Not even her enhanced senses and built-in battle comp could let Sigma see the world fast enough for the coherent light beam to actually slow down. But in her mind, and in her memory the split of a second after, the beam crawled into her.

She saw the turret on the Orion skew and correct, the battle comp directing her to the minute corrections of the focusing lenses behind the protective opaque sphere, the merest opening to permit the beam's passage. She saw the flex of the mirrors and lenses, and the comp spoke to her with the power of reflex to slide aside, to let the beam miss.

But she held, and the lance of energy flexed the glass as it passed through. She saw the atoms in the air fluoresce and bounce away from its power, and the bright coronal flower as it hit her shield. Flat, no planing to deflect. The photons would pile up for only picoseconds before they hammered through.

Through the field, and through her thin armored battlesuit. Through the ablative and conductive mesh under her skin, through the reinforced shells over her organs, and back out through the other side.

A neat hole, right through her.

There was pain. There were internal alarms.

But she had planned for this.

With the laser punching through, the energy dump was minimal against the shield, and thus far less kinetic. Her body burned and screamed, but the pulse of light only pierced her. It did not move her.

The lessons of war she had learned in countless battles had trained her well. The most dangerous time was victory. When you had struck your opponent a mortal blow, the mind rested, the tension dropped. Elation at success overwhelmed you if you had not trained to overcome it.

Sigma had read some of the old books of swordplay that Vasco worked from. One author had written of this and spoken strongly of the need to retreat after landing a killing blow and to throw cuts at the legs of your opponent, who would often continue to attack, not knowing they were dead yet—or enraged, knowing that they soon would be.

Sigma's choice to take the hit was a gamble that whoever was manning the laser was a killer, but the desperation of their actions might mean they were not experienced. A killing blow might make them lapse for a moment.

She didn't wait for that moment, but dove forward through the beam even before the beam pulse had ended. The beam sliced through her belly out her left side. She didn't even slow. Her internal Pook AG drive slammed her forward into the Orion ship, her beams lancing out to crack the shell around the laser. Her hands dove into the steel and wire and lensing materials and ripped them up and off the ship.

She spun, flinging the ruined laser's mass away from her, just in time to see Vasco charge. Time was still slow, and she saw a vast red cloak spread out into the air behind him as round after round ripped through him.

The cloak rose as he hit the first line and leapt over them, decapitating three Outlanders with a backhand cut as he did so. He hit the second line with a visible shock, bowling over troops like kindling... but it was too late.

He was dead before he hit the ground.

The Outlander main force poured through right away. No hesitation. They all knew the risk. The Orion had to be shut down or they'd all be radioactive dust in moments when the first drive charge went off. They poured through the streets and around the buildings.

But that last square, the last run up to the Orion, where Vasco lay, they moved around. They gave his body wide berth.

They were on the still strong remnants of the drop commandos in a moment. Sigma watched as they swarmed the commandos. It was a bitter but quick fight—the Outlanders were too well-trained, too prepared, and too numerous to be stopped. She watched as the last drop commando leader realized this as well, saw him signal the Orion, and turn to fight with his last breath.

The last hatches closed. The Orion was about to launch.

The Orion was a massive pillar on a plate, with the four huge shuttles, one with a hole through its nose cone, winched up and pinned to the top of the pillar, bolted in strong enough to take the enormous blasts that were about to propel the Orion back up the well. Some of the strongest and most well-built engineering in the Polity had gone into those connectors.

Sigma slammed into the ground again, dumping power from her AG drive into the particle beam. Locked the battle computer onto the top of the Orion's pillar, and let the computer pull her shield up and reconfigure it to lens and shape the beam, and fired.

The beam leapt across the brief space, creating an instantaneous arc from Sigma to the top of the Orion launcher. Where it touched, the metal superheated and exploded in a furious roar, spraying molten droplets and radiation at a titanic rate. The Outlanders—all that were left outside of the battling troops—flinched and dove for cover from the intense flash of light and heat. Skin blistered where the light touched.

Sigma let the particle accelerator fire for a second. At maximum output, it significantly hit her power reserves. But after a full second of output, her job was done. The meters-thick pillar was a blasted, pitted ruin. The shuttle connectors hung on by the barest slips of steel. The Orion would never launch. Firing a drive charge now would shake the ship to pieces. Sigma's power dropped precipitously low, but she was safe from counterattack now, with the Outlanders pouring in.

Cave swore and dropped to the deck. The enormous ringing clap and crack of force had taken all the strength out of her legs, making her buckle and fall before she even knew that it was a sound affecting her. The lights flickered. The computers and displays all shut down. She had a moment to realize that only the lights, with their EMP hardening, had survived. The shuttle was built to survive and launch with only the most primitive electronics, and she'd trained for this. It was time to launch. The air was still ringing with the thunderclap of whatever had hit the Orion, but the training was working. She was up and moving to the console to hit the backup mechanical launch sequence initiator.

There was a flurry of something, and in that moment, she realized she must be still deafened because she heard nothing, just saw the flash of hazy sky and daylight as the front of the cockpit was ripped clean away. Her hand was a moment away from the initiator when she looked across the wreck of her consoles and into Sigma's eyes.

Rage filled Cave's heart, and she started to slam down.

Then her brain kicked in. She'd never survive launch. No one in the shuttle would. Each of the four shuttles was crammed full of troops, almost two thousand of them. Her mind raced. Would the internal bulkheads keep the rest of the shuttle safe? They weren't made for this level of stress. The Orion had huge lift potential, but even so, it was built to lift people over equipment. It lacked the redundancy and armor of everything else, freeing up as much space as possible for human cargo.

Cave hesitated.

Looked into Sigma's eyes.

The witch was surrounded by a faint purple nimbus. Suddenly Cave was aware of all the smells—cordite, burning ozone, the rich blood smell of molten steel.

The witch was serene.

There was no hope. All was lost.

Cave raised her hands, slowly, and surrendered.

There was no going home now.

Sigma turned and looked over the city. The square was a wreck. Every building facing in had been damaged in the firefight. Smoke was coming from every quarter, but with the last of the Polity soldiers on the Orion, all the combat had ceased. It was quiet, except for the sounds of fires and yells of troops organizing aid for wounded fellows.

This had been one of the main Sami cities. In the Polity way, they had chosen to make an example of this one, knowing they would likely erase it from the world. The more populated cities were saved for later treatment, if necessary. This city wasn't as large as the others, but it was beautiful. It had numerous parks and elaborately decorated buildings. Each roof and corner was host to intricately carved scenes winding up from the ground.

It had been seconds away from being utterly destroyed.

The evil of the Polity was to obliterate anything that stood out, that was different or refused to be the same, refused to conform to their ideal. The Polity would not have cared one whit for what would have been lost here, only that eventually the planet would come to conform.

The city was safe now. And now that the plan had begun, they could start to free humanity from the Polity. One world at a time, starting on Rumi. This would be the rock, the stone wall from which a change would echo back out through the Polity and bring it crashing down.

There was a coalescence below her.

Sigma looked down and saw the Sami Outlanders carrying Vasco's corpse to her. They knew she was a Walkure and knew what Walkures could do, but this was more than that. She felt their sureness of purpose. They had made their own choice, and even if she had not made the same choice earlier, she was compelled to obey that drive.

The *Alexi* tumbled. Space was bright all around it, lit with the twinkling stars of debris scattered and trailing around it like a halo. What had once been a smooth cylinder, rippling and bumped with weaponry and death all along its hull, was now a rod. A trunk festooned with ragged growths, like some sort of fantastic tree with roots at either end. The Sami Hellbores had been accurate in their damage. The teeth of the *Alexi* had been pulled and its armor stripped. But it could still hold life, and move, and jump again between the stars.

If anyone was left to command it. The giant warship had been built to take on fleets, but no one had ever imagined facing a shotgun blast of multi-ton, near-plasma, atomic-blast-powered metal slugs. The scale of the damage was beyond any level of planning. The redundancies still existed, but scattered and unconnected throughout the ship. With no command, there was no way to know what was needed.

Neruda had been deep at work planning her invasion of Laconia when the Outlander weapons hit. The intelligence pods were buried deep in the heart of the ship, so she'd been in her ship's armor and strapped in to work in the lack of gravity, instead of in the Ring, chasing the Timariot around. The ship had bucked and rung bell-like for long moments, and everything loose had ricocheted within the pod. She'd been lucky to suffer only glancing blows, but she could still see floating rubies of blood all over the pod. At least seeing them had given her the presence of mind to check herself with a pat-down once the bucking had stopped.

She was bleeding from a score of cuts and was patching them when she saw one of the rubies slide through the air at an angle and splat onto her arm. She glanced up to see everything in the air, still moving around, but all of it sliding down toward the deck at the same angle.

Spinning, her brain told her as she stared. The ship is spinning. Or tumbling. She took a minute to orient herself and remember where in the ship she was. She was about a third of the way up from center, toward the bow. Facing the bow, watching the slide for a moment, she realized it was an end-over-end tumble. The stabilizers must be gone. She felt the pull of the coriolis force now, pulling her into her chair like gravity.

She had a terrible moment of wondering if it was actually gravity, if the *Alexi* was now out of orbit and descending down the well. She sensed the slight torque that told her it was coriolis, but the fear wouldn't go. Had the ship been hit hard enough to drop out of orbit? With the stabilizers gone, what was controlling their trajectory? If someone was on the bridge, why hadn't they already fixed it? It was clear the ship had been hit heavily, probably fatally, but she had no idea of the extent.

She unstrapped herself and headed out of the pod. Time to see what was going on.

There was madness everywhere. The dead filled every space, and the living were lost and had no idea what was going on. The experienced spacers were usually working stations closer to the outer hull, and most of the people with combat experience were planet-side, on one continent or another. The Orion should be docking soon for a restock and would definitely bring some much-needed rescue personnel, but so far, the only personnel she'd run across were the kind of menial support staff she'd always hated and avoided.

She moved toward the space bridge, where the Timariot was supposed to be working for this shift, and with this disaster, she knew he'd need her help as soon as possible. Travel was taking forever though. It seemed as though every section she moved through, she had to stop and get all the drones organized and pulling their heads out of their asses.

She got the routine down though. Open the bulkhead, enter, start yelling for reports and getting people to sound off. Designate the first person who answered to get a list of everyone alive. Get them all out and lining up. Find the ones who didn't look like shell-shocked wrecks, get them to make a list of problems that needed to be, and could be, immediately addressed. Get a runner to go back one section and see if anyone needed extra help, or if there were idle hands to help here.

After the fourth section, she'd started sending runners ahead to do the same job, so all she had to do was move into the next section, get a report, shuffle what needed to be shuffled, and yell at who needed to be yelled at.

Slowly she made her way through the ship, and she spread organization with her as she went.

By the time Neruda got to the space bridge, she had a system of runners acting as messengers going all over the ship. There was no way she could get any rapid sense of what was going on, but it was starting to coalesce. The military mindset was kicking back in, so the reports were getting more coherent as time went on. Chaos was still in charge, but it was facing stiff resistance now.

But now that she was on the space bridge, the chaos looked as if it was going to win for real.

Timariot Emil Smith was dead.

His stupid ego had finally killed him. The space bridge hadn't taken a direct hit, but it was a near-hit. The view ports had cracked and shattered and drained the room of most of its air before the safeties had kicked in and sealed around the damage. Even with that, the idiot still should have survived—if he'd bothered to wear his ship's armor. Or if he'd strapped himself in with even a basic tether system. Sure, there was still a chance the debris cloud that had killed so many of the space bridge's crew would have killed him too, but at least that would have been a more dignified death. Instead, the fool was crammed upside down into a workpod with what was probably a broken neck.

Neruda didn't waste much time thinking about that. Dead was dead. Someone had to take charge, and she was close enough to next in line. Anyone who wanted to challenge that could go find the nearest airlock.

She had to find out what had happened and get the damn ship back to running before they all slammed into the damn planet.

Chapter Eighteen: The One Who Slays

Sigma looked down on the mangled wreck that was once Vasco. It was hard to tell what was ship's armor and what was human. Blood and bits of organic matter blended into shattered steel and ceramic composite. There was less the shape of a man left, and more the suggestion of an outline.

She thought back to the last time they had spoken and how she had given him the call to be the warrior he was meant to be. This, as always, was the result. A shattered wreck and a life gone forever. The gift she had given him was to have given his life for others, instead of a life that just faded out or was snuffed in some random twist of fate. He was a lucky man. He'd accepted the gift she'd offered and had responded to the call when the chance came. Now Vasco was hers.

She put her hand into the wreck that was left of his chest. Dead, in the normal sense of the term. The network of his body had broken down, the system no longer connecting to each of the parts. The body was cooling rapidly. Brain and heart had ceased to function. Blood was clotting, and individual cells that were struggling to function with the resulting nutrient loss were dumping acid into the body, making the cells break down. Dead, dying, and already starting to rot. But not all the way. Some parts still clung to their last little islands of nutrients and wastes. Some cell clusters would hang on longer than others. True death would be a little bit yet.

All the damage could be undone.

The protocols were satisfied. The packages buried deep in her body, the final secret of the nanoborg, coalesced and joined together. Sigma's body rippled slightly, and her palm bulged and split as the incubator was formed and ejected.

She completed the process by slipping the incubator into one of the ragged holes in Vasco's torso. The incubator dissolved almost instantly as the nanobot swarm programming kicked in, and it burrowed through Vasco's body.

The secret that Lycurgus, the Laconian founder, had discovered long ago was that the nanoborg process—the creation of a perfect blend between nanobots and humans—was always fatal. But as long as the subject was already dead, the process could complete. With long and brutal experimentation, he'd found the brief window after death that would allow a human to be reborn as a nanoborg and still retain its personality and humanness. It was still a fragile process, and it required a unique personality. A mind that had the focus to surrender its own existence for others. And to do so in righteous battle? That moment of clarity, that focus of self, was the key to rebirth as a nanoborg.

No cold, scientific clinical trial had revealed this final key, but rather the death of a friend in a bitter, last-ditch fight that had driven Lycurgus to give his nanoborg one final try. And that had led to the birth of the first Walkure, and the change that remade Laconia from a barbaric backwater to the most scientifically and militarily advanced world outside of Pook space. As the Polity was going to find out. Vasco would be the key, the first non-Laconian Walkure.

But something wasn't working.

There should have been some signs of life, of localized reconnections, of the nanobots rebuilding. There was nothing. Sigma leaned in closer and activated her diagnostic sensors. The nanobots were active and forming their building blocks, but not interfacing with the organic components.

As she watched, Vasco's body shivered, little ripples running up and down his corpse. She put her hand on him and let the medical comp interface with the nanobots. Diagnostics flooded in, and the comp gave her a quick synopsis. Antibodies. The Creche antibodies were far more powerful than expected. It was almost as if they'd been designed to fight a nanobiotic invasion. The antibodies had been dormant, nascent in Vasco's body, until the nanobots entered, then they'd activated. They weren't exactly organic, but rather some sort of prion-based system that lingered after death in an almost purely chemical fashion.

Sigma couldn't even imagine what in the Creche background has led to creating that defense system. It was a most unpleasant surprise, and it left her with only one option. It would mean revealing far too much, far too early. Was Vasco worth it?

Not even really a question. They'd have to see what could be made of him in the training. The choice had already been made, and if that threw off the timetable, so be it.

She entered the codes in her mind, unlocking the secret caches of computer memory, and activated the communicator. The pulse rippled out, invisible and unknown to any means in the Anubis system.

The *Alexi* was finally stabilizing. Neruda had wrangled and sworn and fought and finally managed to get a semblance of communication and structure going in the ship, and sections were reactivating and repairing. There were pockets that still had active communications systems, and local command-and-control was spreading throughout the ship. She hadn't wanted to stay on the space bridge, but until they got ship-wide coms back up, it was where everyone knew she was. She had to stay put and manage the ship with runners.

"Primus!" yelled one of the com techs. "I've got outside coms back up! Picket-six is reporting in!"

Picket-six was one of the networks of monitor ships the *Alexi* had spread throughout the system. It was on a higher orbit than the *Alexi* and had a greater view of the planet. Its battlespace view should have been wide enough to have caught a glimpse of whatever had crippled the *Alexi*. Neruda wanted that information badly. There had been no ships in space to damage them, and nothing in the system could have generated that much power without them being warned first. It couldn't have been a superluminal weapon because there would be nothing left of the Alexi if it had been. Besides, who would have used one and risked Pook retaliation? Something about that line of thought nagged deep in her brain, but she put it aside as she took advantage of the weak gravity still available from the residing spin and moved to the coms station.

The tech had already put the incoming feed on speaker, and Neruda patiently waited while the tech and picket ship passed info back and forth. The tech was good and asked all the right questions, so Neruda only had to interrupt a few times to get the information she needed. Massive nuclear explosions on the surface, and titanic beams rising from them to smite the *Alexi*. An entire mountain range had been nuked into rubble. Hellbores. Neruda had read about them in some obscure little bit of research from some long-assimilated world. The idea was to use a focused nuclear blast as a charge in a massive cannon to either fire an intense plasma beam or propel a huge slug. Somewhat like an Orion launcher in reverse. There were a million reasons not to build one, and the report she had read had listed all the insurmountable technical details that needed to be overcome. But those were for a mobile weapon.

The Sami Outlanders seemed to have skipped some of those issues by scaling the damn things up to mountain-range size. But how? And how had they managed to aim them? Obviously not perfect aim, because the *Alexi* was still alive, but it was still a tremendous shot. But with weapons that powerful, they should have been able to blow the *Alexi* completely out of commission. But still, how? There was no damn way the Sami, never mind the Outlanders, had that kind of technology or infrastructure.

And then she realized what else picket-six was saying. An inbound Pook ship? What the hell? She reached past the com tech and hit transmit.

"Picket-six, *Alexi*-primus," she said. "Open coms to Pook ship and patch us into response. Put it on the emergency band and request assistance!"

If they could get the obnoxious little bastards to help, there might still be a chance to save the mission. They were an obtuse bunch, but they, like every other spacefaring race, would always come to help a distress call. They absolutely had the tech and the resources to get *Alexi* back on her feet, even in her mauled condition.

The call for help went out again and again, but there was no response from the Pook. Their golden ship slipped closer and closer to the planet.

With the battle over, Cave had been trying to affect what repairs she could and letting the troop leads know that they were stranded, surrounded by the enemy, and had already surrendered. She'd had to repeat over and over what had happened and how the Orion was never to launch. The ground force lead centurion had already started discussing terms with the Sami.

She'd finally gotten coms up in time to hear the chatter about *Alexi*. The shuttle was still busy with activity, but now that they didn't know if they still had overwatch, or any ability to get back to a safe home ever again, the mood was achingly broken. They'd gone from lost to shattered.

Cave had retreated to her TacOps station so she could have a semblance of a job to help keep herself together just a little longer. There wasn't really anything to do except listen to the chatter between picket-six and *Alexi* until the other pickets got back into range. The arrival of the Pook ship had given her a flash of hope, but the repeated calls for help with no response was like a series of repeated slaps in the face.

Cave numbed herself by filling her screens with constantly scrolling log file tails. The stream of data updates soothed her, as it always did, and helped her feel as if there was some semblance of control left to her. Even if it was just seeing the same error messages flowing past like water, unchanged.

Except... not. There was a change. Something... something was different. File update reports showed touch after touch. What the hell? A hack? Someone was in her systems? Who, and why? Why now?

Training kicked in, and Cave opened all her monitoring software and kicked in the honeypots and trap doors that she'd puzzled out and built with Vasco's help. The signature of the attack leapt up almost immediately. Pook. The incoming Pook ship! One of those inquisitive little aliens was making a run on her systems. But why? Why would one of them run on her, but not answer the call for help? Was it a coms issue? Were they missing something?

She opened the next toolbox, the one they rarely used. Just the telemetry tools, mostly used for the odd diagnostic check. She could run a quick sweep of the airways, get a sense of the total traffic going on, triangulate who the Pook were talking to, see who was talking to whom. Maybe they were missing the message? Maybe picket-six or *Alexi* had something broken that was stopping the reply from being heard? She could check that!

There was a signal... no, three signals coming from the Pook ship. There was the hacking carrier reaching out to her, and another to picket-six, and the third was almost the same as the one to Cave's shuttle, but off-axis a little. She let the software clean it up. It was digital coms for sure. Encrypted, and she knew better than to even try to break that encryption. But it was off-axis, not aimed at her, but aimed close? A horrible suspicion hit her, and Cave scrambled to look out the shattered wreck of the cockpit, then back at her deck to confirm.

The Pook were talking to the Sami. Looking down on the mass of them, Cave knew. It was the witch. Somehow the Laconian was in contact with the Pook.

It only took her a moment to bounce a contact back to the *Alexi*.

Neruda was livid. It all clicked into place. The whole fucking thing had been a trap. Every goddamned step of it. It was impossible, but it fit perfectly. The Sami hadn't aimed the hellbores. They'd maneuvered the *Alexi* to be in the right place at the right time. The only answer was the Laconians must have planned the whole thing. The Helots... they must have a whole planet of them that had already figured out the Polity plan to annex them. They must have been working out this whole damn travesty for decades. The bastards!

We walked right into their trap. Right into it, thinking we were winning the whole time.

The single golden Pook ship slipped down the well with no ripple, no sound, as if the atmosphere of Rumi did not exist or as if the ship were just a bulbous shimmering collection of ghostly orbs. Down and down it went, in complete silence, until it hovered over the wrecked and smoking city, directly over the Orion.

A smaller bubble separated and floated down at a speed that should have caused multiple sonic booms. In less than a second, it was floating over Sigma's head, then it drifted off to the side and settled on the ground.

A single Pook emerged. It was everything the Pook were rumored to be. A long-tailed biped, clad from neck to tip of tail in ornately chased and detailed powered armor. Only its head was bare, and it looked exactly like a hairless cat. The single forearm claws added a touch of praying mantis to the look, and its delicate little hands with the tiny, thread-like fingers that hid under the claw were also unarmored.

In those unreal-looking hands, the Pook held a flat, featureless disc made of the same golden Pook metal as everything else about the creature. Sigma stood over Vasco, watching as the Pook made its way over. It stopped, looked at the dead man, then back up at Sigma. They held eye contact for a moment, then Sigma nodded.

The little alien held out the disc and touched it to Vasco's corpse.

The Sami stood watching in a circle, and from that circle emerged hundreds of Weta. There was an odd but unmistakable similarity in form between the Pook and the Weta. A mere echo of physical outline, but enough that all the humans felt it deep within them and felt a little revulsion at the connection between the feline and insect life, a moment of understanding that what they knew as alien was something truly beyond their ken.

Then the moment came, and the Sami and the Weta Listened.

Vasco glowed. At first faintly, from where the disc touched his chest, then his whole body. The glow grew brighter, and brighter still, until it was a ferocious flame that blinded all who tried to look directly at it.

His corpse thrashed and contorted. The tissues rippled, tearing themselves apart and reforming in waves of chaos.

He floated, and the thrashing grew stronger.

He screamed.

The ground shook under him, dust rising in a silent thunderclap.

Vasco's eyes opened, his flesh reformed. He turned his now-rebuilt face and saw Sigma. Looked into her eyes.

His eyes slowly closed, and the glow faded, and he settled onto the ground, whole again.

Sigma picked up his sleeping form, and with the Pook, she walked over and into the golden bubble. After a moment, it rose and merged back into the great golden ship, which swung up and out, leaving Rumi behind.

Neruda saw the Pook ship lifting back out of the atmosphere and stabbed at the transmit button one more time. "Pook ship, this is *Alexi*! We are in desperate need of assistance! Answer me! Damn you! Answer me!"

"Primus Neruda." Neruda froze as she heard Sigma's voice come out of the speaker. "We will not aid you. Your intention was to wage war on Laconia, using the Sami as a steppingstone. We know this. We also know that in your foolish vanity, it was also your plan to use us and our Helots to wage war on the Pook.

"Your plans are done, but the consequences are not. You have your war. Laconia is now the fist of the Pook, and we are coming for you. We have crippled your ship but left you alive enough to flee for home and warn the Polity that we are coming.

"You will be the herald of their last days. The Polity has crushed civilization after civilization, has crushed the natural growth and diversity of life for millennia, but that has now ended. Here, in Anubis, you begin to die. You will die so that humanity can flourish and change and evolve the way it was meant to. Go home, with the last of your people, and let them know their time is done—by their own hand and own actions. When next you see us, it will be in war."

The golden ship vanished.

Neruda sat in her rage. The only thing that stopped her screaming and lashing out was the knowledge that she had been right, and she'd been right to suspect the Laconians all along. She had no idea of the scale of the evil they had actually planned, but she knew that two years behind her was the backup plan she'd carefully worked out a decade ago—two hundred Tatars ready to come through the leap to Anubis.

There would be war all right, but the Laconians weren't the only ones who could play the long game.